A NOSE FOR JUSTICE

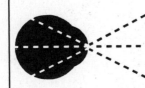

This Large Print Book carries the
Seal of Approval of N.A.V.H.

A NOSE FOR JUSTICE

A NOVEL

RITA MAE BROWN

Illustrated by
Laura Hartman Maestro

WHEELER PUBLISHING
A part of Gale, Cengage Learning

GALE
CENGAGE Learning

Detroit • New York • San Francisco • New Haven, Conn • Waterville, Maine • London

GALE
CENGAGE Learning

Copyright © 2010 by Rita Mae Brown.

Illustrations: Laura Hartman Maestro

Wheeler Publishing, a part of Gale, Cengage Learning.

ALL RIGHTS RESERVED

Wheeler Publishing Large Print Hardcover.

The text of this Large Print edition is unabridged.

Other aspects of the book may vary from the original edition.

Set in 16 pt. Plantin.

LIBRARY OF CONGRESS CATALOGING-IN-PUBLICATION DATA

Brown, Rita Mae.
    A nose for justice / by Rita Mae Brown.
      p. cm.
    ISBN-13: 978-1-4104-3092-2
    ISBN-10: 1-4104-3092-8
      1. Country life — Nevada — Fiction. 2. Corporations —
Corrupt practices — Fiction. 3. Real estate developers — Fiction.
4. Murder — Investigation — Fiction. 5. Dogs — Fiction.
6. Nevada — Fiction. 7. Large type books. I. Title.
PS3552.R698N67 2010b
813'.54—dc22

                                                        2010033310

Published in 2010 in arrangement with The Ballantine Publishing Group, a division of Random House, Inc.

Printed in the United States of America
1 2 3 4 5 6 7 14 13 12 11 10

Dedicated with Bombastic Affection
to
Mrs. Gayle Horn, MFH,
and Miss Lynn Lloyd, MFH,
each of whom showed me why they cherish
the ways of Old Nevada

CAST OF CHARACTERS

Magdalene Reed, "Jeep" — Born in 1924 to a poor, hardworking couple in Reno, Nevada, Jeep was bright but could not afford higher education. While serving as a WASP (Women Airforce Service Pilot) in World War II, she acquired the skills that would make her one of the richest women in Nevada. To her credit, she never forgot her beginnings nor does she ever forget a friend or an enemy.

Magdalene Rogers, "Mags" — She's the great-niece of Jeep. When Mags's parents were killed in an automobile accident, Jeep raised her and her sister, Catherine. At thirty-two, the beautiful Mags has learned some painful lessons as she saw her profession and income disintegrate as a Wall Street broker. She carries great guilt about this although she is hardly to blame for the grotesque irresponsibility of her superiors.

Catherine Rogers — While Mags is beautiful, Catherine is drop-dead gorgeous. She's also a loose cannon, having bounced from being a character actress in Hollywood to an infamous porn star. Jeep could tolerate that. What she couldn't bear was when Catherine tried to force her to disinherit Enrique, Jeep's adopted son, a man in his fifties.

Enrique Salaberry — A Basque by blood, he carries the toughness of his people. He now runs the ranch day-to-day, and loves it. Thanks to Jeep he attended college, where he studied agriculture. He's always open to new ideas about ranching and equipment and has the enthusiastic support of his adoptive mother, whom he loves deeply.

Carlotta Salaberry — Enrique's wife is over the top. Bedecked with bright colors and many adornments if she's going out, she is warm, gregarious and keeps house for Jeep. She loves the old lady for many reasons, one being that when Enrique fell in love with her, Jeep encouraged the match instead of opposing it. That was thirty years ago and most WASPS would have been horrified. Without being obvious, she keeps a close eye on her mother-in-law, who while strong, is still a woman in her mid-eighties.

Deputy Peter Meadows — Although young to be a deputy, the sheriff of Washoe County recognized Pete's ability and his gift with people. In his mid-thirties, Pete is a native of Washoe County, which he loves about as much as Jeep Reed does. Two years ago he suffered a painful divorce, but aren't they all painful? He's getting his feet under him but is still a bit wary of women.

Officer Lonnie Parrish — Pete's sidekick is in his twenties and full of energy. He's got good instincts but needs some seasoning. He's transfixed by the opposite sex.

Jake Tanner — Usually disheveled, Jeep's neighbor, who lives a few miles north of her ranch, has a small business using his heavy equipment to help ranchers. The word nosy was coined for Jake, and one is never quite sure what will fall out of his ever-running mouth.

Twinkie Bosun — In his mid-forties, he works for Silver State Resource Management (SSRM) repairing equipment. There's nothing the man can't fix. Good-natured and responsible, he's one of those wonderful men who just knuckles down and gets the job done.

Bunny Matthews — A year or two younger than Twinkie, he's Twinkie's partner. As much of the work is heavy, and sometimes in unpleasant conditions, the repair teams usually go out in twos, unless it is a massive problem. These two are the number one team.

Oliver Hitchens — He's the head of equipment purchasing and also knowing what kind of pump to put where. He keeps an eye on all repairs and is so good at his job of keeping company costs down that he is endured by his superiors and loathed by those who work under him. He is one of those men who must establish his authority with other men but is a devoted husband who doesn't have a need to be authoritative with his wife. Perhaps like most smart men he realizes it doesn't work anyway.

Darryl Johnson — The president of Silver State Resource Management believes that Reno, now at 410,000 people, can sustain a population of 620,000 people. This is in direct opposition to what Jeep and those concerned with the environment believe. They believe that water will run out. His vision for the future is different from Jeep's, but he is a good man.

Craig Locke — As Director of Acquistions for SSRM, he, too, believes Reno can sustain an extra two hundred thousand people. He's a master at acquiring water rights and could probably sell ice to Eskimos.

George W. Ball — His understanding of equipment, the demands of various terrain, and his ability to identify people who can perform difficult work under tough conditions has earned him the cumbersome title of Director of Internal Resources. George W. cares nothing for titles. He loves his job and gets along well with the guys, like Twinkie and Bunny, who get down there and do the dirty work. He endures Oliver Hitchens with a smile, when possible, because Oliver's ability to save a buck for SSRM benefits the whole operation.

Teton Benson — He's made many mistakes and paid for them. Other people have paid for them, too. He lives in a seedy part of Reno and has a crush on a waitress at the topless bar next to his walk-up apartment. Her assets are considerable.

11

The Deceased

A Russian solider — He died in the late 1800s. Part of this story involves finding out exactly when he died and why.

Dorothy Jocham — Jeep's life partner departed this world at the turn of this century. Her influence on Jeep, Enrique, and the ranch remains as she remains in the hearts of all who knew her.

Daniel Marks — Jeep's other life partner died in 2001. Dan flew fighters in World War II. He and Jeep went into the salvage business together after the war. How Jeep juggled two lovers is a feat as remarkable as how she made her fortune, but one she has no desire to share. People didn't ask such things back in those days. If they had, she would have been truthful. If someone is worth loving, they're worth honoring.

The Ford brothers — Back when Reno was no bigger than a minute, these two farsighted and enterprising men built the ranch that would eventually come to Jeep. They built a house and a barn to last for generations and so they have. They will last for many more.

Wings Ranch — Of course, it's not deceased and could be considered inanimate. I believe places have a personality and may even contain spirits. This ten-thousand-acre spread in Red Rock Valley, just north of Reno, is such a place. It is, itself, a character. Places define us more than we know.

THE SAVIORS

King — This four-year-old shepherd mix possesses intelligence and physical power. He will protect his humans. When Baxter comes into his life, at first he can't take the little guy seriously.

Baxter — A three-year-old wire-haired dachshund, he kept Mags together during the Wall Street meltdown. A dachshund is a hound trained to hunt vermin by scent. If a hound sees his quarry, he might chase it if he recognizes it. But a dachshund will follow the scent regardless of conditions and only give up the chase when the scent disappears. Many people see a dachshund only as cute, but they are far more than that — which King finally, grudgingly, accepts.

CHAPTER ONE

A steady, increasing wind blew dust and sagebrush across the path of Magdalene Rogers. The graceful curving skeleton of a snake long ago disturbed from its resting place formed an S, straightened out, then broke up, its delicate white head carrying four vertebrae with it.

Mags, as she was called, looked down and hoped this wasn't a portent. Putting her hand palm inward to the left of her left eye, she craned her neck upward. Pieces of debris flew harder now. She watched as one small, crooked slip of sagebrush fastened itself to the P-47 propeller in the middle of the high crossbar forming the entrance to Wings Ranch. Just as quickly the brush dislodged, sailing farther into Red Rock Valley. Great sheets of Confederate-gray clouds interlaced with charcoal ones crested the Peterson Mountains, which in essence divided Nevada from California.

Looking west toward that range, Mags saw that the ridgeline at its highest point — 2,250 feet — was already engulfed in snow. Within ten to fifteen minutes the snow's advance guard would be swirling through the Wings Ranch gate.

Baxter, her three-year-old wire-haired dachshund, sat alert in the passenger seat of the rental car. Better Mags stand out there in the cold wind than himself. It had been a long day for the fastidious, very proper canine and he'd hated every last minute of it. The worst was the flight from JFK Airport to Reno. At least that was over — never to be repeated, he hoped fervently.

She flipped up the collar of her shearling jacket — a long-ago Christmas present from her great-aunt who owned this sprawling, 10,000-acre ranch located about twenty-two miles south of Reno.

The first snowflake tentatively appeared as Mags stood under the propeller blade. Aunt Jeep never did anything halfway, so her western entranceway was wide and high. Each spring, the old prop blade would be lovingly cleaned, touched up if needed, and a sprig of evergreen was tucked behind its nose for good luck.

Magdalene was named for her aunt. As Magdalene is a three syllable name, Americans shortened it. Who wants to say a mouthful? Hence, Mags. Aunt Jeep earned her nickname in 1941 when she first began driving Jeeps. She still had an old war issue that ran like a top. If you had any sense, you ran when Aunt Jeep took the wheel. The old lady craved speed whether driving or flying — both of which she had always done with sangfroid.

In the time it took her to fondly recall the sight of her small but imposing great-aunt blasting down a dirt road leaving a plume of dust behind her, Mags was wearing a shawl of snow. Since she wasn't wearing gloves, she rubbed her cold hands together and climbed back into the Camaro. She might be flat broke but damned if she was going to rent something that didn't possess some style. And power.

Closing the door, she reached over to rub the dachshund's russet head. "Buddybud, home. I hope."

"I'd like to eat."

Mags smiled as she heard what sounded like a muffled bark. Then the tears came.

"Oh, Momma. Everything will be all right." Baxter stepped over the center console to lick her tears.

She hugged him. "Damn if I'll let anyone see me cry. Just you." She took a deep breath. "You're the only one who loves me. Well, maybe Aunt Jeep does, too. In her fashion."

She popped the transmission into drive. GM products, while possessing virtues, often had an off-center feel to the steering wheel, a numbness, slowness to respond. The silver Camaro surprised her; its steering wasn't as crisp as a Porsche's, but it was much improved from prior models. She took pleasure in it. Just like her great-aunt, if it had an engine in it, Mags liked it. These days she needed a dash of pleasure.

"Damn, I can barely see the road," she said peering over the wheel. "Everything's different here, Baxter. Everything. You blink and the weather changes. We're in the high desert, but we're in it together."

Poking along at twenty miles an hour she finally reached the old white rambling ranch house. Its first section had been built in 1880, a long time ago in these parts.

Cutting the motor, she sat for a moment, took another deep breath, then brightened. "Hey, I'm not doing great, but at least I'm doing better than my lying, cokehead of a sister."

With that, she jumped out and popped the trunk. Hoisting one bag onto her shoulders, she dragged the other up the steps to the wraparound porch. Returning, she shut the trunk lid and opened the passenger door.

"At your service."

Baxter nimbly negotiated the distance to the ground as snowflakes dotted his wiry fur.

Mags opened the front door, which was never locked, threw in the biggest bag, then set down the other. "Aunt Jeep!"

"In the kitchen," answered a resonant, deep alto voice.

"Who goes there?" King growled as he hurtled himself out of the kitchen to draw up short in front of Mags, whom he knew — although not well — from her infrequent visits.

But what was this low-to-the-ground lowlife with a trimmed Vandyke?

Faced with the shepherd mix, Baxter stood his ground, saying nothing.

Jeep Reed strode out of the kitchen, her slight limp apparent but in no way impeding her progress. "King, he's your new best friend."

"That?" The much bigger dog was incredulous. With a handsome black face with brown points and a regal bearing, he had no patience for what he thought of as inferior breeds. *"I've seen snakes higher off the ground than that."*

Baxter curled back his upper lip. *"And I can*

19

strike just as fast, you ill-bred lout."

"All right, boys. Get along or I'll get out the bull whip." Aunt Jeep wagged her finger at the two dogs as she walked toward her beautiful, thirty-two-year-old great-niece. "Mags, sweetheart, welcome home."

Mags held the lean, fierce old woman close. "I won't be a burden, Aunt Jeep. I swear to you, I won't."

"I know you won't because I intend to work your ass off. Sweat and manual labor should help work free those toxins from Wall Street. I'll fill you in on the details of my latest dream once you've settled in. It's a big dream." She stepped back. "Hang your coat up. You know where. Want help with those?"

"Oh, no. I can manage."

As Mags hung her coat on the peg next to the front door, Aunt Jeep gave her the once-over. "I'm surprised. You didn't turn to fat sitting on your nether regions all day."

"An hour in the gym every day. Five-thirty A.M. Otherwise, I'd be fat as a tick. Walking Baxter every morning and every evening helps."

Jeep's warm brown eyes cast down at the intrepid little fellow. "You and I are going to be friends, Baxter. Did you hear that?"

The little gentleman responded, *"I like you already."*

"You look like you always do." Mags complimented her aunt.

"When you're older than dirt, nothing much changes."

"I think Momma would look like you do now had she lived." Mags smiled.

Jeep laughed. "Honey, your mother was one of the great beauties of her generation. She outshone all those Hollywood starlets vying for your father's attention. If she had made it to eighty-five, she'd have looked better than I did at thirty."

Mags slipped her arm around her much shorter aunt's still small waist as they walked toward the kitchen, heavenly smells drawing them down the center hall.

"You always underestimate your looks, Momma used to say that." Mags swallowed hard. "Aunt Jeep, I'm so grateful to you for taking me in and I'm so glad Mom and Dad aren't here to see — me."

"Oh, shut up, Mags. First off, I love you. The moment Glynnis and John were killed on that awful Memorial Day in 1992, you and your sister became mine. Not only did I wish it, that was your mother's will. Don't fret about that mess on Wall Street. Most of us hit the skids once or twice in our lives and you know something, I feel sorry for those who haven't. Think about your parents; your father wasn't always on the top rung of the Hollywood ladder. He and your mom had plenty of highs and lows, but they loved every minute. What you learn, how you adapt, how you change inside, well, it may be a hard lesson but if you embrace it, you're far better off than when you started. Weaklings ask for an easy life, Mags." She turned toward her great-niece. "Failure is feedback for success."

Mags bent down to kiss the silken cheek. "Then fasten your seatbelt, Aunt Jeepers, I'm heading for one helluva success."

"That's my girl."

As Mags entered the kitchen, Carlotta looked up from stirring porridge at the stove. She carefully laid the spoon on a small yellow plate, then rushed toward the younger woman.

"Baby!"

"Carlotta, oh, how good to see you."

Carlotta, bombastic in her affections, opinions, and dress and much loved for it, proudly held up three fingers. "Three."

"Three what?" Mags looked puzzled.

"I am now three times a grandmother." The middle-aged, well-padded Carlotta beamed, her black eyes sparkling, her black hair still shiny. No gray yet.

"I thought Tommy just had two kids."

Tommy was her only son.

Aunt Jeep wryly commented, "It's a fertile family."

"October twenty-seventh. A girl. Finally, two boys and a girl." Carlotta's eyes darted to her porridge and she hurried back to stir. "We are all waiting for your turn, Mags."

"Oh." Mags waved her off. "I am not getting married."

"Famous last words," Jeep said, pointing to the table. "I'm sure you haven't eaten and if you've eaten plane food, you need help."

"Didn't."

"What about me?" Baxter politely inquired.

"Touch my dish and you die!" King curled back his upper lip.

"Ah." Jeep opened a cabinet door, found a small painted stool, pulled it over, and stood on it to fish out a mid-sized, heavy ceramic bowl. "I've shrunk."

"That cabinet has gotten higher." Carlotta smiled.

Suddenly tired, Mags sat down at the farmer's table.

"Never occurred to me. That must be it." Jeep stepped off the small stool, walked into a small pantry off the spacious kitchen, and returned with a bowl of crunchies for Baxter, which she wisely placed at the opposite end of the kitchen from King's bowl.

23

King's ears shot up. *"Did you give him something better than you gave me?"*

Baxter, famished, made a beeline for the bowl as Jeep shot King a stern look of warning.

Two steaming bowls of porridge were now on the table, along with a loaf of wonderful-smelling fresh bread, a wooden cutting board, and a serrated knife.

Carlotta occasionally ate with the boss, her mother-in-law, but usually returned to her own house, a smaller replica of this house, where she made lunch for her husband. Enrique Salaberry, fifty-eight, had been orphaned in the mid-1950s and then adopted by Jeep and the late Dorothy Jocham. Even after the formal adoption, Jeep had not changed Enrique's last name to Reed. She'd preserved the surname of his unwed mother, a Basque.

In one of her downward spirals, Catherine, Mags's sister, had tried to get her great-aunt to change her will so that only she and Mags (as blood relatives) would inherit Jeep's considerable estate. Jeep's enraged response was to strike Catherine from her will entirely. She sent copies of the revised document to Catherine, Catherine's lawyer, as well as to Catherine's extremely handsome and extremely loathsome husband. That had been

24

in 2000. A long, noticeable silence followed, and had continued ever since.

Either Catherine stewed in Brentwood, a beautiful wealthy neighborhood of Los Angeles, or she was stewed. Ever the actress, she was always ready for another comeback. Catherine, being Catherine, was sure to turn up again sooner or later. She had a talent for picking the worst possible moments to reappear. What made it worse was that she was the spitting image of her mother, Glynnis, which always hit Jeep square in the heart.

Mags carried her mother's high cheekbones, and had that same lithe body, but you could also see her late father in her: the coloring, the piercing green eyes. Mags was wonderful to look at, but Catherine was drop-dead gorgeous. Such striking looks are so often a curse. In Catherine's case, it was a big one.

Jeep rarely mentioned her other greatniece. It wasn't that her name was forbidden, only that the conversation inevitably grew somber. Sooner or later someone would say, "You know, Cath will wind up dead. Someone will wipe her off the face of the earth."

Carlotta leaned over the sink and looked at the sky out the window. Then she walked to the long row of paned glass windows overlooking the wraparound porch. "More is coming."

Jeep turned to look. "The weatherman said two days of snow, maybe a foot and a half or more should fall in the city. That means two or more here."

"Where's Enrique?" Mags asked once she'd eaten a bit. She hadn't realized how lightheaded she'd become.

"The old barn," Aunt Jeep answered. "I've said ever since I bought this place that I'd take it down to the beams and then build it back like the original. Well, it's only taken me fifty-three years. Always one thing or another."

"That will be beautiful. You've sent me the photographs. I was very impressed you used a computer."

Jeep waved off the compliment. "People knew how to build back then. They built to last. For generations. Those hand-hewn beams get me every time I look at them. This ranch's original owners did an incredible job. I can just imagine Ralph Ford and his brother, Michael, one in the pit, one on top, sawing through those huge tree trunks."

"Where'd the Ford brothers ever get the trees?"

While various pines flourished in some spots in Nevada, not much else did.

"Brought 'em over from California by wagon." She shifted in her seat. "In a way, it's my duty to bring the barn back to its origins. I owe it to the Ford brothers. Too much Nevada history has been bulldozed, burned, or smashed to bits." She paused. "Bad as we've been out here, nothing's touched the day Penn Station was destroyed in Manhattan."

"Oh, I bet if there had been a Penn Station around here someone would have said the land beneath it's too valuable, let's tear it down and put up a great big ugly box," Mags critically commented.

"No. Not anymore. We've all awakened on that subject. At least, I hope we have." After a spoonful of the thick porridge, Jeep turned to Carlotta. "Perfect for a wicked cold day."

Carlotta smiled. "Thank you."

"Nobody cooks as good as you." Mags meant it, having tired of food considered as art.

Carlotta waved her be-ringed hand. "Poof."

A rumble stopped their chat.

King barked. *"Trouble."*

Baxter lifted his head from his plate. He'd never before heard such a sound. He specialized in ambulance and fire sirens.

"If those damned kids blow up my mailbox

again, I'm getting out the shotgun." Jeep slammed her hand on the table, stood up, and rushed to the windows at the front of the house.

A brief gap in the snowfall revealed a black spiral of smoke, far from her mailbox, perhaps three miles to the northwest.

Then, just as fast, the snow closed over it.

Jeep scampered back to the kitchen in a rush, her footfalls reverberating on the old wooden floors. She preferred a landline to her cell since reception was spotty in Red Rock Valley. Wings Ranch sat in one of those spots.

From the kitchen's wall phone, Jeep called the Sheriff's Department.

"Lisa."

"Yes, Miss Reed."

"Get me Pete." Everyone knew Jeep. Everyone would take her call.

Mags listened intently, transfixed by the abrupt change — Aunt Jeep was suddenly a WASP, Women Airforce Service Pilot.

Lisa patched her through. Pete's deep voice came over the receiver.

"Pete, there's been an explosion, saw black smoke. I think it's the pump just north of here off Red Rock Road."

He inhaled sharply. "Smart of them. This storm will cost us time. Too much time."

"Bastards!"

28

CHAPTER TWO

"Jesus Christ." Lonnie Parrish grabbed the handle above the passenger door of the SUV squad car.

"You'd rather have Him driving the car?" Deputy Peter Meadows quipped to his partner.

"Well, I've seen you do some incredible things, but you ain't yet walked on water."

"Yet."

Red Rock Road bore evidence of the sudden fury of the blizzard. The hard surface was slick as a cue ball — same color, too. A number of two-wheel-drive cars had slid off the road while the four-wheel ones crept along. Seeing the cops' flashing lights behind them, drivers did their best to get over to the side. Sometimes a shoulder gave them room. No one particularly wanted to drop a wheel off the paved road, but the siren's squeal would send any driver's heartbeat skyward.

Fortunately, traffic was light. The only

times Red Rock Road jammed was when those folks who worked in Reno commuted the eleven miles back and forth. The eleven miles began at the southern tip of Red Rock Valley where the road connected with the Interstate. As it was two-thirty in the afternoon, Pete hoped people had paid attention to the Weather Channel and left work early or had the sense to stay in town. Born and bred in Red Rock and a graduate of Hug High School in 1993, he'd attended the University of Nevada at Reno. His alma mater had provided him with a good education. Sports media tend to focus on UNLV, but as far as Pete was concerned, Las Vegas wasn't really Nevada so his school was the best in the state.

He figured they'd be working all day and probably through the night, too. Law enforcement jobs should have regular hours, but anyone in it knows better. When the snow hits the fan, you stay on duty whether it's your shift or not, if for no other reason than that your replacement may not be able to get in to work.

Many of the officers in the Washoe County Sheriff's Department had grown up here. They cared. Women, Hispanics, Basques, and gays wore the uniform. In the beginning, this was a jolt to the locals. Pete was too young to have been part of the fights to hire minorities. Sure, he'd grown up with prejudices, but not enough to impede his work. When you crouched behind your squad car and a meth-crazed lunatic was firing your way with an Uzi, any minor reservations you might harbor about the man or woman working next to you vanished. That didn't mean a politically incorrect epithet wouldn't now and then fall from his chiseled lips.

A tight curve around a frozen pond caused the SUV to skid slightly. Huddled below, backs to the wind, some heavy-coated Angus looked as comfortable as could be under the circumstances.

Pete checked his speedometer and took his foot off the accelerator. The long red needle dropped back to twenty.

Passing ranch driveways through the snow, he glimpsed bundled-up folks firing up tractors or duallys with plow blades. First they'd work their driveway, then they'd help neighbors or folks who had skidded off the road. None of this was formally organized. With cellphones, anyone severely injured had a chance to get help as fast as possible given conditions. The flipped vehicles were the ones to worry about.

Lonnie noticed the dipping right turn onto

Dry Valley Road. "Four more miles."

"With all this snow, won't be any tracks," Pete complained.

Upon receiving Jeep Reed's call, Pete phoned Silver State Resource Management. If the explosion had damaged their equipment, they'd have a hell of a time doing repair work in these conditions. Pete said he'd call them back if this was the case.

Twenty minutes later they turned left onto the snow-slick road to the pumping station. Up the grade, Pete kept a steady speed, ten miles per hour. A burst of speed would send them skidding down a sharp grade on either side. At the top of the service road, they pulled into an area large enough for service trucks. Pete turned the vehicle around to nose out.

Both officers pulled on their gloves and flipped up their jacket collars.

Smoke from the blown-up Pump 19 rose slightly, then dropped back down, pushed by the low pressure. The pump resembled a metal flower, petals outstretched and sharp. The pipe itself, twelve inches in diameter, hadn't been damaged. Bits of light blue metal could still be seen in the nearby snow. Potable water went out in blue pipes. Reclaimed water flowed through purple pipes.

An impromptu fountain shot upward from

the bottom of the pump, ice already forming at the edges of the water on the ground. A sheet of ice would soon surround the pump.

Standing at the edge of the growing puddle, Lonnie looked down. "Shit."

Neither man was a demolition expert but each had a basic knowledge of homemade bombs, starting with a Molotov cocktail and working up to more sophisticated devices.

Because of the small gusher, Pete couldn't see down into the remains of the machinery.

"Call Silver State and tell 'em it's Pump Nineteen. Find out how far away the nearest repair crew is and when they think they'll get here. If it's within the hour, we'll wait. I'd like to see if we can figure out the explosive device used."

"Silver State will hire its own investigators." Lonnie spoke as he headed back to the SUV.

"That's what I'm afraid of. Make the damned call."

Within minutes, Lonnie was back at the fountain. "Half hour. Big rig. New pump. Looks like Silver State was prepared."

Pete grunted and directed Lonnie to circle to the right of the damage. He'd go around to the left. Both men knew enough not to lose sight of the other. In storms like this, people could get disoriented, even lost, six feet away from a barn door and safety. That meant freezing to death.

Every few paces, Pete scuffed the snow with his right shoe. A scrap of wet paper caught his eye. Kneeling, he nudged it with his gloved forefinger, then picked it up. The ink — ballpoint — was running. He could make out "mil" then below it "butt."

He glanced up and spotted Lonnie through shifting veils of snow. Lonnie looked his way and waved.

Pete smiled. The kid was twenty-five. He showed natural ability for police work, but was still naïve about how the world really works.

Pete walked another ten paces and saw a red bit of cloth against the snow. He picked it up from the frozen ground. Just a red piece of cloth, ripstop.

"Hey, let's go back," Pete called out.

The two met back at the pump. Pete motioned toward the car. They gratefully crawled in, unzipped their heavy coats, and pulled off their gloves. Pete laid his two tiny finds on the center console.

Lonnie added a piece of paper he'd found. It matched Pete's fragment. This ragged bit, fuzzed-up blue ink like Pete's, bore the printed letters, "br."

"A shopping list?" The young man

shrugged.

"Looks like it. Might be nothing. Then again."

Hearing a deep diesel roar, they both looked up simultaneously into the rearview mirror.

"They must have been close by. Let me talk to these guys."

"Always do."

"Yeah, but while I'm talking you study them. Pay special attention when we go over to the pump."

"Okay."

It took the huge truck pulling a short flatbed trailer another five minutes to make it up the hill. Chained on top of the flatbed was a replacement pump.

Behind the rig lumbered a bulldozer, Jake Tanner at the controls, no warm cab to help him, either. The rotund Jake owned a nice spread two miles north of the pumpsite.

Gloves back on, jacket zipped up, Pete stepped out of the car. The rig driver knew his business, swinging the trailer around so the new pump was close to the damaged one.

Goggles on, Jake chugged up behind him, the big bulldozer tracks caked with snow, leaving compressed shards of it in his wake. He left the dozer running as he climbed down, freeing his long beard from his coat collar. "Officer Pete, Christ on a crutch."

"Well, it's not good." Pete smiled.

You couldn't help but like the ebullient, ever-curious Jake, even if he did go three months between haircuts and beard trims.

Two men stepped down from the high trailer rig as yet another SUV climbed the hill. When the Silver State employees spied their boss's Chevy Blazer, the company's silver wave graphic on the side, neither smiled.

Twinkie Bosun, plastic straw clenched between his teeth, was the rig driver. He and Bunny Matthews, his sidekick, lived just outside Reno. While they weren't Red Rock residents, because they serviced and repaired Silver State pumps hither and yon many people recognized them.

Many also knew Oliver Hitchens, earmuffs on, "Silver State" embroidered parka, big boots, as he stepped from the Tahoe — a company vehicle and a good choice for the off-roading he sometimes had to do.

"Prick." Twinkie whispered with a smile.

The other men standing nearby smiled.

Pete stretched out his gloved hand. "Mr. Hitchens. Glad you're here."

Looking at the fountain, Oliver gave the deputy a perfunctory handshake, then slipped and slid up to the pump.

"Bunny, don't stand there like the useless asshole you are. Cut the water," Oliver barked.

Dutifully, Bunny jumped down into the recessed area and wrenched the pump wheel, which was parallel to the ground. It, too, was painted light blue.

"Frozen." Now soaked himself, he shouted above the gushing water.

Oliver motioned for Twinkie to lower himself down. Grunting with effort, the two men finally shut off the line.

Pete could clearly see a three-inch piece of one-inch-diameter pipe. Pipe bomb, he thought, saying nothing, but with his gaze he directed Bunny's eyes to it. Pete looked away as Oliver fast approached the pump now that the water was turned off. Oliver hadn't wanted to get wet. Bending over, Bunny shook as though to shed the water, but he scooped up the metal fragment and slipped it into his pocket. Twinkie, seeing this, engaged Oliver.

"Won't take us too long to unscrew these plates if you've got a little propane torch, you know, a small one. Everything's frozen, Mr. Hitchens. First job is to unfreeze them."

"I'm not in the habit of carrying torches." Oliver sniffed.

Twinkie knew that, and said with relish,

37

"Then you and Bunny will have to hold the big tank steady on the rig while I melt the ice."

Bunny smiled beatifically as unhappiness spread across Oliver's features.

Pete, also savoring the moment, spoke. "A lot of people will thank you fellows. I'm one of them."

Oliver's lips twitched, a remnant of his grimace.

As Pete made his way back to the police vehicle, Bunny followed. He looked over his shoulder to see Oliver struggling to get back up on the flatbed. With a wink, Bunny slipped Pete the pipe.

Jake yelled in the background, "Twinkie, I'm parking my fat ass in your cab until you need me."

"Yeah, yeah." Twinkie yelled back over the wind and the rumble of the bulldozer, which Jake wisely had not turned off.

The way back down proved more treacherous than the way up, but four-wheel-drive is worth the money. At the slope's bottom, Pete headed south down Red Rock Road. Keeping one hand on the wheel, Pete dug in his pocket and pulled out the pipe piece. He put it on the dash with the two shreds of paper and the triangular scrap of red ripstop.

"And what did you see?" asked Pete.

Lonnie leaned forward, peering through the windshield into a whiteout. "The same old, same old. Oliver Hitchens can fart through his mouth. Twinkie and Bunny want to get the job done. Jake — you know, I don't know exactly why Jake showed up. Reckon someone from Silver State called him because they figured they couldn't get another piece of equipment up here fast enough to lift off the pump. Given subsequent water loss and the storm, they might not have made it up there. Pump's not really that big. Jake can do it."

"Look in the pipe. Is it rusted or corroded?"

Lonnie picked up the cold one-inch pipe and held it up toward the road in front of him like a spyglass. "Clean."

"Hmm."

"It's amazing what damage a lead pipe bomb can do," Lonnie noted.

Pete nodded in acknowledgment. "Three ninety-five will be a nightmare."

On one side of the four-lane highway was Washoe County, Nevada. On the other side was California. The Peterson Mountains were the true geographic barrier with less than a mile to the California state line.

"Maybe the state will shut it down."

"Not until an eighteen-wheeler rolls over."

Pete snorted.

"Right." Lonnie shifted. "Did you expect this would happen to Silver State?"

"Sooner or later. If you remember your classes from school, the history of the West is the story of water."

"I remember. That and the Comstock Lode. God, all my history professor ever talked about was the Comstock." Lonnie flopped back into his seat.

"Here's the thing, pardner. Someone blew up a pump. Someone cunning enough to pick a perfectly rotten day for cover. A great many people without water will be inconvenienced. Right now, Silver State's phones are ringing, people are wanting information, some are irate, some will ask for a portion of their bill to be waived. If Twinkie and Bunny can fit up the new pump in this weather, with not much light, it might be five hours before they have water. Could have been a day or two if they hadn't responded as fast as they did, so let's give Silver State credit. So who benefits from this sabotage?"

"Whoever wants to scare people about water."

"Yeah, and maybe even a few more folks will shake loose their water rights. A few ranchers outside of Las Vegas were paid seven point nine million dollars for their water rights. It's happening here, too. Maybe the prices being paid aren't as high, but Reno is greedy for water. Blowing up a pump, cutting off water, that sure underscores the issue."

"Better someone blew up Oliver Hitchens."

Pete laughed as he slowed for a nasty curve, a huge sheet of snow sliding down the east side of the Peterson Mountains as though aiming straight for him. "Someone thinks they will benefit from this."

Just at that moment, passing them in the opposite direction was an SUV driven by Craig Locke, another Silver State employee, the man responsible for securing water rights. Pete saw the vehicle but couldn't make out the driver since the snow required him to keep his eyes on the road.

"Maybe it's a politician," Lonnie said. "You know, someone who creates a big problem so he can solve it, then look like a hero."

"You know, Squirt, I'm starting to think you're growing up. That's a possibility. Silver State is no doubt greasing some palms; that's the great American way."

"Or how about a nutcase who's so pissed off at the fat cats he vandalizes corporate property to let off steam?"

"There's been speculation that the

drought, which finally seems to be ending after five long years, was a conspiracy to limit the water supply. I don't know about that, but there is a logic to cutting off water for three hours a day during a shortage. Scare people while preaching about the shortage as environmental conservation."

Lonnie hadn't thought of that. "Oh."

"One thing I promise you, Lonnie — well, two things — this is the beginning of a water war. And Jeep Reed is right: They're bastards."

"You forgot something."

"What?"

"We're right in the middle of it."

CHAPTER THREE

Three weeks before Pump 19 blew, the newspaper carried a small squib announcing that Horseshoe Estates was finally approved by the Regional Planning Board.

It was to be an upscale development with a thousand homes. The developer, Wade Properties, Ltd., had undergone an arduous process involving lawyers, hydrographers, and surveyors, as well as expensive studies on traffic and the project's wildlife impact. The planning board was duly impressed with the thoroughness of Wade Properties, Ltd.

The developer had learned from observing the Matera Ridge project, which failed to gain approval in 2009. When the county initially approved zoning for 632 homes in Steamboat Hills without requiring the developer to disclose his source of water, residents along Mount Rose Highway protested loudly and effectively. Approval was then withdrawn.

Wade Properties had demonstrated to the board's satisfaction that there was sufficient water available for the homes in Horseshoe Estates. Silver State Resource Management, the firm selected to supply that water, produced compelling evidence. The president of SSRM, Darryl Johnson, provided proof they had acquired the necessary water rights, plus they could renew the water supply with new methods for capturing runoff from what little rain there was, as well as tapping into the snowcaps. This latter contingency plan was attacked as specious by two conservation groups, Washoe Water Rights and Friends of Sierra County, but SSRM still carried the day. Not only had its red-headed president given a presentation, so had Craig Locke, Director of Acquisitions. Also present at the board meeting were Oliver Hitchens and Elizabeth McCormick, although Oliver and Liz did not testify.

Bitterly disappointed at what they felt were skewed facts, the two conservation groups stormed out of the meeting. They'd lost this fight but vowed to lose no more. Their joint press release to the media was ignored by the local papers as were most of the zoning proceedings.

The only part of their statement that was

printed: "If only there were more Jeep Reeds." SSRM countered this with, "While we greatly respect Miss Reed's business acumen and charitable activities, we think she is mistaken in her quest to control usage of water underneath Red Rock Valley."

Since the late 1950s, Jeep had been buying up or optioning water rights in the Valley. Often she paid an annual rent with an option to buy. Her fear was that the aquifer underneath Red Rock Valley would be diverted to Reno and thereby harm cattlemen and ranchers, of which she was one.

Her statements over the years, always brief, focused on sustainable growth and preserving the precious resources of Washoe County.

She had not been asked to comment on the Horseshoe Estates zoning approval.

As it happened, there appeared to be little interest in Wade Properties' victory because the news was dominated by the economic collapse of Nevada's glamorous neighbor, California. Of all the stories in the news, this one certainly concerned Nevada residents the most. They knew they'd be dealing with the fallout.

In fact, Wade Properties' zoning approval went unmentioned on all the local TV broadcasts.

CHAPTER FOUR

The first weekend in December, a massive blizzard blanketed not just Nevada but much of the western half of the country. The eastern edge of this weather monster snowed on Denver as its western edge dumped on Reno. Airports shut down; roadways were deserted. Schools and churches, supermarkets and banks, all closed. Hospitals did what they could, but the best hope for anyone suffering a heart attack was prayer. Ambulances couldn't negotiate roads any better than other vehicles. The storm was so severe that the plows just couldn't keep up with the snowfall. The mile-long drive up to Jeep's house remained buried under two and a half feet of snow. Enrique left the back doors of the stable and sheds open so the horses and cattle could come and go as they pleased. At night he closed the horses in, for the temperatures dropped below zero out in the valley. The cattle, with heavier coats and more fat, could come and go at will.

Basques are tough people. Salaberry is a Basque name. Enrique Salaberry displayed the clean-cut features and the taut small body characteristic of the tough Basque people. Basques played jai alai, a game for lightning reflexes, better than any other people in the world. The Basques — small-statured men who were light on their feet and had incredible hand–eye coordination — dazzled in those few places like south Florida where jai alai was played. Take your eyes off the goatskin ball hurtling at you at 180 mph and you could die. A few players had.

Jeep assumed Enrique's grandparents' generation had fled Spain's tyrannical dictator, Franco. Century after century, Basque hopes for independence were tabled or brutally crushed. The Spanish Civil War and its aftermath, much of it still buried in Spanish and Basque hearts today, pulverized any hopes of self-governance.

Enrique, however, cared little about his genetic heritage. This is hardly uncommon even among those who live in their genetic culture. His world was Jeep's world. She and Dorothy "Dot" Jocham, her deceased partner, were the only parents he had known. Enrique was a Nevada cowboy through and through — with exceptional building and

47

mechanical skills. The ferocious storm was testing them.

The path between his house and the stables was packed-down snow. He'd shoveled it twice already but the continued snowfall convinced him this was futile. So he fired up the 500hp ATV and ran back and forth over the path, packing it down. Then he did the same for a walkway between his house and the main house, another to the cattle sheds, and yet another to the first barn built on the ranch, the one undergoing reconstruction.

Power stayed on. A godsend.

Stock came first. Throwing hay, checking water troughs, and chopping ice consumed the dark day. Low, dark clouds made it feel like six o'clock in the evening. Winter made every moment of light precious, each day another minute lost until the solstice in two weeks.

He walked into the property's original barn, snow still falling. A huge gas tank fueled a heat unit that looked like an open-ended torpedo. The open end flickered red, blue, and white with the gas flame. The flame roared — you couldn't hear yourself think — but it warmed a large area.

"Shit!" Enrique exclaimed as he pushed open the doors so he could get in the ATV.

One of the workers on Jeep's barn restoration had left the heat unit on. Its gas tank was enormous so it kept going. The other farmhands, all trapped in their houses off Wings Ranch, probably wouldn't get to work for a good two days. Enrique figured it would be at least that long before Red Rock Road, then Dry Valley Road, and finally Dixie Lane would be plowed.

Still cursing, he walked over to cut off the unit, stopped, and looked down at his feet. The ground was unfrozen around the heater. That part of the aisle and the back end of a former stall near the gas looked relatively workable. He and the boys had been digging out the stalls and center aisle. They wanted to go down three feet to lay eight-inch-diameter ceramic drainage pipes. Jeep's intent was to restore the exterior of the stable to its pristine form, as well as re-create the interior as it would have looked in the 1880s, with beautiful brass fittings. However, the barn would still be modern and functional in terms of drainage, plumbing, electricity, and footing. Drainage pipes would run under each stall. Each stall would have a pipe on a downward grade to the center aisle. Two large drains in the aisle and a large underground ceramic pipe running the length of the barn would carry waste to a septic tank. The manure would be handled as it had been since before Xenophon, by picking out the stalls.

He plucked a spade hanging on a hook on the wall. Tools hung neatly in a row. This would be changed later when they'd hang in a small storage room off the aisle. People or horses could back into tools not tucked safely away. At this stage of construction there was only the metal sheet exterior covering the original clapboard, which were planks hauled by rail from California, offloaded at Reno Junction, then carried here by mule wagons. To have a clapboard barn screamed filthy rich. The Ford brothers put their money in the front window. Jeep, rich herself, proved more circumspect. Her argument was that Wings Ranch should be what it was in the beginning. Nevada was owed its heritage.

Enrique nudged the soil with the spade tip. The stall had already been dug down two feet. The soil gave way easily. He pulled off his old blanket-lined jacket and started digging. There wasn't much else he could do. The stock would come in the other barns at nightfall. In these conditions, animals could tell better than the humans when it truly was night. He'd have to run over the paths with the ATV again but that was it. Like Jeep, Enrique couldn't tolerate being idle. He also hated being indoors, regardless of the weather.

"Might as well get one stall down to three feet," he thought, tapping the unfrozen part of the center aisle.

If he dug out this stall, he'd have a better idea of how difficult it would be to lay the pipe. These things always sounded easy in conversation or drawn on paper, but then you got into it.

In ten minutes he'd worked up a good sweat. Thirty more and he'd reached a foot down into what would be the front end of the stall. He moved carefully, piling up the sand and small stones mixed in with orovado soil. He turned around to make sure he wasn't too close to the blazing heater. Its loud whoosh and roar irritated him.

As he finished the next section, he started to jam down into the dirt with the spade point, but stopped midair. Laying down the spade he knelt to look closer at something in the hole. He wasn't sure what he was seeing. A tiny LED light hung on the ATV key chain. He ran to the other end of the barn to get it.

The subzero fluorescent overhead lights had allowed him to work, but now he needed something brighter. Plucking the key out, he ran back, knelt down, his face close to the sandy loam. He pressed the button — the breast of buxom woman — on the key fob Carlotta had bought him. The tiny white light shone on a piece of bone.

Enrique had seen plenty of cattle, sheep, horse, and coyote bones. This was human, he was certain. Slipping the fob in his pocket, he dug some more, very carefully. An arm revealed itself, then part of a rib cage, and finally, a hand wearing a tarnished silver ring, which was black against the bony white third digit, and gave an eerie contrast.

He jammed the spade into the dirt right outside the stall. He opened the wide old doors enough to get the ATV out. Firing up the bright red Honda, he sped to the main house.

"Mom!"

In the cozy living room with Jeep, Mags, and the dogs, Carlotta looked up quickly.

Jeep, too.

They heard the urgency in his voice.

"Living room," Jeep called.

He knocked the snow off his feet in the kitchen, leaving two white clumps incised with his boot tread.

Carlotta rose. "What is it?"

But Enrique was looking at Jeep. He said, "Mom, can you get your gear on? I'll drive you to the barn."

She didn't question him. Jeep rarely wasted time like that. She'd find out when she got there. Perhaps this as much as anything else distinguished her from those under fifty who existed in a constant information/conversation swirl, whose continual observations on whatever it was they were seeing or hearing were not necessarily based on reality.

"Honey, you stay here," Enrique ordered his wife. He looked at Mags. "Walk behind us. Take your mind off Wall Street."

Mags, who regarded Enrique as an uncle, took her cue from her great-aunt and kept her mouth shut. The two women quickly bundled up as Enrique grabbed a large nine-volt flashlight from the pantry. Carlotta followed, her eyes full of questions.

"I'll tell you later. It's nothing to worry about." He hoped this was true.

Once outside, the cold hit Jeep and Mags in their faces. Bitter, bitter cold. Whoever said dry cold wasn't as bad as moist cold, East Coast cold, was a barefaced liar.

On the ATV, Jeep wrapped her arms around Enrique's waist as he put it in gear. In a pair of old mukluks Carlotta had unearthed, Mags trotted down the path behind them. King followed her and Baxter followed King, not at all happy with the view.

Given how slick the packed-down snow was, Enrique kept the ATV in second gear.

King stopped a moment to relieve himself along the side of the path.

Baxter observed, then drily said, *"Where's the hydrant?"*

While that made King chortle, it didn't mean he was going to like the fuzzy sausage.

Once at the barn, Enrique dismounted, but Mags reached the double doors first, and with effort, swung one out. He rolled the ATV in and cut its motor. After the dogs scooted inside, Mags closed the door behind them.

Jeep followed.

"Look. Look at this!"

The two dogs sniffed first.

"Nothing worth chewing." King pronounced his judgment.

"I've never smelled bones this old," Baxter said.

"You've never smelled real bones. Bet all you've chewed on is moccasins and Milk-Bones," King sarcastically replied.

"Pissant," Baxter half snarled.

King stood over him, his ruff raised.

Jeep sharply cut through their bull. "Enough!" She knelt down herself and ordered Mags. "Hand me the torch."

Mags did as she was told.

Enrique knelt down next to Jeep. She carefully shined the yellowish light over the exposed part of the skeleton.

"It's human all right. We won't know if it's a man or a woman until we get to the pelvis." Jeep half whispered.

"Shouldn't you call the sheriff?" Mags wondered, standing at the end of the stall.

"In this weather? No. Furthermore, this person has been here a long, long time."

"Maybe the barn was built over a small burial ground." Mags thought out loud.

"Not a chance." Jeep shook her head, deep in thought.

"What about Paiutes?" Mags said. "I mean, we aren't far from an old Indian site and maybe where Fort Sage once was."

Enrique, realizing Jeep's tolerance was fading as her fascination increased, gently said, "Mags, no one has ever found Fort Sage. It's supposed to be west of here. And I don't think the Paiute laid out their dead like this."

She was only trying to be helpful, but it reminded Mags that her great-aunt didn't welcome interruption or personal opinion when riveted by a problem or political exchange.

The blackened ring caught Jeep's eye as it had drawn Enrique's. She handed the flashlight to her son. He held it steady. Mags and the dogs watched intently. Jeep slid off the ring — the distal and middle phalanxes came off with it, but did not disintegrate. She replaced the finger bones.

Jeep looked down before studying the ring. "Good heavy bones, whoever this is — was." She rolled the ring around between her thumb and forefinger. "Silver, a silver horseshoe with the Star of Guard on it. Enrique, got a hankie, anything?"

He reached into his breast coat pocket and pulled out a sullied handkerchief. She spit on it and vigorously rubbed the inside of the ring. A faint glow of interior gold rewarded her. She put the ring almost to her eyeball.

"Yes!"

Mags, driven to distraction, asked, "Yes, what?"

Jeep stood up and Mags helped her out of the three-foot-deep area. "Let's go back to the house and I'll show you. When the storm's over I'll get Pete out here. In the meantime, we've got work to do."

"What kind of work?" Mags's green eyes questioned her great-aunt.

"Tomorrow after the chores, the three of us are going to free what remains of this body from its prison. Now come on."

Back in the house's kitchen, Jeep handed Carlotta the ring and asked her to shine it up. By the time Jeep and Mags had peeled off their layers, Carlotta had already restored the ring, quite a unique one.

Enrique, coat off, gloves off, boots off, dropped to a chair at the big table. All that digging was fatiguing.

Jeep sat at the head, her son on the right, her great-niece on the left of the table. "This is from the Nicholas School of Cavalry, an elite school in Czarist Russia founded by Czar Nicholas I in 1823. It was quartered in St. Petersburg, a fabulous place to be as a young fellow."

"Mom, how do you know this?" Enrique asked.

Sitting next to her husband, Carlotta leaned forward, as eager for the report as the other two.

"I've seen this distinctive ring twice before. The first time was during the war when I found myself with an old, beautifully mannered Soviet colonel. I'd flown a plane to our base in Montana. He always kept on his gloves except once, inside the base's makeshift bar, he took them off. That's when I noticed his ring." She paused. "Sometimes the Russians would come to Montana to pick up planes. They were our allies. Given that he was a colonel, I knew he was here for more than a plane. You knew never to ask."

Mags, a good student of history, held out her palm. Jeep dropped the ring into it. "But Aunt Jeep, if this is the ring of an elite Russian school, wouldn't the Soviet colonel have hidden it? I mean, the royals and aristocrats were killed after the Russian Revolution."

"Most were, but a few threw in their lot with the Reds or possessed such critical skills even Lenin and his bizarre henchman, Trotsky, didn't dare wipe them out."

"I thought Trotsky was a good guy." Mags, who'd read Isaac Deutscher, frowned.

"None of them were good guys. You don't kill millions and come out as good guys no matter how well you write."

"Point taken." Mags hadn't thought of it that way. "The ring is lined with gold."

"Yes. That, too, reflects the ethos of the aristocrats at their best: Hide what is most dear. And to a graduate of this rigorous school, the gold represents one's heart. Nobility, not of birth, but of spirit. Inscribed in Russian is 'Soldier, coronet, and general were eternal friends. 1887.' I can read a little Russian. The colonel I met was Timofev Nilov. Like all the graduates, he was proud of the Nicholas School. It was an even stronger pride than West Pointers have, I think."

Enrique studied the ring. "It's a very simple design."

"So, it was a man?" Carlotta chimed in.

"Couldn't he have given it to a lover, his wife, a daughter?" Mags inquired.

"Highly unlikely." Jeep drummed her fingertips on the table. "Many graduates were buried with their ring or it was kept as a family treasure, but you only wore it if you earned it. The last czar himself could not wear this ring since he had not graduated from the school. Some grand dukes had. And, of course, there were other elite cavalry schools, but the Nicholas School was the oldest — divided into those who would become Cossack units and those who would become light cavalry, like Hussars. I can tell you two things about our skeleton. One, he was likely one hell of a horseman. Two, he had courage, possibly great courage."

"What in God's name is he doing in your barn?" Mags asked.

"Wasn't my barn when he was laid in it. Was the Ford brothers' barn. He could even have been buried before the barn was built, though I doubt it. I don't know why, but I doubt it." Jeep turned to Enrique. "If we can carefully exhume him, we may find out how he died. Dollars to donuts, his was not a natural death."

Mags eyes widened. "And why not?"

Jeep took back the ring and slipped it onto the third finger of her left hand. "Odd. It fits perfectly." She took it off. "I don't have the right to wear it." Then she suddenly slipped it back on. "But I will."

The Star of Guard stood out on the flattened silver nailhead. Jeep felt as she had felt before flying a mission: a sharp current of excitement, laced with an undertow of joy. Once she and her copilot were strapped in, if flying a big bomber to its last stateside destination, once she cranked the great engines, she always turned to Laura and said, "Tits to the wind."

CHAPTER FIVE

They started at six in the morning on December 8, the birthday of Mary, Queen of Scots in 1542. Jeep kept a calendar in her head of such events. Enrique and Mags finally exposed the entire skeleton by one that afternoon. While it remained embedded in the soil, the entire human figure could be clearly seen. Jeep feared if they tried to pry him loose, they might destroy the bones or damage something that could later provide a clue to his identity.

Carlotta helped by feeding the cattle, chopping ice, and checking and feeding the horses.

Jeep, her beloved Hasselblad in hand, took careful photographs. She had learned about photography while in the service, though she'd been so poor upon discharge she couldn't exactly afford it as a hobby. Many of the WASPs, when mustered out, had to pay for their own bus tickets home. That ticket from Texas to Nevada had depleted her little nest egg. Still, she had built her own darkroom to help with costs, taking great pleasure in snapping what she called "Nevada-scapes" — especially from the air. She flew an old World War I Curtiss JN-6H, called "the Jenny" — a plane she shared with Danny Marks, another young World War II vet. You might even say it was because of this hobby that she made her fortune. It had been her day to crop dust over Lassen County, California, a far more fertile area than around Reno. That day in 1949, Jeep had just enough fuel left to indulge herself and laze over the Kumina Peak area. A seam of land caught her attention.

Later, the large two-inch images taken by the Hasselblad further intrigued her. She drove to the desolate area in her old truck, along the way every filling in her teeth rattling. She then pinpointed what she had seen from the air. Even more barren than the usual high desert acreage, the land was privately owned. Quietly, not even telling her folks — still alive and hardworking back then — she investigated. An elderly widow, living in Sacramento, owned five thousand acres. The adjoining pieces were also privately owned. One by one, Jeep tracked down the owners of these properties. Ultimately she pieced together ten thousand acres of what was considered pure trash. Without a cent of her own, but enormous drive — the same drive that sent her into rolling thunder in the skies — she pushed onward. She sold the old truck, sold anything she could, except her one-eared dog, a many-times grandmother of King. No one would have wanted Daisy anyway. She borrowed from friends who had a bit put away, making them wealthy, too. Not that anyone knew that then. Jeep never forgot a favor nor forgave an insult.

Not one of the owners wanted to hold on to their land. When she offered a modest sum, in one case offering only to pay back taxes, Jeep became the proud owner of what most folks would have considered nothing. Even Danny, who knew her well and loved her, was shocked when she showed him her recently acquired land deeds. He shook his head in wonderment that such a smart woman could be so dumb.

The land — now called the Reed tract — contained a deep vein of gold with many off-shoots, some of which contained silver. As methods of harvesting had improved by the 1950s and continue to improve, the find was monumental. That was only the beginning of her fortune, but it gave notice that Magdalene Reed was ready to take more than physical risks. Funny, though, how some people think. Jeep, ignorant about mineral extraction, studied and made a deal with a mining company. She owned the land and took thirty percent of the profits. The mining company paid an annual rent. Once operations began, it took two and a half years for profits to materialize. Jeep was often discounted because she was young, quite pretty, and feminine. Rather than become overtly angry at this treatment, she used it to her advantage. Over the decades she got even with those who'd insulted her. Conventional thinkers can usually be defeated by unconventional thinkers. Jeep was unconventional.

She piled Pelion on Parnassus. Once she had money, she founded, with Danny, a salvage company called Marks and Reed. She graciously put Danny's name first. He put up sweat equity. Marks and Reed dismantled defunct mining sites, tore down wooden buildings — dismantled anything useful. Then they bought a few acres near Reno, Carson City, Virginia City, and Elko. People flocked to the salvage yards for below-cost, good materials. A recession followed the war. Everyone was looking for a bargain. By 1955, double-digit millions in profit showed on the books of Marks and Reed.

In Nevada people began to say, "The Reed touch" instead of "The Midas touch." By 1960, no one thought to discount the slender, still very attractive Jeep born in 1924. Most people liked her. Those who didn't were generally those who had been stupid enough to belittle her way back when. And people being loyal to their own tragedies, bewailing of their fate — a fate they created but would never accept responsibility for — became part of the family jewels, so to speak. Every one of the Filberts, Isadores, and Larsons hated her. At least now they had sense enough to fear her. Good thing.

The war taught Jeep Reed that anyone who acts like an enemy is an enemy. Kill the enemy. That's the job of a soldier, sailor, airman, marine. Remove the threat to your people. That kind of thinking is now considered antiquated, but Jeep still believed it. She wouldn't kill her enemies physically but she crushed them otherwise.

Peering down at the skeleton before her, she thought, *This man had been someone's enemy.* Three ribs on the left side bore distinct, smooth, deep incisions. He'd been stabbed twice by someone powerful. The deceased had heavy bones, was around five foot ten inches tall, and symmetrical in form with large good teeth.

He lay faceup.

"Must have had a killer smile." Jeep steadied the camera box with both hands, focusing on his skull.

"If he graduated in 1887, he would have been what, twenty-one or twenty-two at graduation?" Mags, like Jeep, was falling under the spell of this long-dead man.

"Somewhere around that. To make it easy, let's say twenty." Jeep placed the camera on the broad, cold seat of the ATV parked next to the grave. "He was probably in his thirties, at the most early forties, when he met his Maker. His teeth are all there. Given the time in which he lived, most people lost a few or all by the time they reached middle age."

"Here's the thing." Mags looked down, then at the surrounding earth where the other stalls once stood. "When a body decays, it blows up full of gas. He was only three feet down. Why didn't the earth swell up? And dogs would smell him down there. We can't, of course."

King, laying near the heater, raised his head. *"She's not so dumb."*

"I trained her." Baxter barked on the other side of the heater.

In his four years of life, King had somewhat gotten to known Mags on her visits,

67

which were usually just long weekends. He liked her just fine but he figured she was like most of her species: limited senses, limited sense, and appallingly self-centered.

From down below in the hole, Enrique considered Mags's point. "Well, the horse, shod, moving around in the stall, that would keep tamping the earth down. That's the only thing I can think of."

Jeep knelt at the edge of the grave for another shot. "The boys should be back to work tomorrow. Roads have to be a little better now that the storm's passed. I'll call Pete. I imagine at this point we'll be low on his to-do list, but that's fine with me."

"Wouldn't be fine if it was a crisis." Mags teased her.

"Then I'd be number one." Jeep smiled back.

"Whoever killed this guy laid him out with respect." Enrique stepped up and out with a hand up from Mags. "He wasn't dumped facedown or rolled onto his side. He was laid flat, faceup, legs straightened and arms by his side. Respect."

"Curious." Jeep sighed.

Mags studied her old great-aunt for a long moment. "You've seen so much death. Isn't this just one more body?"

Enrique looked at his mother. He'd never

really thought of that.

"You get used to death as you age. Doesn't mean I like saying goodbye, but I've learned to celebrate the lives of the departed. Do the same for me when my time comes."

"Mom, don't say that." King loved his human.

"I guess we should enjoy the interludes between goodbyes," Mags said.

"They seem fewer and farther between as you get older, but grab what you can, Babycakes." Jeep looked at these two people whom she loved beyond measure, even when saddened by them at times. "Here I am, about two years older than dirt and I can't tell you why but I feel young; I feel this incredible rush." She looked down at the skeleton. "He speaks to me. I must find out who he is."

"What does he say?" Enrique felt a pull, but not as strong as Jeep's.

"Find my killer."

"Well, his killer is long dead, too." Mags stated the obvious.

"That doesn't mean I can't find him."

Baxter whispered loud enough so King could hear. *"More old bones."*

King couldn't help it. He laughed.

CHAPTER SIX

That same evening, the icy roads of downtown Reno could be negotiated if a driver rolled along slowly. Fourth Street, seedy but not without edgy energy, was denuded of pedestrians as was all of Reno. The topless bar called Jugs, however, did entertain some patrons.

Teton Benson lived in a sparse apartment walk-up next door to Jugs. The doorway to both the apartment building and the bar was recessed. Neither landlord wasted money on good lighting — an advantage for the bar; a disadvantage for the residents of the walk-up. Teton carried a small flashlight.

He knew most people on the block. He was friendly and good-looking in a worn-down fashion with his sandy hair, straight teeth, clean jeans and sweater. He sat at the bar.

Next to him, tenuously perched on a barstool, sat Egon Utrecht, towering above Teton at six foot four.

"Thought you'd be at work." Tets sipped a Coke.

"Bare bones crew. It's a good night to take off. And it gives Lisa" — he mentioned his assistant chef — "the chance to run the show without too much stress."

"She's good-looking." Tets smiled and nodded at one of the working girls, a triumph against gravity, as she teetered by on high heels.

She kissed him on the cheek. "Sweetheart."

As Teton never had money to lure the girls or buy more drinks, he knew Lark, her stage name, had purposefully sauntered by because she wanted an introduction to this prosperous-looking man.

"Lark, this is Egon Utrecht."

She squealed, "The famous chef!"

Egon nodded. "The same."

"Oh, my God, oh, my God, I can't believe you're here." She moved her most prominent feature closer to his chest.

"Teton and I know each other." Egon fished a twenty out of his pocket. "Next time I'm here, I'd like to know you better, but for now I need to talk to Tets."

Smart girl, she took the money, then ran her right hand suggestively up his forearm. "You're very generous. Thank you."

She left with Teton's eyes following her. "Lark's a good girl. This is a tough place to be."

"If the heating ever fails, it will be more than tough." Egon half smiled. "Thank you again for the business tip. I'd like to do more business. I'd like to meet your contact."

"Well, that I can't promise. It's up to him, but he's working on a new deal. It won't turn around as fast as the last one, but it will be big."

"I want in."

"I'll tell him." Teton's eyes again followed Lark, who apart from her Silicon protuberances, looked much more natural than the other girls.

"You made enough money. Buy her some earrings. Spend a little. She'll lay down for you," Egon urged.

"If I spend a little, everyone on Fourth Street will know. Not a good idea."

Egon considered this. "Good thinking. Hadn't thought of that." He then suggested, "But what if you gave her something for Christmas that wouldn't be a tipoff? You could tell the bartender and uh —"

"Lark."

"Tell Lark that you've been saving."

Teton smiled broadly. "Might work."

"Can you tell me anything about the

new project?"

"Only that it's north of Reno. I'll let you know when the time is right to buy in."

"Good." Egon checked his Panerai watch, its simple clean blackface contrasting with the steel bracelet.

Teton observed watches, rings, belt buckles, and boots — indicators of a man's willingness to spend bucks if he had them. This watch announced that Egon was not on food stamps nor did he run with the pack.

Teton asked, voice low, "You doing okay?"

"Yeah, sometimes the stress at work gets me. I'll drink champagne but I won't toot. One thing at a time. I miss the coke, don't get me wrong. I like the lift at about eleven at night but I'm sticking to my promise. Next year, I'll try to give up the drinking."

"I don't know if it will make us live even longer but it sure will seem longer." Teton laughed.

Egon laughed with him. "Yeah. What about you?"

"I'm okay. When I hear from my contact I'll let you know. I figured we could meet here tonight because no one is here really and my place is as cold as a witch's tit in a brass bra."

"Buy Lark some sparkly earrings. Warm you right up."

CHAPTER SEVEN

Reeking of the self-importance that made him so loathsome to others, Oliver Hitchens placed a thick report on the desk of George W. Ball, overlord of all equipment for Silver State Resource Management. George was called George W. to his face.

It usually provoked a tiny smile and much-used comeback: "I'm the Decider."

People working for utilities, waste management, or what Silver State termed "resource management" usually had to get to sites or the office, no matter what. In Silver State's case the resources being managed were water, water rights, and delivery of water to customers.

In a state where the average annual rainfall was seven inches, water was as valuable as Jeep's gold. Given the rush of immigrants from California, which is how locals thought of them, water was becoming an even more critical issue. Even without these people abandoning the disastrous state of California, the longtime residents of Washoe County already stressed the environment and services.

"Had a devil of a time." Oliver sat across from George W. without being asked. "The escaping water turned to ice, the big lug nuts were frozen stiff. Had to use a propane torch to just get the ice off while being careful not to melt any metal. I was filthy by the time it was over and as cold as I've ever been in my life."

George W. knew what Oliver was. Distasteful as he found Oliver's personality, and his penchant for taking credit for other people's work, he got the job done. He drove those under him mercilessly. He did not swell payroll and he was often right about just when to keep an old piece of equipment running and when to replace it. Oliver saved the company money. George W. also noted that Oliver made no mention of Craig Locke who, in the area at the time, had braved the weather to see if he could help. Oliver curtly dismissed him since he had no engineering expertise, instead of thanking him.

George couldn't help tweaking him. "Twinkie and Bunny weren't up to the job?"

Shifting in his seat. "Good as they are, they have to be managed."

Since Twinkie and Bunny had cellphones with cameras, they had taken the precaution of sending photos of themselves the minute Oliver drove away or, more accurately, slid down the hill so George W. could see them encased in ice. They sent on a photo of Jake, too, snow covered, as well as Craig Locke who was in the area and had stopped by to see if they needed anything, like a hot drink. Craig knew little about equipment repair.

"Quick thinking getting Jake Tanner out there." George W. threw Oliver a morsel of a compliment.

Oliver puffed up. "What an old gossip he is. Worse than a woman."

"Oliver, according to you, that's not possible." George W. continued to check the contents of the folder. "Maybe he's on estrogen. Estrogen poisoning."

"Next time I'll call him Jennifer." For Oliver, this was ribald humor.

Moments passed.

George W. closed the folder. "I will read this carefully. I do thank you for responding to the crisis swiftly, in terrible conditions. I'll make sure Darryl knows," he said.

"Thank you." Oliver felt wonderful.

"The pump was bombed. Why not the line?"

"A pro would have done as much damage

as possible. I'm thinking this was a disgruntled person. We've come under a lot of criticism." Oliver lifted both hands and made quotation mark signs around his words. "We haven't stolen anyone's water. We have legally bought the rights."

"Do you know how it was done?"

"Not yet. All I know is that the explosive device was small. No chunks of large metal were around."

"The ground is still covered with snow. Once it melts, go back up. It would be easy to miss something in those conditions."

"Already planned to do so," Oliver replied.

"Last question."

Oliver straightened. "Shoot."

"Any ideas?"

"None that I can prove."

"So how about some you can't prove?"

Quickly dropping the cagey pose, Oliver said, "California. I think it's Friends of Sierra County or Washoe Water Rights."

In 1889, California refused to recognize Nevada's claim to manage water on the eastern flank of the Sierra Nevadas. Since the headwaters of the Truckee, Carson, and Walker Rivers are all located in California, this created problems that flared up to this day.

When George W. didn't respond right

away, Oliver grew more vehement. "Millions upon millions of dollars can be extracted from right under Sierra County! Given the economic crisis in California especially, that state might get over its jealousy over its water when citizens realize the money that water could bring in. The water sent to Reno — that's what they're all after. Some pose as conservationists and all that shit, but those people are ruthless. And they never give us credit for recapturing used water. I hate them."

"So why blow up our pump?" asked George.

"It makes a point, doesn't it? The point being that Reno needs water bad. I'm willing to bet this isn't the last problem we will have and I'm not so sure there won't be some problems in Sierra County."

"Those ranchers are pulling their own water out of the ground."

"Yes, they are. And those ranchers who still want to ranch and who have enough cushion to weather California's meltdown, if that's possible, will fight."

"We're always the bad guys." George W. peered over his expensive tortoiseshell glasses.

"I'm proud to work for Silver State," Oliver boasted. "We manage carefully. Our leadership understands that wiping out ranchers is not in the long-term interest of this state, or even our profits ultimately. Wild as it sounds, a company such as ours could be nationalized, for lack of a better term. If enough public pressure is brought to bear, we could be taken over by the state government — or far worse, the federal."

George W. folded his hands together. "That's a pretty outrageous scenario."

"Outrageous times," Oliver shot back. "But we are well managed. That is a shield."

George W. wanted to believe that but lately he was harboring quiet doubts. If more water could be sent into Reno, the profits would eventually climb into the billions. It would take an unusual Board of Directors, a remarkable CEO, to put other needs first, like agriculture.

"Right," George W. said softly.

"And one more thing. Some residents of Sierra want our money. The county in California next to Las Vegas wants to sell its water, too."

"Las Vegas is so close to California, why don't we cede it to them?" George W. chuckled, glad for a moment not to consider the ramifications of Oliver's thoughts.

"I like Las Vegas. Nevada enjoys a healthy revenue stream from Las Vegas."

Inwardly sighing, George smiled tightly. "You're right, Oliver. Time I get over my prejudice, but I have a hard time taking seriously a place where men have pectoral implants and then gyrate on stage with shirts open to their navels."

CHAPTER EIGHT

By Friday, things had reverted back to normal in Washoe County. The airport had reopened on Tuesday. Flurries continued, and flights had been cut back or planes had sat on the tarmac thanks to fluctuating visibility. By now the storm was headed into Kansas, finally blowing itself apart on the westernmost ridges of the fertile Ohio Valley — Johnny Appleseed country.

Roads were cleared, though a few back roads, like Dixie Lane up in Red Rock, could still send one spinning. Pete and Lonnie returned to their normal duties: traffic arrests, drug busts, domestic violence, and investigating suicides in hotels and motels in the big town.

Although Reno was famous for its divorce laws — after mining diminished, the true impetus to the beginnings of prosperity on the Truckee River in the twentieth century — the city was now becoming infamous for its epidemic of suicides. The Chamber of Commerce published no statistics, nor was this peculiarity mentioned when the area was touted, but the numbers were close to double the national average.

Pete and Lonnie had been called to one just at the end of their shift yesterday. They viewed the usual middle-aged male who had chosen to blow his brains out in the Jolly Roger Motel. A nautical theme seemed out of place in the high desert, but in this case the skull and crossbones wasn't.

As it so often happened during these sorrowful events, a motel maid discovered the body. She screamed, knocking over her cart as she flew down the dimly lit corridor to find the manager, Kyle Kamitsis. Himself in his early forties, he'd managed this dispirited place for six years. This was his thirteenth suicide. Maybe it was the skull and crossbones.

The deceased had used a .38 with a silencer, which made it better since the hangings, slashed wrists, and shotgun blasts created a much bigger mess. And like twelve of the other stiffs found at the Jolly Roger, this man had driven over from California to end his life.

Those who committed suicide were generally unconcerned over the trouble or shock to others, which made the silencer odd.

"Didn't disturb the other guests," Lonnie quipped when he spotted the silencer. The gun was gripped in Samuel Peruzzi's right hand. His wallet and car keys rested on the nightstand along with his rings, one glass, the newspaper, and empty beer bottles.

Pete thought that in most cases suicide was one of the most self-centered acts in which a human could engage. Then again, he reminded himself, he'd felt despair, pain, remorse, grief, and anger, but perhaps never the spiral downward that a suicidal person felt. He figured he'd never know, but he devoutly wished those residents of the Golden State would kill themselves back across the border.

On the following day, there'd been no suicides, no wrecks, and no petty thefts by ten A.M. After Pete called the dispatcher, he had headed to Pump 19 in the police vehicle.

Lonnie, fiddling with his pocketknife, grumbled from the passenger seat. "How did I squash the bolster?"

"Is it nickel?"

"Yeah."

"Must be your impressive brute strength."

Lonnie opened the blade again, hearing the slight scrape as he did so. "Balls."

"Exactly."

They both laughed.

The slick incline up to the pump caused the SUV one small skid. Twinkie and Bunny, in a regular Silver State Resource Management vehicle, awaited them. As Pete pulled up, both doors opened simultaneously.

Pete and Lonnie climbed out and were greeted by the frigid air. Then the group walked over to the pump.

"Where's Oliver?" Peter wondered.

"Didn't tell him," Bunny answered.

"Smart move." Pete smiled. "I'll call on him at his office. Make him feel important."

"You're a good man." Twinkie smiled.

As the official stenographer, Lonnie flipped open his notebook. He took off his right glove and looked imploringly at Pete to speed it up.

"Have either of you two seen any trucks or cars around here? I know you check these pumps regularly. Anyone ever come down the drive whom you didn't know?"

"Nah. If they did, we'd stop them," Twinkie responded. "No one ever comes up to these pumps but us."

"Lynn Lloyd's been up here," Bunny contradicted Twinkie.

"Oh, yeah. Forgot about her."

Lynn Lloyd was the master of a pack of foxhounds, called appropriately enough,

Red Rock Hounds.

"Bunny, that was a year ago," Twinkie said.

"Looking for hounds?" Pete knew the master.

"Yeah. Found 'em later. But I don't think she has much interest in our pump." Twinkie offered his opinion.

"I don't, either, but I still need to ask these questions. Has anyone threatened you?"

"Me?" Twinkie was surprised.

Bunny smarted off. "Twinkie believes he is universally loved."

"Fuck you," Twinkie replied without malice.

"What about you, Bunny?"

"Only my ex-wife."

"Which one?" Twinkie enjoyed a swift revenge.

"Number two."

"I know the feeling." Pete nodded. "Has anyone to your knowledge ever threatened Silver State? A letter, an email, text?"

"The usual." Twinkie put his gloved hands in his pockets as his fingers were getting numb.

"What's the usual?"

"Protestors who say the company's trying to buy up everyone's water rights. That's standard, but every now and then we'll get a complaint that a pump site is an eyesore and can't we landscape it?" A flash of indignation crossed Twinkie's ruddy face. "Landscape them with what? One newcomer from across the border suggested we plant maples. Maples in high desert! Jesus, why don't these people go home?"

For a second Pete recalled the sight of yesterday's corpse sprawled in the motel room. That one had gone home all right. Funny, how most suicides who shoot themselves do it in bed.

Bunny piped up, "We've been asking ourselves who would blow up Pump Nineteen. All we can come up with is — what's the phrase now, the bullshit phrase, oh yeah, someone mentally incapacitated or suffering complications from Asshole Syndrome? This was a nutcase. That's all I can figure."

"Silver State has plenty of detractors." Pete folded his arms across his massive chest, which was made even larger by his coat.

"Yeah, any company turning a profit does these days." Twinkie agreed. "But Pete, this fight's reflected in the letters to the editor or the state house. You know, someone writes in about how we're bleeding dry the good people of Nevada."

Bunny feigned surprise. "You read the letters to the editor?"

"Unlike you, my lips don't move when I do

it." Twinkie teased him back.

"Personally, the way my fingers feel right now, I don't think I'll ever write again," Lonnie's low voice informed Pete.

Pete looked down at the stenographer's book. Lonnie's penmanship deteriorated the farther down the page he read.

"Hell with it. Put your gloves back on. We'll remember." He turned to Bunny. "Apart from our shared opinion of Oliver Hitchens, could he know something he's not telling?"

Twinkie and Bunny looked at each other, then back at Pete, the lawman.

Twinkie spoke first. "All the time, but if you mean is he crooked, no, I don't think so. What do you think, Bun?"

"He's a shithead, but he's straight up. I mean Oliver isn't stealing from the company in some way or making deals behind Silver State's back."

"What kind of deals?" Pete, alert now, lifted his chin, which he'd dropped into his mouton collar for warmth.

"Oliver knows where water rights are being purchased, where someone refuses, that kind of stuff. He's always on Craig Locke's tail, asking about what and where have we bought. He's nosy, but then again, after all the bigwigs look at the aerials and the topo maps and decide where a pump has to go in, Bunny and I usually go out with Oliver because he has to make the equipment call. We don't use the same kind of pump each time. There's a lot to this. How deep do we have to sink the shaft, what kind of drill bits? What will be the draw on the pump? How many gallons per minute during peak use now and what about projected peak use five years from now? Plus you never really know what you're going to hit when you go down. So the truth is, the three of us figure it out. Much as I hate his guts, Oliver's good at it.

"If Oliver wanted to, he could have bought up the water rights to some small parcels, some properties that didn't cost millions. He's shrewd with his money, but he never sneaked around like that," Twinkie finished.

"We'd know," Bunny said resolutely.

"How would you know?" Pete asked.

"Oliver's not a big spender, but little things would show up. He's in love with his wife. Not a bad-looking woman. He'd buy her a new car or earrings or something," Twinkie offered.

"And he'd yank his kids out of the University of Nevada–Reno."

"Bunny, why?" A devout Wolfpack man, this touched Pete's pride in his alma mater.

"Snob. If he could afford it, he'd put those

two kids of his in Yale or some East Coast school."

"Stanford." Lonnie spoke up.

"Oliver thinks the East is best. I sure as hell don't. It's those East Coast buttheads that got us all in this mess." Bunny snapped his lips shut like a turtle.

"Got that right." Twinkie nodded vigorously.

"Let me go back to one more question and I won't take up too much more of your time. You said Oliver kept things from you but you didn't think he was — what did you say — crooked?"

"Oh, he likes to hint there are rumbles in the office, George W. is going to make a change, stuff like that. It's a snide way to try and scare us into working longer and harder for no overtime claims. We're onto it."

"George W.?" Pete asked Twinkie.

"George W. Ball, head of equipment. I think his official title is some more bullshit like Infrastructure. Anyway, he makes all our purchases, everything down to the last wrench. He's an easy man to get along with, one of those techno guys. He's up on the latest, whether it's a computer or better pumps. Guess he has to be."

"I don't know him. Not that that means anything." Pete recognized that while he knew many people in his own generation and his parents' generation, Reno was big enough that he wouldn't know all the natives and he sure couldn't keep up with the newcomers.

"He's from Elko. Grew up by the Ruby Mountains," Bunny added.

"I like Elko," Pete said offhand. "Last question. Jake Tanner. He's a talker. Did he say anything, you know, how his neighbor hates Silver State or he's seen a blue truck he doesn't recognize? With Jake, you'll get everything, including the last time he slept with his wife."

"October." Twinkie quickly said as the three of them laughed with him.

"Jake ranted on about the weather," said Bunny, "about who might blow up a pump, but nothing out of the ordinary."

"Hey, thanks a lot. For the record, I won't report our conversation to Oliver. Given his need to constantly stress how important he is, it wouldn't go down so well with him that I'd spoken with you first."

"Thanks," they responded in unison.

"If you should think of anything, even if it seems crazy, let me know," Pete asked.

"We're good at crazy," Bunny replied.

"I'm counting on it." Pete waved as he headed back to the SUV.

Back down on Red Rock Road, Lonnie asked, "What do you think?"

"They're telling the truth."

"Hey, we did our duty." Lonnie checked his watch, then checked the time on the SUV clock. "We might find out who blew up the pump. Then again, we might not. It won't hurt us if we don't."

"Why do you say that?"

"People don't care all that much what happens to a Silver State pump. Neither does the department." He meant the Sheriff's Department. "Solving murders, robberies, that's what gets the headlines and that makes the department look good."

Pete tilted his head slightly. Lonnie was right.

They rode in silence.

Lonnie noted it. "What's on your mind?"

"I, well, I don't know, but I feel like we're standing at the edge of an arroyo and we think the ground is solid. Then it starts to slip. You hear a little slide first, see a few rocks. Can't shake it."

"Hope you're wrong."

"Me, too." He turned left onto Dry Valley Road.

Jeep had called earlier about the skeleton and they were just now getting to it. Given recent events and the fact that Jeep felt this was quite an old skeleton, it wasn't first on their list.

Lonnie brightened. "Jeep?"

"Um-hmm."

"Isn't that something? Finding an old skeleton in the barn?"

"Yes. And going back to what you were saying, if we find out who that old body is and then find out who killed him, that would make the news, but probably no one will much notice if we catch our bomber."

Lonnie smiled broadly. "Crazy."

CHAPTER NINE

"How's that strike you?" Standing next to Pete in the barn, Jeep cast her eyes upward to meet his warm brown ones, eyes much like her own.

"Sounds like a plan, but you know I'll have to run it by Sheriff Haley." Pete was a deputy sheriff and a young one at that — testimony to the regard in which Pete was held by his superiors.

"They should give the human bones to us." Baxter felt strongly about this. He looked from Mags to Jeep to Pete and Lonnie.

"I can find better bones than these." That said, King did not disagree with the wire-haired dachshund.

Baxter glowed at his small social victory. Given the few phone calls he'd overheard Mags make back to New York City, he realized they would be at Wings for a long time. Of course, Mags had told him that, but hearing it over and over in her conversations drove the fact home. He knew he'd better work out some accord with the shepherd mix.

He agreed with King. *"Bet you can."*

"Easier when the snow melts." King sniffed Lonnie's shoes.

Jeep suggested to Pete that given budgetary restraints and the fact that this murder most likely occurred one hundred and thirty years ago, at least, it wouldn't look good if the department spent taxpayers' money carefully unearthing these remains. Better to let the UNR do it and keep the whole story quiet until they found out who he was, if they could. No telling what kind of gold diggers would show up, claiming this was their long-lost great-grandfather.

As did all Reno residents, Jeep referred to the University of Nevada–Reno as "UNR."

"Do they have an archaeology department?" Mags inquired, as this was the first time she'd heard this idea from Jeep. Not that her great-aunt discussed her ideas all the time.

"Yes, ma'am." Pete smiled. "Mostly they work with Native American sites, sometimes abandoned mine towns. This would be different. A novelty, maybe. Great idea, Miss Reed."

"And they'll be careful." Jeep motioned for the two men to follow her out of the building. "Come on, let me warm you up. I know you've got a million things to do, but fifteen minutes in my kitchen won't put you that far behind. And, Pete, if you call me Miss Reed one more time I will beat your ass with a wooden spoon. I've known you since you played second base in Little League. You're old enough now to call me Jeep to my face. What you call me behind my back, keep to yourself."

Before Mags could step up to Aunt Jeep, a grinning Pete gallantly offered his arm. Lonnie offered his to Mags, not sure whether this big-city girl would take it the right way, but she slipped her arm through his, so he relaxed.

In the kitchen, Carlotta fussed over the officers, taking their coats, pouring coffee, offering cinnamon rolls freshly baked that morning. She was vaguely acquainted with both of them. Everybody loved Carlotta; Pete and Lonnie were no exceptions.

"You keep telling me you're going to find me a wife just like you." Lonnie kissed her on the cheek.

"Give me time. Give me time. You're special."

Now seated, Pete drawled, "Lonnie, that

means bullheaded. Will take a special woman."

"Takes one to know one."

"Anyone tell you two that you're getting like an old married couple?" Jeep poured half and half into her coffee.

Lonnie wrinkled his nose as he looked at Pete. "Too hairy."

Even Mags burst out laughing at this.

Jeep had shown the policemen the Nicholas Cavalry School ring. She'd also handed them an envelope with photographs of the ring for their records since she wished to keep it. Pete said since it was found on her property, and given the time frame of the crime, why not?

Pete knew Sheriff Haley would readily concur. He was a practical man. Allowing the university to remove and study the bones would save his department money. It wasn't as though the murder occurred yesterday.

"Haven't talked to you since I called you about that explosion," Jeep said to Pete while pouring herself another mug of coffee. "What happened up there?"

"Someone blew up the pump." Pete was enjoying Carlotta's coffee. "Our department has a pretty good explosives expert, part time. I gave her the fragment and some paper bits Lonnie and I found and she was able to come back with answers." Pete stirred his coffee after Carlotta refilled his cup. "It was a small pipe bomb. Small enough that you or I could have slid it into our coat pocket. Residue inside indicated that whoever did it had access to high-grade materials and knew what he was doing."

"That's hardly consoling." Jeep sighed.

"Based on her conclusions — oh, I forgot to mention, he used some paper wadding."

Lonnie chipped in. "A grocery list."

"It wasn't me!" Carlotta held up her hands in surrender.

"Carlotta, you'd throw a grenade instead." Jeep laughed.

Pete continued. "But here's the thing, again according to Mindy, our explosives expert: The perp didn't want to cause a great deal of damage. Just enough."

"Enough?"

"Either to divert our attention or as a warning. Then again, this could be a fruit loop."

"Fruit loops with pipe bombs usually do things like ride buses to take out a lot of people, isn't that right?" Mags joined in.

"More or less, ma'am. We've not had to deal with anything like that in Reno and I pray we never will; people whose sole purpose is to kill others they don't even know.

This is something else entirely and I don't know why it happened. I could try and impress you ladies with solid-sounding theories, but I just flat-out don't know what motivated our bomber." Pete didn't sound frustrated so much as puzzled.

"No one claimed responsibility," Lonnie added.

"Why would someone do that?" Although Mags had spent periods of time throughout her life in Nevada and knew more about the state than most, she wasn't up-to-date on recent politics or problems, whereby a radical group would claim a bombing.

"For political gain," Jeep answered. "If a movement, say environmental — labor in the old days — is extremely well organized, well led, there's always an arm that is violent. The main group disavows this fringe element but actually directs its actions."

"Why?" Mags wondered, and so did Pete and Lonnie.

"Violent or outrageous acts, whether from the left or the right, make any nonviolent position appear more reasonable. It's another way to move the center off center, shall we say? Forty years ago the center of American politics would seem quite leftist now. The Republican Party's conservative wing has managed to move the center rightward with great success. Of course, now they're fighting among themselves, but that happens. Not just their problem. It's an old strategy and a very effective one. You know, these days Nixon would be considered too liberal by his own party."

Lonnie thought out loud, "Someone bombs Pump Nineteen. Eventually claims that this was done to protect water rights for all individuals or something like that. Everyone is shocked, right?" Jeep nodded, so he continued. "The politicians push harder to limit Silver State's control of water."

"Seems to me if that's the drill, it's better than one well-trained person acting alone." Pete wiped his hands on a napkin.

"It is. There's governance within the group, but one person alone does whatever they want. Even if they aren't mentally unstable, one person without any feedback from others ultimately presents a greater danger. At least that's how I see it." Jeep tapped her forefinger on the table.

"Last thing we need, another self-righteous bastard." Pete said low, then blinked. "Excuse me, ladies."

Jeep smiled. "As I recall, I used that very same profanity to describe this creep."

Walking the men to the back door, Jeep

put her hand on Pete's shoulder. "How's Rebecca?"

"Good. She goes every six months for her checkup and she's great. Thank you for asking."

"Give her my love."

"I will."

As they drove away, Mags asked, "Who's Rebecca?"

"His mother. Had a bout with colon cancer. I don't remember this much cancer when I was young, but don't worry: I'm not going to sing that tiresome tune about the good old days."

Mags said, "No. I agree with you about cancer rates. It's like an unacknowledged epidemic."

King looked down at Baxter. *"He liked her."*

Baxter twitched his neatly trimmed moustache. *"She liked him, too."*

"They don't know it, of course."

"Can't smell a damned thing. The odor is quite sweet. No wonder they make such a mess of it." Baxter plopped down on the kitchen floor.

"Kind of sad, isn't it?"

"King, if Mags would have listened to me, or if she had any kind of nose, she'd know the last fellow she liked wasn't worth an old Milk-Bone."

100

"You like Milk-Bones?"

"Not as much as Greenies," Baxter promptly replied. Nothing was better than gnawing on those dog biscuits.

"Greenies really are the best, but expensive. Mom complains about the cost." King laid down next to Baxter, a sign of acceptance.

"Jeez, your mom has more money than God."

"Doesn't stop her from complaining." King laughed, put his big handsome head on his brown-tipped paws, and fell asleep.

Jeep and Mags sat in Jeep's office, paneled in cypress. The cypress, at four hundred pounds a tie, had been used for railroad ties in the 1930s in Mississippi. When some were torn up, Jeep — who was beginning to see some return on her business — bought the lot of them and had them shipped to Reno. She took them to a sawmill to be cut into planks for her office. She'd always loved the soft platinum glow of cypress.

Unlike many offices, hers was shorn of plaques and displayed no degrees (she had none) or photographs of so-called important people. A large Frederic Remington painting hung over the fireplace. That was trophy enough. A small Frederic Remington sketch hung on the wall and one was in the hall, too.

The smaller ones were often overlooked. People not conversant in the arts did not recognize this important artist's distinctive gift.

In her bedroom, photographs of Danny Marks; Dot; Jeep's beloved sister, Sarah; Mags; Grandmother all reposed in silver frames on a table near her bed. A large picture of Glynnis Rogers; John, her husband; Mags and Catherine as grade-schoolers sat on her dresser, along with a photo of a wonderful old quarter horse she had purchased with the first profits she made from the mines. Framed photos of various deceased beloved dogs and cats filled a table, along with a picture of Thor, a now-deceased attack goose, who lived in the memory of everyone who'd had the occasion to be chased by him. The bird's hissing alone scared the bejesus out of most people.

Her office was for business. A big sofa at a right angle to the fireplace gave Jeep a spot to read. She liked curling up with a book as the fire crackled, looking up from the pages to see the flames. She thought of books as kindling for the mind.

Jeep directed Mags to the chair behind the desk and computer. "Find the graduates of the Nicholas School from 1887."

"Wouldn't the revolutionaries have destroyed the records?"

"That's your job. Find out. But I'm willing to bet you a new computer there are records somewhere. Those that lived, escaped, might have been able to take their yearbooks with them or what passed for yearbooks then. Graduates from this prestigious school were very proud."

Mags wiggled in the chair, pretty comfortable. "Your computer is getting gray hairs."

"Which is why I bet you a new one. Get whatever you want if I win."

"I thought if you won I'd have to buy one."

"You don't have any money."

Mags lifted her chin, squared her shoulders. "For now."

"You might pick another line of work."

"Aunt Jeep, how was I to know the stock market would go down in flames?"

"Arrogance, sweetie, arrogance. Your generation has only known fat years. All the signs were there for you and everyone else to see. The generation older than you — pretty spoiled itself — ignored them, too. If nothing else, learn not to follow the herd."

"God, Aunt Jeep, I feel like such a fool. I feel awful. I lost people millions."

"You did, but unlike others, you tried to use your own money to pick them back up. In business terms, that was stupid. In terms of the heart, I'm proud of you."

Tears unexpectedly rolled down the pretty woman's smooth cheeks.

Jeep crossed the room and put her arm around Mags. Bending down, she kissed her on the cheek. "There really are things more important than money. You've only known me with money, but I come from hunger."

"That's what Momma always said."

"I know what money can do for you and I know what it can't. If you lose your soul, no amount of cash can buy it back. You die with the Devil waiting with an outstretched hand. Now come on, dry the tears, go to work. It will all turn out right." She paused. "It may seem cruel for me not to carry you financially, other than to feed and house you, but Mags, a weakling does the world no good. Yes, you will inherit this estate, you and Enrique. Much of it is tied up, which I will explain some day — the charities, the trusts — but you will be well-off. However, if you don't fight your way back, you'll be just another rich toad with no mother wit."

Mags raised her eyes to Jeep's. "I know. I really do know." She took a deep breath. "A question. When we found the ring you said you'd seen it two times. You never told us the second time."

"I didn't, did I?" Jeep walked over to the

fireplace, leaning against the mantel as the yellow and red flames curled upward. "When I was at Sweetwater, Texas, I delivered all types of aircraft to Alameda, California, and Great Falls, Montana. I made a lot of friends. Usually, we'd turn around and fly back to Texas. Sometimes we'd stay over in the barracks. In Montana, the planes were flown over to the Soviets, over Alaska. But a few times, the Soviet pilots came to Montana. Most were women pilots and they flew in combat. Their English was about as good as our Russian, but we all got along. One of those women wore this ring. I recognized it. She was surprised. It was her father's, inscribed 1910. She wore it defiantly, too. I often wonder what happened to her, if she survived the war, if she survived the aftermath."

"Must have been wonderful here after the war."

"It's a funny thing, it was wonderful during the war in so many ways. God, yes, I saw terrible things and lost friends, but I was young and we felt a great shared purpose. I can't tell you how that felt and it's sad to say but I don't believe Americans will ever feel it again."

"Not even if we get attacked?"

"We have been attacked!"

Mags sat quietly. "You're right. Pearl Harbor galvanized us, but the Pentagon and Twin Towers didn't."

"I'm sure some intellectual somewhere will pluck out the many reasons why, but I'm pretty basic: attack my people, you're the enemy and all of us band together. That kind of spirit is gone, Mags. That kind of pulling together is all gone."

"We seem to be awfully good at pulling apart."

Jeep let her hand drop from the mantel and looked up at the fabulous painting of cowboys trying to herd rampaging cattle. "The real sorrow is there are so few men left, real men."

Mags got up from the chair, went over to her beloved Aunt Jeep, and gave her a little punch on the arm. "But there are real women."

"Yes, there are."

"I remember what you used to say to me when I was little, when I was scared." Mags lifted her eyebrows.

"What was that?"

"Tits to the wind."

Jeep dissolved in laughter. How funny to hear her battle cry from her great-niece.

At the edge of Reno — past a low-lying flat

area on the left full of snow devils twirling upward — Lonnie took a call so Pete could keep his hands on the wheel. All department communications were on a specific frequency.

"Hey," said Lonnie.

"Hey back." Sergeant Perez's voice then said, "Got the lab report on the corpse at the Jolly Roger. There were no fingerprints on the gun. 'Cause of that and the silencer, we're changing the status of this case to murder."

"Right." Lonnie frowned. "Any information on who he was other than his name?"

"Owned a muffler franchise in Susanville. It was making money. He belonged to a lot of environmental groups. Things like Ducks Unlimited, the National Wildlife Federation, stuff like that."

Lonnie relayed this to Pete.

"The murder is our jurisdiction," Pete said. "Can the Chief find someone in Susanville to interview his wife if he had one?" Lonnie repeated all this to Sergeant Perez.

Susanville was in California. Two prisons were there — High Desert Station Prison and California Correctional Center — both operating way over capacity. The prisoners' families often moved to Susanville so it was an irregular community, to put it nicely.

"He's on it." Perez stopped a moment. "Your report says there were no weapons in the dead dude's car, no ammunition, only a few unopened bills, the electric bill."

"Saab hatchback, tidy." Pete inhaled. "We've got more work to do."

Perez signed off.

"Suicide would have been so easy." Lonnie sighed. "Oh, well. No fingerprints and no gloves on his hands. This guy pissed off someone."

They drove down into an old part of town, turning right by a sex shop — videos and the like.

"Jeep's great-niece is a looker." Lonnie smiled, the sex shop provoking his thoughts on the opposite sex.

"Uh-huh." Pete, knowing Lonnie well, smiled.

"Remember people saying that Jeep was in love with Dan Marks? Mom used to comment on it. She never married him. Then others said she was in love with Dot Jocham." He waited, then said with conviction, "I don't care if a woman's gay."

"That's big of you, Lonnie."

"I only care if she doesn't sleep with me."

Pete laughed. "Me, too."

CHAPTER TEN

"You never fail to remember." Standing at the open front door, Jeep viewed the foiled pot of massive red poinsettias.

On the porch, Craig Locke inclined his head in a slight gentlemanly bow. "A courageous and lovely woman should always be remembered."

"What a smoothie." King chuckled from behind.

"I smell cigar smoke." Baxter wrinkled his nose with distaste. *"Why do they do it?"*

"It's their version of bones."

"Ah." The little dog put his head on his front paws.

"Craig, am I courageous because I keep outmaneuvering you in Red Rock Valley?" She smiled.

"Well, there is that. I certainly admire that you never back down from a fight. And to think that you flew those B-17s. That took a lot of guts."

109

"Did take a lot of strength." She opened the door wider. "Please, come in out of the cold. It's your annual Wings Ranch visit."

"This is heavy. Where would you like it?"

"Right there on the hall table. It will be the first thing people see when they visit. Now, come and have a drink. Coffee, tea, hot chocolate, or maybe you'd like a stiff one this morning?"

After placing the beautiful flowers on the table, he held up his hands. "If I had a drink you'd likely find me under this table. How about hot chocolate?"

Carlotta served them in the living room, fragrant with the pine smell from the den, where a huge Christmas tree stood, yet to be decorated.

"How's the family?" Jeep asked, perching on an easy chair while Craig sat on the sofa.

"Growing. One in college. One still in high school." He sipped the chocolate, the top smothered with whipped cream. "You know my visit comes with SSRM's annual request?"

"I do." Jeep smiled. "And I again politely decline to sell my rights."

Clasping his hands over his right knee, his right leg crossed over his left, Craig said, "The Colorado Supreme Court in 1979 passed the first antispeculation doctrine. You

110

know, eventually the Nevada Supreme Court will come down hard on that issue. Some then might accuse you of hoarding all your water rights."

Jeep, voice confident, fired back. "The Vidler Tunnel Water Company case, yes, I know it. First, this is Nevada. We aren't going to follow Colorado, Utah, California, you name it. We'll do things our own way. Second, I never seek to profit from my water rights. I own them to protect agriculture. That's that."

"What about your heirs? You've hog-tied them. What if they need the money?"

"Craig Locke, you know better than that." She smiled slyly. "One, Enrique, Mags, and I are as one on this issue. Two, they will be rich, in plain words, and they will be responsible with their bounty." She paused. "Now tell me, how long did it take you to come up with that angle?"

He did have to chuckle. "A month of research before my Christmas visit. I came armed this season with a new tack and a big poinsettia." He nodded to her. "But you're always a step ahead."

"I try. I love Nevada. I especially love northern Nevada. What are the latest population guesses? Another one hundred million people in our country by 2034? Something like that. More environmental damage, more harm to wildlife, and what is frightening to me, more city dwellers who do not understand and feel superior to those of us who are ranchers. You know as well as I do, forests may be renewable, water is not. I've tried to protect Red Rock Valley and a few other places hither and yon. I don't fault you, really. SSRM is prepared for and needs growth. I'm certain it will destroy us. I'm an old, old Nevada girl and I will do all I can to save and protect the ways of old Nevada."

He listened respectfully. "I know you will. We just see the future differently."

"Well, at least we're both thinking about tomorrow. Plenty don't." She reiterated, "I won't sell any land. I won't sell or transfer water rights that I rent from other ranchers and I will fight the transfer of water rights from agricultural to municipal use if Reno begins to covet Red Rock Valley."

"Well, we got that out of the way." He laughed. "You know, water really is a fascinating subject all over the world."

"That it is. I wonder about China and India, all those people, their controls don't seem to be very stringent, the pollution." She shook her head. "Unless they do something about it, it will be their undoing."

"That goes for us, too. We have our problems. But I like to go back and read the National Reclamation Act of 1902. That was a visionary statement."

"Yes, it was. We will never have a president who loved the West as much as Theodore Roosevelt. He brilliantly combined development, ecology, and common sense. Can you imagine where our nation would be without him?" Jeep dearly loved the Rough Rider.

"Even Teddy couldn't have foreseen the population explosion out here, though. At the turn of the last century, Reno had only fifteen thousand inhabitants — and even then water issues began to arise."

"It is amazing. You know, I have some of the papers and the visitors' book of Ralph and Michael Ford from 1880 onward. I once read them all and I need to do so again. I'm afraid I've forgotten much of it. They dug drainage ditches and irrigated the land from Campbell Springs. They also dug two deep wells. Those two planned ahead, for which I'm certainly grateful. I'm still using what they did."

"Know that."

"I bet you do." She smiled at him. "Then again, that's part of your job."

"It is. I think the struggle over water is like everything else in Nevada's history. When times are good, people forget. When they're bad, then they remember because they're looking for other ways to make money. Remember, Nevada lost half its population from 1880 to about 1990 when the mines began to play out."

"Now it's California that's playing out." From her seat, Jeep reached down and petted King, now at her side.

"California would be better off if they declared bankruptcy."

"You've got a point there. I just hope that mess doesn't spread here. We have our problems, but we seem to be ahead of them. Well, we never exploded like they did nor did our state government make promises to the various unions like they did."

"Well, on our side, gambling's down," Craig mentioned. "And we lead the nation in foreclosures."

"If the economy keeps tanking, it will get worse. How sad to think of people just walking away from their homes."

"Think so? Most of that disaster is in Las Vegas." He rubbed his knee. "But we have our share here."

"So then why on earth build Horseshoe Estates?"

She caught Craig off guard, but he recovered. With Jeep, it was never wise to forget whom you were dealing with. "The abandoned properties in Reno will be trashed. Vagrants and the like will live in them." He seemed to be evading the subject.

"Even without electricity?"

"A place to sleep is better than the streets." He finished his hot chocolate. "The banks will have to write off those properties. We need new, good housing. Maybe not as much or as expensive as Wade Properties thinks, but I wonder if some of the California refugees will actually get out with their money. If so, they may well buy here. We have no state income tax and Nevada is extremely business friendly."

"For which I am extremely grateful."

They chatted a bit more, then he rose to leave. She walked him to the front door.

"Thank you for your hospitality. It's always bracing to talk to you."

"Likewise."

"I think of us as the best of enemies." He took her hand and squeezed it. "Merry Christmas, Jeep."

"Merry Christmas, Craig."

CHAPTER ELEVEN

Christmas rarely brought out the best in people, as the Reno police force well knew. The shopping mall parking lots overflowed, but this year folks kept their wallets more closed than open. Sales clerks were run ragged trying to please shoppers. Some gave up, but perhaps they never much cared in the first place. A fight broke out at — of all places — Macy's men's fragrance counter. The combatants, not male, assaulted each other with bulky purses.

Back on the freeway after this incident, Lonnie flipped his notebook closed. "Purse used as an assault weapon."

"That should look good in the report." Pete pulled into a parking lot near the multilevel downtown library.

While outsiders derided Reno as a nadir of culture and learning, the library employees knew otherwise. This town was full of voracious readers. The bookstores sold books, fat

116

times or lean. For other cultural diversions, Trinity Episcopal opened its doors Friday afternoon for free organ concerts. The pews were filled with enthusiastic music lovers.

The casinos, however, were emptier than usual. This unfortunate addiction paid the state's bills. As gambling revenues diminished, lawmakers grew anxious. Since government is zero profit, those in it have no idea how to make money. They sure know how to spend it, however.

One always has to eat, though. Trying to get in the habit of eating better, Pete and Lonnie decided they'd shun fast food for the Christmas season. While Pete hit the gym regularly and kept in good shape, he knew he wasn't doing himself any favors at the table. He didn't eat a lot, but he ate poorly.

Lonnie was still too young to care.

After giving their orders, they relaxed. A huge TV played behind the bar. A soccer match between the Netherlands and Spain looked like a good one. In summer, the patrons of the Wild River Grille could eat outside as the Truckee River gurgled by. The interior, sleek, was pleasant in any season.

"Replay." Lonnie diverted his eyes from the screen. "Want to bet on it?"

"Hell no."

"I'll give you good odds."

"Since you obviously already know who won, no odds out of your mouth are good odds."

Usually the two couldn't enjoy a good lunch, but they'd called in and were temporarily unavailable. If there was a fender bender on Fifth Street, someone else would take the call. Tomorrow, they'd return the favor for someone else. Every now and then a body needs a small break from routine, especially from the frayed nerves of the holiday season.

After polishing off a salad with steak strips for Pete, a huge rib eye for Lonnie, they sipped coffee. Lonnie ordered New York cheesecake. Pete liked the look of it, but refused to put on weight over Christmas.

"Haven't had time to go over the report from Susanville together," Pete mentioned.

"I read it, though."

"Glad I didn't have to question his widow before the holidays." Pete, like most law enforcement people, hated bringing dreadful news to folks who — until the police knocked on their door — assumed life was normal.

"Yeah, I'm glad to have missed that." Lonnie carefully cut a piece of rich, chocolate-drizzled cheesecake with his fork. "I'm learning a lot from you."

Pete peered over his raised coffee cup. "I'm waiting."

"No, really. When we went to the motel, you saw something I didn't. I looked at the corpse, questioned the manager while you questioned the maid. Forensics showed up and I got out of their way."

"What'd you learn?"

"I made a crack about no noise because of the silencer. No guests would be disturbed. You didn't elaborate, but you didn't agree with me."

"Well, as I've said before, when we go on these suicide calls, it's usually open-and-shut; one person's last self-indulgent act. A suicidal person probably *wouldn't* be thinking about other guests."

Lonnie savored the delicate flavors of the cheesecake. "This is great."

"Don't tempt me. You know the average American gains five pounds or more over the holidays?"

"Not me."

"Wait until you turn thirty. The pounds sneak up on you. That's why I go to the gym at five-thirty. I don't want to be one of those men who has a tank over his nozzle."

"Ever notice that the tank is always full? Means they probably aren't using the nozzle." Lonnie speared another piece of cheesecake with delight.

Pete laughed. "Tell it to Jake."

"Wait long enough and he'll tell you how he maneuvers his tool. Jake will tell you just about anything."

"Wonder if his wife knows that?"

"She's almost as fat as he is," said Lonnie. "Must be like —"

"Hold it right there. Go no further. I don't want to think about Jake Tanner's sex life." Pete drained his cup. "Okay, back to what Sergeant Evans sent down from Susanville. Sam Peruzzi, our victim, married, four children. Two in their teens, two in grade school. Owned a muffler shop, as you know. Well liked. No stories of marital problems or fooling around — nothing of the sort of thing that might set off another jealous husband." He paused. "A husband who could get a silencer."

"Hey, the guy's name's Peruzzi. Maybe he pissed off someone in the mob?"

"Antidefamation will get you for that." Pete could understand the sentiments of Americans of Italian descent. Still, the mob had indeed been created by Italians — very, very smart ones.

"Right."

"Those Mafia guys are so sophisticated nowadays they don't have to take out people.

Not saying it doesn't happen now and then, but they have found more elegant solutions."

"Didn't mean to get off the track," Lonnie said.

"Okay, here's the rest of it. Mr. Peruzzi was well liked. Strong supporter of high school sports, as his older son was on the football team, his older daughter on volleyball. Wife also a community leader. The whole family was passionate about environmental preservation. One of the things, uh, Sergeant Eades from Susanville mentioned is that Mrs. Peruzzi kept repeating how they'd never see the whales. The family had planned a trip to see the whales off the California coast."

"Funny what people fixate on."

"Yeah, it is."

"Mr. Peruzzi appears to have had no enemies, perhaps a disgruntled customer from time to time, but no more than any other person in business. Maybe less. There is one thing, though."

Lonnie looked up. "Oh?"

"Peruzzi had recently raised the issue of *foreigners*, as he called them, buying up water rights around Susanville and throughout Sierra County. This was in connection with Farmland Trust — another advocacy group of which he was a member. He attended zoning requests in Sierra County and Reno. Seems he was a regular at hearings."

"Why don't they call it Ranchland Trust?"

"Started out East. Anyway, his point was that while we are focusing on human consumption and misdirection — *his* words — of water, what about the wildlife? What happens to them when the water table is used up? Peruzzi was supposedly working on a report outlining the problem, identifying those ranches at risk."

"Huh." Lonnie pushed his plate away and leaned back a little in his chair.

Pete checked his watch. "Apparently he was passionate about this."

"So maybe one of the groups he was involved in somehow channeled this passion."

"Maybe." Pete frowned. "When there are millions or even billions of dollars to be made, some of those environmental groups will be bought off one way or another. The bad guys get richer and money sanctifies everything."

A patron rose from a nearby table, three business associates with him, giving the officers the eye as he walked past their table. Middle-aged, self-satisfied, and carrying his own gas tank, he said to the public servant, for the benefit of his compatriots, "You guys sure are living high off the hog. I'm paying your salary and I only come here as a treat."

Lonnie smiled beatifically. "We could eat shit and die. Would that make you happy?"

One of the big mouth's associates laughed. The disgruntled taxpayer turned beet red and hustled out of the restaurant.

"Lucky he didn't write down your badge number." Nonetheless, Pete had enjoyed the exchange.

For different reasons, lunch over at Wings Ranch was also enjoyable. Mags had contacted Sotheby's in New York where she had associates. Her former brokerage house manager, while raking in millions, often attended the auctions and he'd taken Mags with him.

"Isn't that stupendous?" At the table, Mags opened the auction catalog for a recent sale of Romanov heirlooms. She'd had the fancy publication overnighted via FedEx.

The auction of the lost inheritance of Grand Duchess Maria Pavlovna had been November 30, 2009, in London.

Catching Mags's eye on page thirty-five, a gorgeous Fabergé wood cigarette case with silver-gilt mounts bespoke the marvelous workmanship of Fabergé. Created in 1859, the auction estimate in U.S. dollars was

$4,200–$5,900. This was one of the more modestly priced items, other objects priced well into six figures.

Mags told Jeep what she'd learned about the Grand Duchess. Born in 1854, died in 1920, she'd married the brother of Czar Alexander III, Grand Duke Vladimir Alexandrovich, who lived from 1847 to 1909. Much as they would have hated being called such, they were what Americans would dub leaders of the "smart set." With limitless resources, exquisite taste, and the expectation of getting her way, the beautiful Grand Duchess was an unforgettable figure in pre-Revolutionary Russia. When the Revolution swept away elegance, refinement, and human life, she escaped, not by hiding, but by leaving in great style. The Bolsheviks didn't break her spirit but the strain most likely brought her goodbye to life. Then again, if one has lived as the wife to the brother of the czar, then as the aunt to the current czar, perhaps the Soviet's Brave New World looked tatty and rude, so why bother?

"I wonder if there's anyone still alive who can create objects like these in this book?" Jeep asked.

"I certainly hope so." Mags grinned, revealing very white teeth. "There's got to be some beauty still being made in the world."

"One hopes there are still dedicated crafts-men and artists out there."

"Twenty-one-year-olds with tiny tools carving cigarette cases," Mags said. "Well, everyone has to have a passion."

"What's yours?" Jeep caught her off guard.

"Don't laugh."

"Why would I laugh? Anyone without a passion is half dead."

"I used to love fixing motors, cars. Daddy kept saying there's no real money in that and girls don't get covered in grease."

"Your father was a good man, but an unimaginative one. Odd, isn't it? He was surrounded by creative people."

"Some movie producers are creative. Not Daddy. It was profit, profit, profit. The ac-tors, writers, directors, were all a means to the profit, like cattle to ranchers. He used everybody. I don't mean he didn't like them but I guess ranchers like the cattle they drive to slaughter, too."

"Well, may he rest in peace and have an ac-count book in heaven where everything is in the right-hand column. So, anything more to say about Maria Pavlovna?"

"Sotheby's has such incredible connec-tions. The people who mounted this auction contacted her descendants. Perhaps one of them knows a descendant of the cavalry school. Maybe someone has a scrapbook."

"Good thinking."

CHAPTER TWELVE

Wings Ranch rested on both sides of Dixie Lane, down which Jeep roared along on her ATV. To the naked eye, the landscape appeared barren save for the sagebrush, but she knew better. A narrow creek running north and south had stunted trees and some brush along it, which turned silver-green in spring. Thin feeder creeks, most of which dried up in the summer, interlaced through Red Rock Valley. While the land looked barren, a deep aquifer undergirded the valley.

Naturally, Jeep had known that when she bought the Fords' property. Back in 1905, the Nevada legislature devised a permit system. Early settlers established rights to water flow just by usage, even if diverted from a streambed. Over time, that property had rights to that water, especially if this was established before 1905. The Fords did this, so Jeep inherited these flow rights, plus she owned the water underground. In Nevada terms she had a "vested" water right. Easterners always own the water underground. In Nevada, it's another form of gold. Whoever owned water rights could sell them to the Sultan of Brunei if they wished.

Back in the mid-fifties when Jeep bought the various parcels that became her ranch, Reno consisted of 35,000 souls, give or take. Even into the early 1960s when the population topped 50,000, the ownership and resale of water rights festered as a recurring problem. Never satisfactorily resolved in the nineteenth century, it remained subject to interpretation in the twentieth and now the twenty-first.

Some people can see beyond their immediate needs. Jeep was one of them. She would never have dug into her wallet for any piece of land to which she did not own the water, and she was farsighted enough to buy up water rights to land she did not own. The key was not owning land without water rights. It always comes back to water. The human race bred past the food supply in some continents while heedlessly emptying out its water table. Americans kept their breeding at reasonable rates, yet some areas of the country were teetering dangerously close to exhausting groundwater. Eventually blood would flow rather than water.

Intelligent as she was about land, water, and business, Jeep could be stupid about other things. She appreciated the arts, but evidenced little creativity in that sphere. Had it been up to her, the ranch house interior would consist of a kitchen table, chairs, a desk and a chair, a sofa, if she thought of it, and a bed upstairs. Then again she'd have been just as happy sleeping in a bedroll. One of the reasons she loved her Army days was the spartan barracks. Uniforms suited her personality.

The warmth of the ranch — its colors and artwork — reflected Dot's sensibility. Jeep had readily handed her a checkbook and let her go to it. She didn't even balk at the gorgeous Remington painting, which she thought pretty costly even back then. The amount of joy she gained from looking at that beautiful work could never be measured in dollars, but Jeep hadn't been aware of that.

Jeep steered the ATV to the top of the Sand Hills at 1,660 feet near her ranch. She looked down to the edge of the Bedell Flat. Behind her was Mags on a camouflage ATV. Snow arced behind the wheels as Jeep drove along the wide path, dodging large rounded stone outcroppings. She stopped, nose pointing north.

"There." Jeep pointed.

Mags pulled up behind her. "On the north side of the Dogskins?" Mags looked at the truncated range, which ran northeast to southwest at an odd angle.

"When you were little, your mother and I drove you and Catherine up there to have lunch by Dry Valley Creek. April. One of those unbelievably clear days. You know, I haven't been back up there since 1973. No reason to, but every now and then I get curious about it because that's where many people believe old Fort Sage was."

"Strange really, that an army supply station could vanish."

" 'Tis, but a lot of very strange things happened here in the eighteen eighties and eighteen nineties."

"Pretty close to the Indian site."

"That may or may not be a coincidence. One of the things I learned back in the forties was that all government reports are written to enhance the contributions and value of the author. Even today's students can learn that from Julius Caesar's *Gallic Wars*."

"I don't think they teach that anymore." Mags, forced to take Latin by her mother, now realized her mother had been correct that Latin was the founding pillar of all Western society, law, politics, literature, and especially engineering.

"If that's so, our society deserves whatever they get." Jeep spoke this without malice. "The past is prologue. I know I'm not the first to say it. What are those reports from J.C.? The Romans fielded a highly trained, technically superior army facing more primitive peoples. The Gauls and primitive tribes, the Romans learned, were hell to conquer. What has changed since then?" She waved her hand. "I don't give a damn anymore, Mags. If we dumb down our schools, if we turn our backs on the lessons of the past, we deserve to fail — and guess what, we are. All progress is built on prior knowledge. By the time this country winds up in the trash can, I'll be dead."

"Oh, Aunt Jeep, you've been saying we're going to hell in a handbasket since I was in college. And whatever happens, you always rise to the occasion."

"Flatterer." But Jeep liked hearing it. She looked north to the Dogskins, then west to Seven Lakes.

Mags followed her gaze. "I used to really think there were seven lakes. Seven ponds is more like it."

"You got spoiled back East squatting between the East River and the Hudson. I never saw so much water in my life until I entered the service. You know the government said we were really civilians, not members of the service. We never got the pay and benefits given to men." She shrugged, then continued. "I'd never been out of Nevada. I mean, we never even drove to see the Pacific. The biggest body of water I'd ever seen was Pyramid Lake. It wasn't until I saw how fertile the Midwest and the East are that I understood how easy it was for them to ranch compared to us. For one thing, you don't need as much land. The forage is rich. Well, beautiful as it all was to me — and remains, I pray — I couldn't wait to come home. I belong right here."

"I hope I do in time."

"Me too. You asked me about Fort Sage. Now the goddamned wind has picked up. Want me to drive you over there?"

"On the ATVs?"

Jeep laughed. "No."

"Let's wait for a slightly warmer day, but I would like to see it again. There's something romantic about a lost fort. But if you brought me up here looking, you must have something in mind."

"Well —" Jeep twirled her hand around, put her left land on the starter button, but didn't push it. "I've been thinking about buying up some land that borders Dry Valley Creek."

"Cost a fortune now."

"Prices are falling precipitously. Might be a good time."

Mags grinned. "Which means you think it will shoot back up again in time."

"Well, if I'm successful, it will."

"All you have to do is hang on."

"I have even more in mind, Mags. I've been thinking about food a lot. I've focused on the businesses and the ranch, my true love, really, and I've been fortunate, kissed by the gods. When I offered you a place to rebuild your life I told you I had a dream and that I'd tell you about it in time."

"Of course I'm wildly curious but before I forget to say it, you may be blessed, but you've also worked for every penny."

"Yes, I did, but there are millions of people who work yet can't get ahead. Fate. If you work hard and have a bit of intelligence most times you will progress, but there's always that element of fate. So now that I am the Ancient of Days, I've been turning my mind toward how to take care of people who are struggling, who are trying their damndest. How does one give them a hand up? Note that I said hand *up,* not hand*out.* Failure can become a habit. And what about their children? Are we breeding in failure?"

"I don't know." And Mags didn't.

"The only time I have ever seen government programs work in terms of preparing people for the task at hand was during the war. We were trained and we were *well* trained, too. And a lot of what we learned in the service carried over into civilian life."

"Aunt Jeep, forgive me, but what does any of this have to do with food?"

"Think I'm getting dotty?"

"No, but you're on the roundabout." Mags teased her great-aunt.

"Hard to resist when one has a captive audience. Okay, here is my conclusion: We were fed. We had a mess hall. People who are hungry have difficulty thinking clearly, much less learning new skills. If I can find a way to remove the middleman, to get good food grown locally to Reno markets, we can at least begin right here in Nevada."

"I never connected food with performance."

"People who have never gone hungry or seen hunger don't. We didn't win the war just because we were right. That sounds great, but you win wars with firepower and food and the will to win. The United States had all in abundance. We still do. I'm no longer sure about our collective will, but I'll spare you that sermon. I'll tell you one thing the history books won't tell you: The German troops were the best army in the world at the time and their air force was incredible, too. But war wore them down, thanks to the enormous sacrifice of the Russians on the eastern front. Toward the last year and a half of the war, Germans didn't have the nutrition we had. Neither did the Russians, but they were defending their homeland. If we could have fed them, I think the war would have been shortened by at least six months. It was impossible to feed them, I know. At least that's what one old Army fly girl thinks. Start with nutrition."

"Buy the land, rent it out?"

"First, I have to irrigate it. If I can't buy it, maybe I can fashion long-term leases or buy the water rights. As you know, I own a lot of water rights in Red Rock Valley. If I can't buy land along Dry Valley Creek, I might be able to purchase water rights. The value of land and water will escalate, but a lot of money has to go into pulling the water up, spreading it on the land."

"The people who own that land, what's private, probably don't own the water rights."

"Some do. Some don't. Step one: take a thousand acres of my land and irrigate them. Step two: let people see how it works. Step three: hold their feet to the fire."

"Whose feet?"

"The company or companies that own some water rights along Dry Creek. Whoever owns what I can't buy. If I can convince them to irrigate those acres, then they'll look ever so generous and public spirited."

"Oh, Aunt Jeep, that will be a hard sell."

"We'll see." She put her hands on her hips. "I think this will be my last great fight."

"I hope not the last." Mags meant it, too.

"Well, that's a happy thought, but if it is my last, I'll be glad I can go down swinging. I've gotten a little too comfortable, you know. Then again I always had Dot and Dan beside me. They gave me heart. Both could get me back on course if I veered off. You know, I never realized just how much I depended on them until they died — and within a year of each other. I just sat down in the middle of the road. Took me a good two years to get up again." Jeep used an expression for grief.

"Two thousand, two thousand one. Seems like yesterday."

"Does. I had two wonderful partners in my life. A business partner can be as close, sometimes closer to you, than a life partner, you know. I was a lucky, lucky woman."

Before Mags could reply that she thought

Dot and Dan were lucky as well, Jeep hit the start button; the motor roared and she flew down the ridge. Mags had a hard time keeping up with her while dodging the large sagebrush and trying to avoid those rocks still covered in snow.

As they pulled up to the back of the house, inside King barked, followed by Baxter. Mags hurried off the ATV to open the door. Out flew the two dogs.

There was still enough snow down that Baxter had to follow behind King. He longed for the snow to melt so he could run ahead just to see if the larger dog could keep up with him.

"Hurry up, boys," Mags ordered.

"Maybe I'll pee on her," King suggested.

"She has a temper," the dachshund warned. *"And she's watched* The Dog Whisperer."

At this, they both cracked up. Then again, why dash human illusions that they trained canines instead of vice versa?

On the back porch, the two women peeled off their layers. When the dogs returned, Mags opened the door and they trotted in, leaving little snowprints.

"Aunt Jeep, you think partners are fate, too?"

"Sure."

"Any suggestions?"

She ran her eyes up and down Mags's lovely body. "Two. You have a beautiful figure. Show it off. And don't look."

"What do you mean, don't look?"

"The minute you look for a partner is when you will find Mr. Wrong. Go about your business and fate will send you Mr. Right."

"I'd settle for Mr. Right Now."

CHAPTER THIRTEEN

Shopping offered as much appeal for Pete Meadows as a rectal exam, but given that his two sisters were arriving very soon with husbands and children to stay with his mom and dad, and it was his day off, it was now or never for getting presents. Bewildered in the middle of the upscale Summit Shopping Center, he plucked the list his mother had made for him: Lucky jeans, an Arizona Cardinals football jersey with "Warner" on the back, and two pony halters for the twins. Rebecca had carefully written sizes and styles; everything he would need.

Pete's two older sisters, Jamie and Audrey, had married well — in Jamie's case extremely well. She lived in Greenwich, Connecticut. He'd visited her two years ago, needing a compass to find his way from his bedroom to the kitchen. Her twins had ponies — hence the halters. Audrey had married a careerist in the Defense Department. When the Republicans returned to power, the rumor was that Bryson would be named Undersecretary of Defense as he'd be too young to be the Secretary. They hoped to win the presidency in 2012. Failing that, it would be 2016. Americans grew bored with whoever was in power for eight years. Dress it up in issues, scandals, personality, it really came down to boredom. Time for a change.

Once Pete asked Audrey if the Washington life was tough.

She said, "You have no idea." Then she brightened, adding, "But I meet the most interesting people."

His older sisters rarely missed a chance to boss him around, even after he'd developed into the broad-shouldered, heavily muscled, handsome young man he remained. A star athlete in high school, Pete was deemed too small for college ball, but he had played baseball for UNR and was a standout. He had a chance at the Minor Leagues, but somehow knew he wasn't cut out for professional sports. Pete loved Nevada. He wanted to stay home and he wanted to do something worthwhile.

To an outsider, Pete might look like the failure in the family. Law enforcement was rarely deemed a suitable or lucrative career. However, his sisters strongly supported his choice. His mother feared for him. His father was quite proud. The family was still close, even though scattered geographically. Traditionally, the Meadows enjoyed their big family meal the evening of December 25. The kids would have opened their presents in the morning. And the night before, all would have gone to Trinity Episcopal together.

His sisters suggested they buy Mom a bracelet inset with every child's and grandchild's birthstone. Jamie took charge. Neither Jamie nor Audrey told Pete the true price. His slender means were so overmatched by their own, both sisters agreed to lie, telling him he had to ante up $200 and they'd give Mom her gift when all were together at Christmas dinner.

Audrey, closer to Pete in age, being two years older to Jamie's four, had asked their mother to take photos of his small cottage. When Pete and his wife divorced two years ago, Lorraine, his ex-wife, took everything. The good news was he didn't have to pay alimony since his ex had made more money than him. No one in his family suggested he ask for alimony. The Meadows did not think that way.

Everyone knew he was lonely. While he kept himself busy — played ball in the summer, worked out in the winter, read voraciously — he still needed a partner. The human race marches in twos.

No one had particularly disliked Lorraine. They'd met in college, she was in journalism, switched to media studies, and now was on the nightly news. Lorraine, quite pretty, could also be quite self-centered. Pete usually gave way, but what really split them apart was that they'd agreed to have children once established. As her career took off, she decided against this. A woman who doesn't truly want to be a mother shouldn't. Pete finally realized Lorraine wouldn't backtrack. He also came to understand that she would wind up in a much larger market than Reno and he'd be left behind. It was a matter of time.

By late in the afternoon, he'd bought everything his mother had listed. Frazzled, he turned his dark blue Jeep Wrangler toward UNR. As a student, the Getchell Library had served his research needs. With the university's growth, a new library had been opened in 2009, the Mattheson, IGT Knowledge Center.

Once inside, Pete was as lost as he was at Summit Shopping Center. However, the librarian pointed him to the Nevada history section.

Glad to be in a quiet place — a nearly empty place since Christmas vacation created the usual diaspora — he draped his coat over a chair, pulled a notebook out of the inside pocket and a pen, too. What he wanted were the names of Reno residents from 1887 to 1900 with Russian surnames. With help from another librarian, after an hour, he had fourteen names, including one Romanov who surely had been a crook.

Then, like Mags, he tried to find what he could about the Nicholas Cavalry School. Not much.

Leaning back in the chair, refreshed by not hearing various renditions of "Jingle Bells," he wondered why it mattered to know about Reed's Russian, which is how he thought of the skeleton.

Pete had joined the police force to prevent crime, to help people in severe distress. If a crime had been committed, then his job was to find the perpetrator. He had known early in his career that justice rarely followed but, like everyone else in law enforcement, did his best and tried not to despair at the aftermath. If ever found, there could be no justice for whoever killed Reed's Russian yet some form of peace would follow — for Pete, anyway. And it would make an old woman happy, a woman he admired and one who had helped his family even before he and his sisters were born.

A flash of Mags made him sit up straighter. He pushed the image back. He wasn't going to think about a beautiful woman who wouldn't look at him twice.

By seven, he was hungry. He picked up his notebook, slipped his bomber jacket back on, then stopped by the reference desk.

"Ma'am, do you have copies of the Reno newspaper from 1887 to 1900?" He held up his hand. "Don't want them now. I know it's late and it's the holidays. I'll come back later."

"We have everything on computer from the *Gazette-Journal*'s morgue. So does the public library downtown if that's more convenient for you."

"Thank you."

As he drove to his place he turned on the radio and "We Three Kings of Orient Are" blared out at him. He listened a moment, then smiled and sang along, suddenly ridiculously happy without knowing why.

CHAPTER FOURTEEN

Racing across the frozen sandy loam to the original barn, King called over his shoulder. *"Can't you keep up? It's those dwarf legs of yours."*

The snow had melted in places, packed down in others. The dry high-desert air blew steadily over the frozen terrain, gradually making movement easier for man and beast.

"I'm watching out for the footing." Baxter, insulted, called forward.

"Yeah, yeah." King broke into a lope to further torment the dachshund.

Now angry, Baxter hit a good stride and passed the shepherd mix. *"Can't you keep up?"*

King, ears pricked up, dug into the ground to draw alongside the small dog. Almost to the barn, King finally nudged ahead of the surprisingly fast Baxter. He veered from the closed big side doors to the side where the old exterior tack room door was, a dog door still in place. He bustled through. Baxter followed with a little whoosh of air.

Although not ready to admit it, King liked having a companion. Oh, he loved Jeep but human limitations occasionally plucked his last nerve. Finally, another truly intelligent creature, even if he was a sawed-off shotgun.

Vapor streams flowed from the dogs' noses and mouths as they inspected the rectangular space where the Russian had lain. His remains, dusted, photographed, and measured by university students, had finally been moved to the university for further study. The students had left behind piles of dirt, which rested like rounded berms at each corner of the grave.

King stopped in front of the northeast pile, looked at the other three, put his front paws in, and started digging, throwing dirt everywhere.

Baxter, puzzled, observed the mostly black dog with glossy thick fur, grinning as his paws rapidly made a mess.

"Whoopee!" King stopped. *"What's the matter with you?"*

"I was about to ask the same thing." Baxter sat on his haunches.

"It's a pile. You dig." King stepped back a moment. *"Take the pile opposite me."*

"Hmm." Baxter walked around the pile in a

semi-circle. If he'd completed the circle he'd have fallen into the grave. No point in hurrying that process. Tentatively he put one paw into the dirt, then pulled it backward. Didn't hurt. Felt pretty good.

"Is there a reason I'm to do that?"

"You're a dog." King was incredulous.

"I've never seen a dirt pile."

"There's no dirt where you come from? How can there be no dirt?"

Baxter lifted his bushy eyebrows. *"Concrete. There's some dirt in the parks but you can't dig. And you have to walk on a leash. You can't even run in the parks. I mean, you can try but someone gets pissy about it."* He sighed. *"I never raced another dog before now."*

"That's awful. How can your human be so cruel?"

"She's not cruel." Baxter took offense. *"We lived in a giant city. She took good care of me, but that's just the way it is. At night you can't even see the stars because there's so much light from the buildings."*

"All night? There are indoor lights on all night?" King just couldn't believe it.

"I only know about stars because every summer Mags rents a place in the Hamptons. I saw them then, plus I could walk along the ocean with her. No leash!"

"Saw the ocean once with Jeep. Too noisy."

"Mine is a different ocean but it's noisy, too. I like it here. I like not having people everywhere. No sidewalks. No horns or traffic. Being a dog in New York City is dangerous." Baxter cocked his head, looked at the pile, then jumped in the middle of it. *"This is fun."* He jumped out, shook himself, and began digging with a vengeance.

Five minutes passed. The two stopped to admire their progress. King walked over to Baxter's pile while Baxter checked King's.

"What's this?" Baxter noticed some tiny colored square bits spread about.

King returned, touched one with his nose. It wasn't even as big as a piece of square kibble. *"Old bones."*

Baxter touched it. *"In little squares? What kind of animal is that?"*

King again touched the little squares, one white, one red, one faded blue. *"Don't know, but, see, they're cut. This isn't natural. They've been dyed. There are no blue bones."*

"Greenies." Baxter so loved his Greenies.

"Not real bone."

"Oh. Well, King, this is your world. What's the point of tiny bones cut in squares and dyed?"

"Jeep will know. She knows things I don't. Not about animals or weather or real stuff, but human stuff. She also knows what's under the

earth. It's almost like she has a nose that can smell things like gold, silver, copper. Stuff we don't much need but they do."

"What's it like to live with a human that old?"

"I never lived with a human that's young. Even Enrique is half old. Mags is young. I like her. She moves without pain. Jeep hurts, but she doesn't whimper. She'd be furious if anyone noticed. She hides a lot. She is very, very old, really. She plays ball, though. She never gives up. I love her."

"I love mine, too. She's pretty dumb, though."

King laughed. "They are what they are. All you can do is love them." He thought a long time. "Let's get Jeep to look at these odd bones. You know these ones didn't come from the skeleton they took away."

"How are we going to do that?"

"Baxter, we start with barking. I'll show you all the steps. You haven't properly trained your person. But then," King said in a kindly voice, "you didn't have an older dog to teach you. I had my mother and she knew every trick in the book."

"I barely remember my mother." Baxter mentioned this with little emotion.

"Follow me and learn," King said bursting through the dog door at the back of the house, Baxter on his heels.

Taking a deep sniff, King realized Jeep wasn't in the kitchen.

"What's the fuss?" Jeep called out from the den.

King hustled through the kitchen door and down the hall, skidding out as he turned into the room where Mags, at the desk, peered at the computer screen. Jeep sat by the fire-place, replacing a worn headstall on a still-serviceable bridle. As her fingers stiffened, she forced herself to do more and more of what her mother called "close work," to re-tain some nimbleness.

"Come to the barn." King barked up in her face, then called to Baxter. *"Go do the same thing to Mags."*

The wire-haired dachshund scurried over and stood on his hind paws, placing his front paws on her thigh. *"You'd better come with me. King will be upset if I don't get you out of this chair."*

King turned in small circles, sat down, whined, turned a few more, then yelled, *"Baxter, turn in circles, jump up and down. Make noise!"* Then as an afterthought, *"But don't pee on the floor."*

"I would never do that!" Baxter did turn a few circles, which made him dizzy, so he pat-ted Mags's leg again.

"King, will you stop barking!" Jeep shook

her finger at him.

"It's really important." King circled, ran to the open door of the den, ran back to Jeep.

Jeep put down the bridle and stood up. "I wonder if the coyote have come close?"

Mags pushed away from the desk to follow. "I hear them at night but I didn't think they'd come up to the house."

"If you hear one, there are many more. If they're hungry enough they'll root around or kill anything you haven't made safe. I imagine it's been slim pickings since the storm."

"Come on. Come on." King danced. *"Baxter, you have to make it very obvious."*

"All right. All right." Baxter dashed ahead of Mags, stopped, looked up at her, then dashed ahead again.

Jeep grabbed her heavy jacket, then yanked on a wool lumberjack cap. Mags did the same and the two women followed the dogs from the house.

"Look for tracks." Jeep ordered Mags. "Like a dog's, but, um —" She paused. "King's. See how King's are wide? The coyote print is more narrow."

"She's not completely stupid." King waved his tail.

"Right." Baxter agreed.

"We can run way ahead now," King said.

The two ran to the original barn and dis-

151

appeared through the tack room door.

Jeep, relieved, noted the location. "At least it's not the cattle barn. We don't have any heifers due but sometimes they abort. That brings in the marauders if food is scarce. I swear they can smell that hot blood for miles. And if enough of them get in the barn —" She paused. "Coyotes can hunt singly but they prefer to hunt in a pack. The larger the pack the bolder their actions. If they're desperate enough, pumped up by numbers, they'll go in the barn and start killing."

"Can't you shoot them?"

"Yes. But I haven't had much trouble and we've shut up the horses at night and some of the younger cattle."

The two women slipped in after opening the big doors a crack.

"What have you done?" Jeep spoke to King when she saw the large pile tossed all over.

Baxter's modest efforts didn't provoke comment.

Both dogs stood by the small colored bone squares.

Jeep and Mags walked over. Jeep noticed that King did not drop his ears or look chastised. Having lived with dogs all her life she had mastered their basic communication methods, although the more refined ones escaped her. But then, they did most everyone.

King barked again. *"Look! More bones!"*

At first, neither woman spotted the object of King's excitement.

Mags bent over, then dropped onto one knee. She plucked out a tiny red square, handing it up to Jeep. Then she began smoothing over the dirt, picking out a blue one, a white one, then a cracked one.

Jeep, with the small squares in her hand, whistled, "I'll be damned."

Mags stood up to peer into her great-aunt's palm. "They're cut in almost perfect squares."

"They aren't glass, either." Jeep took her right glove off and stuffed it in her coat pocket, then nudged one. "Tiny, little cut bones for decoration." She looked up at Mags. "Guess those college kids didn't sift the earth as carefully as they should have. Well, lifting out our Russian with minimal damage was more important, I reckon. These were in there with him."

"Could have been there before he was buried."

"Hmm." Jeep touched the squares again. "Delicate work making something like this."

"Told you she'd know something." King sat next to Baxter.

Jeep, hearing the comment, looked at her beloved dog. "King, good dog."

"He certainly was excited. Tearing apart the pile took a lot of effort." Mags laughed.

"Yes, it did." Jeep held one square up between her thumb and forefinger to see the small hole pierced in it. "These were woven into something."

"A necklace?"

"Could be, or some kind of talisman. What intrigues me, apart from the fact they were in our Russian's grave, is they are genuine — not glass beads, which a lot of Indians used once they had access to them. These were carved, then colored. They had great meaning for whoever created them and probably for whoever received them."

"Our Russian?"

"You know he didn't make them and I find it quite a coincidence that something like this could have been in the soil. Our man was held in high esteem by someone," Jeep mused.

"Aunt Jeep, I'm going to get Carlotta's flour sifter. I'll go through these other piles."

"That's a good idea." Jeep then cast her eyes down at the packed floor. "And I think I'd better get Enrique to use the ditch witch to dig down two feet on both stall sides, then have the boys do the last foot by hand. It's a lot of work, but I think he planned on doing it later anyway. We haven't had time to discuss this. Who knows what else is down there."

Mags shivered slightly. "Nothing, I hope."

"I do, too, but then I never expected our Russian."

After having to promise Carlotta she would go to town and buy her a new flour sifter tomorrow, Mags carefully sifted the earth. She found six more colored bones and one faded cracked one. After replacing the piles, she walked back to the house, Baxter at her heels. King stayed at the house with Jeep.

Mags dropped the six colored objects into Jeep's hand.

"Two white, three blue, and one red." Jeep then put the three she had with Mags's six.

"You're wearing his ring." Mags sat down at the kitchen table. "I'd like to wear these."

Jeep smiled. "You, too?"

Mags nodded. "I don't know why."

"Me, neither, but I can't resist the urge."

CHAPTER FIFTEEN

One wall of George W. Ball's office was covered with U.S. Geological Survey maps, the topographical lines showing elevation. While the information could be pulled up on computer, George wanted Washoe County in front of him at a glance. Also spread out were maps of the eastern part of Sierra County, California, and the western part of Churchill County, Nevada. On the adjoining wall were some topo maps of down south toward Lake Tahoe.

He'd marked with colored red pins where each of the Silver State Resource Management pumps were. Those pins had small flags with the pump number as well as a code for the type of pump. They were long pins, too.

Shorter pins with blue heads identified privately owned aquifers. Those owned by SSRM had a yellow flag.

At a glance, George W. could see Reno's

present and possibly its future water supply. Wings Ranch sprouted blue pins everywhere — not that George concentrated on them.

With a blue marker he'd drawn wavy lines on these maps where creeks ran above-ground. A dotted line indicated an under-ground creek. There was actually a lot of water flowing under those arid acres. Of course, the trick was getting it up and out.

The weather report announced Washoe County was under a winter storm watch. Some snow would fall beginning in the mid-afternoon but it wasn't projected to be a storm like the monster that had hit earlier in the month.

It was Monday, the winter solstice. He'd just walked into his office after having taken his secretary, Christina, to a Christmas lunch.

She buzzed him. "Mr. Ball, you need to take this."

Christina's voice told him it was urgent. He clicked on his multiline phone. "George W. Ball."

"Pump Twenty-two," said Twinkie. "Boss, someone blew it. Sheriff's Department couldn't find you so they found me."

"Dammit," George said softly. "Okay. I'll get down there. I'll get there as fast as I can." He paused. "Has anyone seen the

157

damage yet?"

"No. The sheriff said a nearby resident reported the explosion, saw the smoke, and drove to see where it was but he didn't know what he was looking at."

"Better take a new pump and pipe. I'll get extra support. You got Bunny along?"

"Yep."

"All right, then. Will take me about forty minutes. Traffic is a goddamned mess. This is a goddamned mess."

"Yes, sir."

Given that Pete Meadows and Lonnie Parrish had been at the scene of the Pump 19 explosion, the Sheriff's Department wisely ordered them to the crime scene.

CHAPTER SIXTEEN

When the two officers pulled into the parking area for Pump 22, the wasted water spread over the area, a small jet shooting straight up from what remained of the machinery. The temperature hung at a relatively balmy 36°F, melting snow still filled crevices, but most had already seeped into the ground thanks to a few days in the mid-forties. The nights remained bitter. Although the day was better than the conditions that had greeted them when Pump 19 was blown, they weren't great. An exploded pump still meant bone-chilling cold water.

Pete and Lonnie arrived at the site first. Again it resembled a pale blue flower, jagged edges curling outward. Pete motioned for Lonnie to walk to the right. He'd search to the left.

A scrap of paper fluttered by in a slight breeze. Pete stomped on it and picked it up. Again, indecipherable writing. A bit of red caught his eye. Twenty paces away he recovered a small piece of red ripstop fabric. Placing the paper and fabric in a plastic baggie, he rejoined Lonnie. "Looks like another shopping list." Lonnie pointed to "Tide" written on one of the paper scraps he'd found.

"What does this guy do? Stop at the supermarket for a six-pack of Coke on his way to his bombings?" Pete opened the plastic bag for Lonnie to drop in his paper fragments.

The two men scanned the surrounding area. Anything of a bright color stood out against the palette of sand and beige, light gray rock outcroppings. The sagebrush added brown to the mix but there was nothing remotely bright to it.

Pete folded over the top of the baggie, putting it in his pocket before the two men returned to the damaged pump.

"How many people are serviced by this pump, I wonder?" Lonnie looked down for loose fragments. "Hey." He pointed to a blasted piece of one-inch pipe lodged in one of the outward metal petals of the pump. Water fell back on it from the jet, but the piece of pipe was quite visible. The recessed pump housing was filling with water. So far, there were perhaps six inches on the floor.

"Looks very much the same as last time

but best not to jump to any conclusions." Pete got down on his hands and knees, oblivious to the frigid water falling on him from above. "Looks welded or wedged in there. Don't think we can pull it out." He stood up and shook himself.

"Same M.O.?"

"Sure looks like it. I wish we had Mindy here."

The part-time explosives expert was only called to a location if a bomb threat came in. She'd accompany the team to the site, they'd try to locate the device, then she'd defuse it. However, the only bomb threats the sheriff's office had received in the last few years were fake. Each of the various high schools throughout the school year spawned some clown who thought this an excellent strategy to get out of class. It was, too, until someone squealed or the prankster couldn't resist bragging. The media wallowed in irresponsible youth stories, angry comments from teachers, fellow students, and the usual bewildered mother denying any wrongdoing by her darling son, it was always a son. Occasionally, some other news angle would be inflicted on the television news. Perhaps during the bomb scare a cafeteria worker dropped a large bowl of peas, slipped on them, and broke her hip. And, of course,

Mommy's angelic son would never get good recommendations to college unless he crawled on his belly to perform endless community service.

Pete had answered enough of these sort of calls to find some slender amusement in them, as long as no hips were broken. This business of attacking folks' water supply, however, was not amusing. The south side of Reno toward Lake Tahoe contained some of the wealthiest neighborhoods in the county. This particular service disruption would create much more of a furor than Red Rock had. Whoever was doing this had upped the ante.

Pete kept these thoughts to himself. Sooner or later the department would feel the public's wrath along with the loud complaint from Silver State Resource Management. As this was Pete's case, he could expect full helpings of the same.

Lonnie knew this, too. "Pete, we need to pick up a map of all the pump sites from SSRM."

Pete nodded. "Right."

The low rumble of the big diesel engine told them Twinkie and Bunny would soon make the turn. With the land flatter here it wouldn't present as many difficulties as Red Rock. Also as the pump wasn't on high ground, maneuvering the replacement equipment on the big rig would be somewhat easier.

At the wheel, Twinkie, ever-present plastic straw clamped between his teeth, barreled down the service road, swung that big sucker around, and put the rig's bed right alongside the blown pump.

Twinkie and Bunny scrambled from the cab. As much as this worried Pete and Lonnie, it worried them more. They both had many years in water management under their belts. Hostilities over water rights happened at public hearings, not at the equipment sites. This was new. It was not only an attack on SSRM, it was an attack on people's basic need: water.

Twinkie waved at Pete as he surveyed the mess.

Bunny, alongside Twinkie, shook his head. "Shit."

"Might find some of that there, too." Twinkie half-joked.

Pete said, "Be washed away now."

As if on cue, Oliver Hitchens's white company car came into sight.

"Our very own company turd. Old Faithful couldn't wash him away." Bunny laughed derisively. "All right, Twink, where's my slicker?"

"Behind the seat. Grab mine, too," Twinkie called.

"Twinkie, there's a piece of one-inch pipe wedged down there." Pete pointed. "When you cut the water, if you can dislodge it, give it to me for our explosives expert."

"Sure enough."

Bunny urged, "Let's get down in there before Shithead can issue his orders."

Twinkie dropped into the recessed area, careful with his feet. Sharp pieces of metal might be hidden by the water rising from the concrete floor.

A jagged piece of metal could cut through most soles, even good work boots. Twinkie tapped his toe every few inches as he moved toward the pump.

Thanks to the lessons learned at Pump 19, the two had come prepared. A new pump, chained to the flatbed, along with sections of pipe, bore evidence to that. They carried wrenches and heavy tools as a matter of course, but this time had two small propane torches, too.

Both reached the wide horizontal wheel. Since the temperature was above freezing, it was only cold, not frozen, and with effort they managed to cut the water flow.

Oliver got out of his parked car and slammed the door, angrily acknowledging the two officers with a curt nod. He hurried to the pump and looked down at the two men in the pit. "You should have waited for me."

"Mr. Hitchens, there's only three and a half hours of light left. It's easier to work in natural light and I think we can fix this," Twinkie replied honestly.

Oliver stared down. "How bad is it?"

"About the same as Pump Nineteen."

Oliver ran his hand through his thick hair. "ETA?"

"Five hours. Part of the pipe is damaged. We have to seal it, cut it out, replace it. Didn't have to do that up in Red Rock. So we're going to need artificial lights."

"How long before the lights get here?"

"An hour at the most."

Oliver turned his head at the crunch of approaching tires.

George W. Ball pulled his car right next to the pump. Getting out of another company Tahoe, he approached with a grim expression. "Officers, thank you for being here."

"George W.," Twinkie looked up. "Pump's ruined."

"Figured." George W. turned to Oliver. "Glad you made it here so quickly."

"I can handle this, George W. I know you have a lot on your plate."

"Nothing more important than this. I called Darryl. There will be an emergency meeting of department vice presidents tonight at seven. One blown pump was bad. Two is a trend." Ball reached out his hand to Pete, whom he perceived to be the senior officer. "George W. Ball, easiest way to describe me is head of equipment."

"Deputy Peter Meadows and this is Officer Lonnie Parrish. We responded to the first blown pump."

"Any ideas?"

"It appears to be the same M.O." Pete pulled out his clear plastic bag. "Bits of paper, a red sliver of ripstop fabric, and there's a section of one-inch pipe wedged down there in your pump." He paused. "The department has an excellent explosives expert. She was in demolition in Desert Storm."

George W.'s eyebrows raised. "Pipe bombs are easy to make."

"Yes, sir, they are. The first one contained high-grade explosives. That's why I want that section down there. I'm hoping there's some residue left," Pete said.

"Ah, that is just terrible." George looked down at Twinkie and Bunny checking the damaged pipe.

"Bunny, what's the floor like?" George

W. asked.

The water had stabilized at seven inches once the wheel shut off the flow.

"Wet." Bunny smiled up at him.

"Metal shards?" George W. asked.

Twinkie glanced up. "I pushed some to the side with my boot. If you're coming down, it's safe around the pump and the pipe."

Without hesitation, George W. lowered himself into the cold water, heedless of his fancy wingtip shoes and tailored trousers. The people who worked for George W. loved him at moments like this. He was right in there with you.

"Three's better than two." George sloshed over to the pipe. "Hey, Bun, you've got gloves on, see if you can wiggle this out." He pointed at the pipe fragment. Looking up at Oliver, "Go get the propane torches and a channel lock wrench."

Hoping he wouldn't have to get down in the water, Oliver fairly sprinted away.

"Got it!" Bunny triumphantly held up two inches of pipe fragment.

"Give it to Deputy Meadows," George W. ordered.

"Thanks, Bunny." Pete placed the pipe in another bag and handed it to Lonnie, indicating he should put it in the cab of the squad car. "If you find anything once the water recedes, let me know," Pete asked.

"Will do." George, examining the damaged pipe, a little water spritzing up in his face, replied, "Boys, you cut off the valve. This is what's left. I think we can section it out now."

"Could put in a new pipe," Oliver said.

"We will in the spring," George W. replied without looking at Oliver, his attention riveted on the pipe. "Have to dig out a twelve-foot length. If we can make a clean cut here, measure and cut a refit, use our rubber seals. We might have some leakage, but it won't be too bad. There's no way we can take the day needed to lay a new length of outtake pipe."

"Well, you're right about that." Oliver saw a mobile television news unit make the turn. "Oh, no."

Lonnie nudged Pete. "Vamoose."

"Why, you don't have on your makeup?" Pete's desire to talk to the TV news was low, but they'd pass the mobile unit on the way out. They were trapped.

Last thing the department needed was officers appearing to be uncooperative with the media.

Oliver informed the three men down in the pump enclosure that the TV news would arrive in approximately three minutes.

George called out, "Deputy Meadows."

"Yes, Mr. Ball." Pete walked over.

"Any ideas who is doing this?"

"All I know is it's someone intelligent and motivated. While we're working hard, sir, we don't have enough evidence yet to have a suspect or even a person of interest."

George W. grimaced. "Chances are this isn't the last we hear from this idiot."

"Let me ask you something, sir. Has there been equipment damage before, something less serious that you didn't report?"

"No. Absolutely nothing."

Pete saw the on-air reporter checking his gorgeous mane of hair in the mirror before approaching them.

Michael Carruthers wore a heavy short jacket with the station numbers embroidered on it. His haircut was perfect, his dental work blindingly white. For all that, he didn't seem like too much of a twit.

"Deputy." Michael walked toward Pete, camerawoman right behind him. "May I ask you a few questions?"

"Of course. And this is my colleague Officer Lonnie Parrish," Pete said, nodding at Lonnie, who looked alarmed at the attention. "You can ask him questions, too."

"You look better on TV than I do." Lonnie demurred.

Focusing on Pete, Michael inquired,

"We've been informed that this is the second pump bombing. Any suspects in this string of crimes?"

"No. We are still gathering evidence. It's too early in the investigation to draw conclusions." Pete prudently turned toward the three working in the pump enclosure. "As you can see, there is a fair amount of damage."

Taking his cue from Pete, Michael walked over to get footage of the men at work. Oliver, useless as tits on a boar hog, stood idle beside the rig.

Much as Oliver wanted to appear on camera, he had the sense to stay put.

Pete and Lonnie slipped back into the squad car.

George W. looked up and noticed the journalist. "Mike, you can ask anything you want but we have to keep working. We're going to start losing sunlight soon. We've got to repair this as fast as possible. It is the holidays." He blew air out for emphasis.

"Right." Mike motioned for his camerawoman to circle the pump site.

"How much damage is there?"

George W. replied, "The pump is completely destroyed as is part of the outtake pipe." His pants and shoes were ruined. It was cold in his workday clothes but the sight of a Silver State department head working with two well-equipped servicemen would be decent PR for the company. Darry and the Board of Directors would be grateful, too. But that wasn't why George W. was down there.

The growl of the approaching big rig caught their attention. The camerawoman swung around to catch the large truck lumbering toward them, huge worklights on the bed.

"Thank God!" Twinkie exulted.

"Who is that?" Mike asked.

"Twinkie Bosun." He identified himself and smiled at an imaginary TV audience. "That means we'll get this pump repaired much faster."

"Any ideas who might do such a thing?" Mike asked all three.

Bunny piped up. "The Grinch who stole Christmas. Trying to ruin people's holiday. We won't let him."

The other two laughed, as did Mike.

"Mike, can you move your van?" George W. requested. "Our driver is going to need a wide arc to get to us."

"Sure. We'll shoot all this, if you don't mind."

"Not at all. Perhaps Silver State can purchase your footage since I know only a bit will be televised. I think our corporate officers should see the damage and what it takes to repair it."

"Hey, no charge. I'll email you the digital file." Mike left, then walked back to move the truck.

George W. yelled out, "Oliver, call Christina. Ask her to call my wife and have her bring a change of clothes to the office. I'll make it just in time for the emergency meeting. Oh, when you're done, bring us those rubber seals, will you?" George W. knew Oliver didn't have his home number in his head but he knew all the company numbers, had them stored in his phone.

Reduced to a gofer, Oliver did as told.

Another SSRM vehicle churned toward the site. Parking out of the way, Craig Locke hopped out of his SUV.

He identified himself to the newsman. "Craig Locke, Development. I have nothing to say. This isn't my department. I just happened to be driving up from Wellington. My secretary called and told me about Pump Twenty-two so I thought I'd stop by. It's not my department," he repeated.

George W. called out, "Craig, come here."

Craig hurried over. "Jesus Christ, George W., you're soaking wet."

"Yeah. I'm still hoping to make that meeting but if I'm late, make my apologies and tell me what happens, will you?"

"Of course." Craig then asked Twinkie and Bunny, "Can I get you all coffee or anything? There's a convenience store a few miles back." He turned to the reporter. "What about you?"

"No, thank you," Michael Carruthers answered.

"Craig, we got a hot thermos in the rig, but thanks," Twinkie called out while twisting a wrench around a big lug nut.

"All right, then. I'll leave you to it."

That night watching the news together in the living room, Jeep and Mags moved toward the edge of their seats when the story came on about Pump 22.

"Not another one!" Jeep exclaimed.

"He's good on camera." Mags petted Baxter in her lap.

"Who is?"

"Pete Meadows."

"Yes, he is. Handsome, too." Jeep smiled. "Good people, his family."

"Married?"

"Divorced. You can watch her on the other channel, Lorraine Kaine, she never took his name when they married."

173

"Standard practice in the biz," Mags said.

"I suppose."

"Know why?"

"Why what?" Jeep's mind had returned to the pump explosions.

"Why they divorced."

"The usual. Ambition trumps love."

They watched the rest of the news, King snoring loudly as he lay in front of the fireplace.

"Aunt Jeep?"

"I hear an important question coming my way." She laughed.

"Were you ever in love?"

The old lady threw up her hands in delight. "You're thirty-two years old and only now you ask?"

"Well" — Mags blushed — "you aren't exactly someone who invites personal questions. My mother told me to never bother you about anything really — not just this particular subject."

"Yes, I was in love. High school crush. In Sweetwater, Texas, I fell in love with an airplane mechanic. Didn't last long. That's pretty much the sum total 'til you get to Dot and Dan. Loved them both deeply, and in different ways. Satisfied?"

"Uh —"

She laughed. "You want to know if I slept

with those two, is that it? Mags, come out with it."

"We all wondered."

"I see. So I was the hot topic of discussion at the Rogers dinner table?"

"I wouldn't put it that way, but —"

"I'm not a total fool. Dot was gorgeous, Dan was divine. Of course I slept with them." She held up her hands for silence. "Not at the same time."

"And they knew about each other?"

"Yep. There were a few dicey moments. He suffered more, really. Dan was a sweet, rather conventional man. He was sure sooner or later I'd come to my senses and marry him. He asked me over and over."

"And?"

"I'd patiently explain that if I married him I would still keep Dot as my mistress."

"And what about her?"

"Same explanation, sort of. Well, after five years Dan understood I was telling him the truth. That's when he married Renata. I adored her. We all did. She bore me no ill will nor I her. I'd had my time with him. He needed a wife, the kind you stand with in front of a minister or at the courthouse, the sort to have children. She gave him all that. In the end, he came to see I loved him truly. Had I married him, eventually both of us would have been wretched. I could be a Mrs., but I couldn't and can't be a wife. I say *can't* because you never know, now do you?"

Mags laughed. "No, I suppose not."

Mags's cell rang. She got up and left the room so as not to disturb Jeep. Returning five minutes later, she cheerlessly dropped in the chair.

"You look like you're suffering a severe gas pain."

"That was my dear sister, Catherine."

Jeep immediately straightened up. "And?"

"She's in Reno." Mags held up one hand, palm outward. "She knows you won't let her on the ranch. She's not even asking to come out, but she wants to see me."

"What on earth is she doing in Reno?"

"She has a boyfriend in Las Vegas and they were coming through to check up on one of his businesses. She says she'll tell me about it tomorrow. I said I'd meet her for lunch."

"She has all the appeal of a puff adder, but she is your sister, I can understand why you'd agree to lunch."

"Noon."

"Take a stiletto."

CHAPTER SEVENTEEN

"You're driving a Camaro?" Catherine's flawless features registered shock. Mags, one long leg out of the car, swung out the other, and got out of the good-looking muscle car. "What of it?"

"Well, it's, it's so working class." Catherine kissed her sister on the cheek and took her hand to lead her into the small, chic Beaujolais Bistro. "This is on me. Heard about your crash."

"You don't have to pay." Much as she wanted to hate her older sister, Mags couldn't quite do it. But that sure didn't mean she'd trust her one bit.

After being seated in their booth, Catherine folded her hands in front of her on the table, the deep green of a five-carat emerald ring announcing this was a woman of means. "You look great, Mags. It's been a long time."

"Thanks. And you always look great. Like

Nanna," Mags said, referring to their grandmother Sarah, Jeep's sister.

"What a compliment. Nanna was so beautiful. Did you ever see photographs of the Empress Elizabeth of Austria, Sissy?" When Mags nodded that she had, Catherine continued, "Don't you think Nanna looked a lot like Sissy?"

"I never thought about it, but yes, I guess she did."

"How's Aunt Jeep? She was pretty much a looker, too. Not as glam as Nanna, of course, but no slouch."

"She's herself."

"Still hates me?"

"You're not her number one relative."

"And you are?" The jet-black eyebrows arched over the green eyes; same eyes as Mags.

"Oh, we get along, but Enrique is closest to her heart and now she has great-grandchildren. Carlotta, as always, is terrific. How one woman can wear so many colors at the same time and pull it off, I'll never know."

"I miss Carlotta." Catherine sighed a practiced, dramatic sigh. "Miss the Old Dragon, too. She taught me so much and after all, she did manage us when Mom and Dad died."

"You were at Skidmore and already unmanageable," Mags teased.

"Well, you were in your senior year at West-lake." Catherine named the tony private school in Los Angeles. "When Jeep transferred you to that private school in Reno, I remember the letters I got filled with angst and the fact that no one knew how to dress."

Mags flushed. "What a little snob I was. Got over that, thank goodness." She glanced up at the young, pleasingly plump waitress waiting to take their order. The woman did not give her name and utter those fateful words, "I'll be your server today."

"Martini, olive please." Catherine motioned for her sister to order.

"Tonic water with lime."

"Be right back." The waitress placed two menus before them that had been handwritten that morning, always a sign that the fare was original. Well, one was supposed to think so anyway.

"Still drinking?" Mags said, trying to keep the judgment out of her voice.

"Yep, however, I don't take smack anymore. That was a major mistake."

"Learn anything from it?"

"Sure." Catherine's eyes sparkled. "It worked wonders for Louis Armstrong but didn't do a damn thing for me except make me nod out. Ruined my acting career."

"And?"

"And what?"

"Any jobs on the horizon? Are you going to auditions?"

Catherine waved her bejeweled hand. "I got a small part on 'Flame Out.' It's a sitcom about stock car racing. I don't know if it will turn into anything bigger or not. I've got a lot to overcome."

"So do the bosses at 'Flame Out' know about the movies you made using the name Camilla Littleton and wearing the worst red wig imaginable?" Mags shook her head.

"Was a fright, wasn't it?" Catherine said as the two sisters laughed.

"Catherine, how could you do it?"

Taking another sip of one of the best martinis she'd ever tasted, Catherine leveled her gorgeous eyes at Mags. "Look, Shortcakes, I was in big trouble. I'd blown what Mom and Dad left us. I was making good money, had no idea it could ever run out. I had gofers, hairdressers, masseuses. Buyers were calling on me from department stores, jewelry stores, car dealers, telling me what great deals they had just for me. And all the while I sat in my trailer waiting for the next scene. I was going to be the next Sandra Bullock. Maybe I was a fool, but I'll tell you one thing, I have fabulous, fabulous memories. To be young and rich, fawned over by sultans, famous baseball players, and too many politicians to shake a stick at, I *loved* every minute. Totally, completely, loved it! Unfortunately, somewhere along the way, I lost all common sense."

Mags leaned back in the restaurant's comfortable booth. "I did, too, but in a different way."

"Great sex in the Wall Street world?"

"Ha!" Mags exploded. "Great egos who think they're God's gift. Most of those boys who think they're men are soft as the Pillsbury Doughboy. Baldness I don't mind, but spare tires turn me right off. You can bet they all made passes at me, especially the married ones. Unlike you, I didn't fall for it. But then you had better material."

"Didn't I? Revolting as Bobby is" — she named her ex — "he was gorgeous, well hung, and knew what to do with it. Other than that, he's my candidate for all-time slimeball. Okay, maybe I exaggerate. I guess Hitler and Stalin were a bit worse."

"Funny you should mention Stalin. Last week, Aunt Jeep said something about Trotsky. They were all monsters, that was her word, 'monsters.'"

"We don't seem to spawn that sort of evil pathology over on this side of the pond. I can't decide if it's lack of imagination or if

Americans really are more stable. Well, I'm hardly a good example of a stable American, am I? Born to privilege, grew up with a wonderful family, movie stars were our parents' best friends. We had every advantage in the world. I wound up in porn. Easy money. I could have afforded a better wig."

"Why red?"

"Lucille Testicle Red."

Mags laughed until the tears came. "What would Desi say? Poor Lucy. I doubt she would have wished to be your inspiration for those roles."

"Remember how good-looking she was?"

"Yeah, Dad took us to meet her and she must have been seventy. We were so excited. I truly loved Lucy. Great bones, carriage. Ah." Mags smiled when the food arrived for she was hungry.

"Are you done with it?"

"Porn?" Catherine raised her eyebrows, something she did often. "Never say never, but I hope I am. Fast money. Paid off my creditors. At least now I'm not wallowing in debt. Sometimes I drink too much to forget. I don't incline toward uppers. I prefer 'the soothers.' It's in the family genetically, you know."

"I know. Dad's side seems to be an unbroken string of drunks. We're hardly doomed.

Not everyone falls victim to it. Dad didn't."

"Well, I did. There isn't a substance I'm not willing to ingest or inhale." She smiled, suddenly embarrassed. "In moderation, of course."

"Who's the boyfriend?"

Catherine put down her fork to use both hands for effect. "Not handsome but sweet, hardworking, and built. Really fantastic shape. Jorge Batista."

"Batista Funeral Homes?" Mags mentioned a large chain throughout Nevada.

"He inherited the business from his father. It's a rags-to-riches story. Aunt Jeep would adore him."

"Where's the rags?"

"Migrant workers, the Mexicans. When they died, they wanted to be buried in Mexico. So Miguel, Jorge's father, who was working as a mop-up boy in a funeral parlor in Las Vegas, volunteered to accompany the caskets to wherever they would be shipped into Mexico. He learned a lot, was good with bereaved people, saved his money, and went to school to be an undertaker. When he started his business with a tiny chapel, the Mexicans came to him. As they say, the rest is history, but like so many business success stories, it started with a need that was unanswered. Now the traffic goes both ways across the border. Some Mexican citizens want to be buried near their family up here."

"That is remarkable."

"Look at Aunt Jeep. Discovering the gold seam was a combination of luck, her sharp eye, and her sixth sense — she really has one. Anyway, it was the salvage business that answered two needs: deconstruction and cheap materials for people. The Old Dragon is a genius. Dan was smart, but we all knew she was the real brains."

"Few people have vision and even fewer the determination to see it through. She still has dreams."

"Aunt Jeep?"

"You'd better believe it. She wants to find a way to feed the poor, to remove the middleman." Mags did not trust her sister with any more details than that.

"I'll be damned."

"She thinks you are." Mags leveled her gaze at her sister.

Catherine remained silent a moment. "I don't think you've ever been as desperate as I was. And I was a fool." She paused, eyes welling up. "I burned so many bridges. I don't know if I can ever repair that damage and I can't even promise that I won't be stupid again, but I just hope the only person I hurt this time is myself."

"I forgive you, if that's any help."

"It is. It so totally is." Catherine reached over to grab her sister's hand, tears spilling over.

"Here." Mags offered her napkin.

"Got my own. Right here in my lap." She dabbed her eyes with the burgundy cloth napkin. "God knows, enough else has been in my lap."

At this, the two laughed some more, Catherine's tears turning to tears of laughter.

The plump waitress returned.

Mags looked up. "We're having a sisterly moment."

The young woman nodded. "Couldn't live without mine."

"Coffee with half and half," Catherine ordered.

"Tea." Mags smiled back at the waitress and wondered what the young woman's chances were in life. "Have to tell you about Baxter, the male in my life. He's a wire-haired dachshund. Had him for three years. Couldn't live without him."

"Really? I can't have a dog, I'm not home enough. I still think about Spot." The dalmatian they'd had as kids had been named with a lack of originality but not love.

"Without Baxter, I don't think I could

have gotten through that bloodbath back in New York. It was such a disaster. Pretty much everyone on Wall Street refused to read the handwriting on the wall. I suppose we'd suffered a kind of dreadful optimism. We'd been high so long no one thought we could come down, you know?"

"Of course I know." Catherine refolded her napkin.

"I blame myself. Of course, there's plenty of blame to go around, unfettered greed going for broke, literally. You'd think Congress would get serious about financial reform after such an unmitigated disaster, but, of course, they're all on the take, too."

Catherine smiled. "They make my sins look tiny."

"Well, your sins are far more exciting."

"That's why they turned the camera on. Hey, we're all sinners, right? What's church but a workshop for sinners?"

"You're going to church these days?"

"Not exactly. By necessity, Jorge spends a good deal of his time at chapel services, so I go with him. I'm inching into the fold. If Mary Magdalene could do it, why not me?"

"Magdalene." Mags exhaled. "Ah, my distinguished namesake."

"You and Aunt Jeep bear a very interesting name. Hell, make the most of it." Catherine laughed another deep, throaty, provocative laugh. "With a name like Catherine, I should be ruling Russia."

"You still might." Mags happily sipped her tea.

As untrustworthy as Catherine was, Mags appreciated how good it was to have a sister. They shared memories, little catch phrases, even facial expressions — these things forged hoops of steel binding people together over generations. Perhaps that's why no fight is as ugly as a family fight.

"What are you going to do now?" Catherine asked.

"Help Aunt Jeep with her dream. Last night at three in the morning, when the coyotes woke me up, I decided I'm going back to school."

"Really?"

"Auto repair. I want to work with my hands and I've always loved motors. I want to fix a problem and see it work. I don't want paperwork or phone calls or BlackBerrys, breakfast meetings or ritzy expense account lunches and dinners. I don't want to go to parties that are just an extension of business." She leaned forward toward Catherine. "There's a mass delusion on Wall Street where everyone is convinced of their own importance. When I cut the lights off in the garage at the end of a workday, I want to leave my work there. I guess Dad will turn over in his grave."

"Nah, he would be proud of his little girl. He was wrong to make fun of you back then. You always had a gift. I remember when you took my bicycle apart and put it back together. Got grease all over Mom's living room chair, too."

"Someday I'll open my own garage specializing in restoration. Solid machinery built before computer chips. Machines where parts hummed, slid against one another, beat out a rhythm. Machines built by human hands, not robots. I don't give a shit if anyone thinks I'm crazy."

Catherine looked down at her folded hands, then up at her sister's brilliant eyes. "Mags, go for it. Mom and Dad, Nanna, and even Aunt Jeep did what they thought was right. They prepared us to fit into the world. But I don't think either one of us ever really wanted to fit in. We just wanted to be ourselves. Aunt Jeep gave us the most freedom but she's a creature of her time no matter how independent. Nanna was born in 1922. Aunt Jeep in 1924."

"Never really thought about it that way, being prepared to fit in. Well, I'm not going to fit in now."

"Do you think she'll ever forgive me? You know, about Enrique?"

Mags looked across the room, to the window outside. "I don't know, Catherine. He's her son. I don't know what possessed you to try and get him cut out of her will." Mags turned back to her sister, and their eyes met. "Jesus, there's enough for all of us."

"I was strung out, marriage coming apart, whole life going up in smoke. All I thought about was me."

"If you're asking for advice, I can offer some or I can keep my mouth shut."

"No. What? Tell me what you think I should do."

"Do nothing. Let another year pass. Once you've been on your feet for a while, write a letter of apology. Don't call. By that time Jeep's dream just might be reality. Then she'll be most likely to make peace."

Catherine watched the half and half swirl around in her coffee cup as she'd added more with a refill. "All right. God knows if she'd give me some money, a small part of what should be my inheritance, life would be easier. I'm tired of all the worry."

Outside the restaurant in the parking lot, the air was cold.

"The Camaro is rented. I'll have to take it back. But it's a good car and really affordable. The engine note is heaven."

Catherine laughed. "Only you would notice an engine note."

Just then a hearse pulled up: an attractive man in his mid-thirties emerged from the driver's side.

Catherine greeted him with a kiss. "Mags, this is Jorge Batista. Jorge, my little sis."

"Pleased to meet you." He noticed Mags's eyes scanning the hearse. "Taking the departed to Los Angeles. Since I have some business here, when this drive was mentioned, I thought I'd do it myself. Also, it was an excuse to keep my princess at my side. She wanted to come and see you."

Catherine gave him another kiss, then turned to Mags. "Like I said, people want to go home." She nodded at the hearse. "This was a frat boy. Killed auto surfing. One thing I've learned through Jorge is that there are so many ways to die. A lot of them are bone stupid."

Pete checked the clock on the wall. Off duty, he stayed behind to read a report from the Susanville Sheriff's Department. Since he was going to pick up Audrey and her family at the airport there was no point in going back to his cottage.

The Susanville department had gone

through Sam Peruzzi's files, his computer at work, too. The deceased, an obsessive researcher, had identified the aquifers on both sides of Highway 395. Those lots that were still privately owned were marked. He also had maps of Sierra County and Washoe County, in which he had marked areas recently rezoned for development.

Among a huge amount of amassed information, Peruzzi had listed those local companies involved in water purchases and management. All the employees of Silver State Resource Management were listed along with the Board of Directors. The salaries that Peruzzi thought they earned were put alongside the employee's name with question marks, noting stock options since that would not be noted as salary. Each board member's business, school affiliations, and charities were neatly listed, along with supposed net worth. Compensation for those politicians working for more water for Reno were also noted.

Sam Peruzzi carefully listed those plants, animals, and agricultural pursuits that would be most negatively affected if water became scarce, paying a great deal of attention to Jeep Reed's ten thousand acres. Peruzzi had written in the margin that Jeep's property was filled with wildlife and harbored a lot of water underneath. He had placed a big star by Jeep's name, but Pete couldn't infer its meaning. Another document showed individuals selling water rights and others purchasing some. Yet another document identified acreage or parcels where the state engineer granted water rights being changed from agricultural use to municipal.

Sam Peruzzi's death was not the result of stupidity. He'd gotten too close to something, or someone. Pete looked more carefully at the pages of names and companies, wondering.

He looked at the clock again, closed the folder, and hurried out. He didn't want to be late picking up Audrey. Good thing he'd borrowed his dad's car. The whole brood would not fit into the Wrangler.

On the way to the airport he kept returning to the blown pumps and Sam Peruzzi. They were linked by water. Then he couldn't help but think about Mrs. Peruzzi and their children spending their first Christmas without Dad.

Chapter Eighteen

After picking up odds and ends her great-aunt requested from town, Mags pulled into Wings just as the sun set behind the mountains. A few long diffuse rays pierced the valley through the *V*s in the mountains. The winter light, so soft, faded as a thin gold line above the range slowly turned a lavender blue.

How beautiful, Mags thought to herself, a shopping bag in each hand as she stepped onto the porch. She paused to drink in the various shades of blue, pink, mauve, and deep purple — all in straight lines across the sky as though painted by a giant using a straight edge. The moment the sun dropped so did the mercury. She'd rarely seen a sunset when she lived in Manhattan, but had enjoyed the sunrises over the East River. After her gym workouts she'd return to her apartment in the east seventies and get Baxter. The two would run as close to the river as they could. The buildings in Queens would turn from light gray to soft pink, the East River tagging along in the same colors. But when the sun finally crested, a path shone over the East River, deep red, then scarlet, and finally molten gold. By the time she and Baxter would turn back toward home, the windows in all those east-facing Manhattan buildings shone gold, too.

She wasn't morose but she missed the city; its steel canyons, the traffic lights blinking, headlights, lights in shop windows, the wonderful colored lights atop the Empire State Building changed to celebrate various events, but always red, white, and blue on July 4. Other big buildings, too, sported tops awash in colors. She loved the brashness of it. She did not, however, miss the noise. As to the famed rudeness of New Yorkers, Mags never found them any more rude than anyone else. The pace meant fewer extraneous chats, but most New Yorkers were matter-of-factly kind and helpful.

It was pretty much this way in any American city and, observing the changing shadows, the slashes of Prussian blue now over the range, the darkening gray shadows on the steep sides of those Petersons, Mags thought she knew why. The first emotion the early settlers felt, whether they came on their own hook or as slaves, was loneliness. They encountered a vast land filled with wildlife and other strange humans, with not one castle, crossroad, or livery. Virgin. Even when the East Coast hosted one million people in 1776, one had only to go a few miles west of any city to again be facing deep forest. As the decades wore on, American settlers moved west but the loneliness followed. To see another person, to find out the news, to offer what little you had as hospitality, for you must, created what we are. Hold out your hand, and another American will grasp it and pull you up.

A lick of wind brushed her face, tears welled up. Seeing Catherine had brought small arrowheads of emotion to the surface. She wondered why she'd never given much thought to that core of loneliness. She'd felt it in herself, even on Fifth Avenue and Fifty-seventh Street. No amount of urbanization could eradicate it.

Nevada, seemingly barren itself, stripped you bare. In a place like this, it was up to each individual to find their inner riches.

Mags knew crime and old prejudices still existed. The prejudices were fading like the light, but there remained pockets, like those deep-gray slashes on the east side of the Peterson range. Every society had them. Didn't matter if it was the Athens of Pericles, a rollicking London in 1664, or today; still, she thought, We are a great people. We are a good people. We've lost our way. I know I did. We'll find the road again.

The tears streamed down her cheeks, stinging cold. If only she didn't love Catherine, then she'd never be betrayed, hurt, wretched. That was another revelation: Pain is a purifier. Mags reckoned she was getting quite pure in every area. Wiping her tears, she heard Baxter barking, King, too.

She opened the front door, her little fellow on his hind legs, front legs pawing in the air, so happy to see her. She set down the shopping bags, lifted him up, hugged him and kissed him.

Then she bent over and solemnly petted King. "You're too big to pick up, King, but I'm so glad to see you."

"Likewise," King replied.

"Jeep, where are you?"

"Hiding." Her great-aunt's voice filtered down from upstairs.

"I'll put your bags on the kitchen table."

"Be down in a minute."

And she was. Jeep opened the shopping bags wide.

"Ready for your scotch and water? Sun's down." Mags volunteered to make it for her.

"Excellent idea. Let me take this upstairs and I'll be right back."

"I have a better idea. I'll carry the bags upstairs. You make your drink."

"No. You can't go in my bedroom. I have presents on the bed. Still have two to wrap."

"You weren't supposed to get me Christmas presents."

"Who said they were for you?" Jeep winked at her, looked in the bags again. "Oh, you found those socks. The ones were you can pull down that little extra layer on the top of your work boots. Hooray."

"Right where you said they'd be, on Kuietzke Lane. Prices are good in that store, too. The other good thing is the sales people actually want to help and know the merchandise. How refreshing."

Jeep laughed. "I'd be naked if it weren't for them. You know, old as I am, I'm in good shape."

"You're in fine form."

"You'd better believe it. Had some success today. Tell you about it after I make my drink. Are you having one?"

"Blanton's."

"Good. A lady hates to drink alone."

"Which one of us is a lady?" Mags handed her the bags, which Jeep handed back.

"Touché," Jeep said. "Go ahead. Take

them. Just leave them at the top of the stairs."

"I'm going with you." Baxter padded after Mags.

"Careful you don't scrape your belly on the stairs." King followed Jeep.

"One of these days you'll be glad I'm made the way I am." Baxter made a swift retort. *"I can do things you can't."*

"Name one."

On the stairs now, Baxter poked his long nose through the railing. *"I can go into dens and kill varmints. You can't."*

Stumped for a moment, King trotted to the base of the stairs for the two had already reached the top. *"You can go in. Can you get out?"*

Saucily, the little dog barked. *"I can do anything!"*

Mags looked down. "You're talkative."

Back in the living room, drinks in hand, dogs by the fireplace, Jeep asked, "Well? Let's get a report."

"The usual, charming, funny, self-deprecating Catherine."

"How'd she look?"

"Drop-dead gorgeous." Mags took a swig. "Don't worry, I know the leopard doesn't change its spots. Well, I suppose some do or those rehab clinics wouldn't stay in business."

"Still on drugs?"

"Seems to be under control, but she's never going to give up partying, Aunt Jeep. She was a social butterfly when we were kids. Catherine lives to be the center of attention."

"She's succeeded in some ways." Jeep put her feet up on the hassock. "I can feel the cold in my hip. Funny. Anyway, thanks for taking the bags upstairs. I'll climb them when I have to."

"Hurt?"

"It's just the damn cold goes so deep. Why I waited so long to get my hip replaced I'll never know. I thought I'd magically rebuild my joint through willpower. Anyway, that was" — she paused — "six years ago. I do have a little hitch in my giddyap."

"Not noticeable." Mags fibbed, for there was that slight roll to Aunt Jeep's walk now.

"Um. Want to hear about my day?" She held up her drink.

"She sat at the desk all day. Boring. Boring. Boring." King grumbled.

"She hummed while she did it," Baxter added.

"Humans can't sing." King spoke with authority. *"They try but who sounds better than a dog? Be honest."*

"They do rather squeak." Baxter agreed, which made King happy.

"What worlds did you conquer today?" Mags meant it.

"Pulled out my old books, early Nevada history stuff. Studied the photographs and colored drawings. Our beads were probably part of clothing or a swagger piece. I think of them as swagger pieces. You know, a fellow has a crop and a beaded tail hangs from it. The beads are Lakota. I have no idea what specific tribe. If we had the entire artifact, we might be able to figure it out."

"Isn't that something?"

"Our Russian, let's call him Nicholas, may have worn or owned this piece, or the beads dropped from whoever buried him. Maybe there was even a struggle before Nicholas was killed. Curious, but we are learning a little more."

"He was stabbed from the front. The marks on the ribs were right where his heart would be."

Jeep studied her. "Yes."

"Why are you looking at me like that?"

"I'm afraid I often underestimate young people. It's the sin of age."

"Just because I noticed where the marks were on the rib cage?"

"Uh-huh."

Mags continued, "Now whether or not he struggled, I didn't see anything else. No broken jaw, knocked out teeth. I wonder if he knew who killed him? I hope, for his sake, Nicholas landed at least one blow. And, in a way, I have some sense of his killer."

"Why do you say that?" Jeep raised her eyebrows.

"He didn't sneak up on him from behind."

"Ah." Jeep exhaled. "Could have been an explosion of tempers. Want to hear what else I discovered today in my research?"

"Yeah. Sure."

"You know Ralph Ford lived in this house with his wife, Antonia. His brother Michael lived with his wife, Pauline, in Enrique and Carlotta's house."

"They got the short end of the stick?" Mags said.

"No. That's a nice house, but Michael and Pauline were childless. Ralph and Antonia had four children. Two survived childhood. The remaining son was killed in a ranch accident at twenty. The daughter, Felicia, married an English colonel, a baron, and moved to England. He was posted all over and she often followed him. The English side of the family would come for a visit every year. They had more money than Croesus. Felicia Ford Wavell — her married name — seemed to love her mother and father, but had no wish to settle back here. I guess when you marry a baron, Nevada dims by comparison. Anyway, I'm getting off track. When I was young, I used to really hate it when old people would do that, and now here I go. It's just awful."

"Aunt Jeep, this is fascinating."

"Antonia Ford kept a visitors' book from the day she married Ralph. She kept everything: letters, photographs, theater programs, tickets to the rodeo. Anyway, I went up to the attic and rooted around in the old trunks and found six visitors' books."

"Any Russian visitors?"

"Haven't gone through all of them. But in book two, you'll never guess whose name I found."

"Who?"

"Buffalo Bill."

"No kidding."

"The book's on the desk. Would you bring it here?"

Mags put down her drink and hurried across the wide hall, returning with the gilt-edged Moroccan bound book. She handed it to Jeep.

Jeep opened to the page where she had placed a Post-it note. There in florid, masculine handwriting was "Buffalo Bill and Boys.

September 5, 1902."

"Just a few lines above is Colonel and Mrs. Wavell. Felicia met the old showman. Must have been quite a gathering," said Jeep.

Mags ran her forefinger over Buffalo Bill's signature. "He was something, wasn't he?" She returned to the deep, inviting chair. "Somehow, those days seem more vivid than now. Things have gotten tepid."

"In some ways." Jeep enjoyed the taste of her scotch. "If you are passive, allow yourself to be entertained, that's tepid. If you go out and make your own fun, that's still plenty vivid."

"You're right. 'Course, Buffalo Bill entertained all over the world." She stroked Baxter's back on her lap. "He brought the romance of the West. If you think about it, by 1902 the frontier had vanished. It was nostalgia that sold, I guess. That and showmanship. Wish I could have seen it." Mags looked at other signatures. "Wonder what Buffalo Bill thought of the Wavells?"

"Buffalo Bill had hobnobbed with princes and kings. I'm sure he could handle a baron who was a colonel. Plus, I believe he had English officers in his show."

"The Fords must have been the social hub of Reno."

Jeep laughed. "Think they were." She wiggled her toes, switched gears. "Thursday's Christmas Eve. Carlotta always cooks with her daughter-in-law. The little ones are really too little to do much. But it will be fun."

"I look forward to it."

"I bought everyone presents and put your name on the tags. Don't worry about it."

Again, tears moistened Mags's green eyes. She couldn't control herself. She'd never thought of herself as a particularly emotional person, but lately she was feeling a bit tender.

"Aunt Jeep, I'm so sorry. Let me pay you."

"With what?" Jeep sighed. "Kleenex in the porcelain painted box. Next to you."

"Oh. That's pretty. Does everyone cry who sits here?"

"No, but in winter we get a lot of runny noses. Now look, sweetie, remove your ego and what do you find?"

The lovely young woman thought a long time. "A spoiled person who basically means well."

"I wouldn't put it that way. Even those raised without the luxury that you two had — I mean your whole generation — look horribly spoiled to those of us left in mine. I didn't think it could get any worse than those loudmouthed protestors in the late sixties and early seventies. I was wrong." She clinked the cubes in her glass. "Those awful tie-dyed clothes and wild hair but, you know, they did end the war. I'll give them that. It was so different for my generation. Our purpose was so clear. Sometimes the execution was terrifying, at times exhilarating, but we were never in doubt. I knew that I wanted to help end the war and I wanted to fly. Most of us girls ferried planes. I envied those Soviet girls for being in combat. When I came back home, I didn't expect a damned thing. I knew I'd figure it out. When I look back on it, in so many ways, we had better lives. Maybe everyone thinks that when they start singing, 'Nearer, My God, to Thee.'"

At this, they both cracked up.

"Aunt Jeep, you loved Nanna, didn't you?"

"My sister really was one of the most lovable, witty, charming people to ever walk the earth."

"What if she had turned out like Catherine?"

This provoked a long silence. "I might have cut her out of my life, but I could never have cut her out of my heart." She paused. "There were drugs back then. There's always been booze, and women straying off the path were ruined. I don't think Nanna would have fallen but then again, maybe there but for the grace of God. I think I would have fallen before Nanna."

"Mom used to chide Catherine, 'Enough is never enough for you.' Then she'd turn to me and say, 'And you're becoming a little grind.' Funny."

"There's a lot of life left. Who knows how it will all turn out?" Jeep reached over to run her hands through King's silky hair as he'd just put his head on her thigh. "Better we don't know. Not because we'd see the pain coming, but because all the suspense would be gone, the thrill, those moments of charged excitement. I don't want to know what's around the bend. I want to live through it all."

"You've had an amazing life." Mags held up her glass.

"Now it's your turn. Keep your eyes on the doughnut, not the hole. You'll do just fine."

CHAPTER NINETEEN

Walter De Quille — late sixties, wavy gray hair, running to fat — opened the door of the small storefront office to greet Deputy Meadows and Officer Parrish.

"Come on in." The president of the advocacy group, Washoe Water Rights, beckoned the policemen to sit on a tattered and worn sofa. Nearby, the file cabinets brimmed with documents, shelves were crammed with reference books and three-ring binders.

"Thank you for meeting with us." Pete sat down, feeling sucked in by the old cushions, hearing an odd squeak.

Lonnie also became enveloped by the broken-down sofa.

Walter smiled as he sat in an upright wooden ladder chair. "Don't worry. When you want to get back out, I'll give you two a hand. When you're a nonprofit, you take whatever donations you can get."

Pete smiled. "Better than sitting on

the floor."

"You two gentlemen finished with your Christmas shopping? Tomorrow's Christmas Eve. By then, even the teetotalers will need a drink. Which reminds me, can I offer you two anything?"

"No, thank you, Mr. De Quille."

"What can I do to help you?"

Lonnie flipped open his notebook as Pete, in his genial manner, began questioning. "Can you tell me the purpose of Washoe Water Rights? I read your brochure, but I'd like to hear you explain it."

"To intelligently plan and use our water supply with regard to animal as well as human consumption. That's as succinctly as I can put it."

"You're a 501(c)3?" Pete referred to non-profit, charitable status.

"We are. We're fifteen years old, but WWR has really grown in the last five years. Before that, very few people took our mission seriously."

"Why do you think this has changed?"

"Two things, well, three: new leadership, which is more vigorous. Then there's the increasing population, some of which is caused by California runaways. And lastly, young people today are much more environmentally savvy than their parents. In fact, the

university here contributes a lot to aware-
ness of the issues involved, both with their
curriculum and other green initiatives."

Pete smiled. "My alma mater." Pete rarely
referred to written notes. He studied someone's bio, if he had time, before questioning
them, so the process felt more like a conversation, less like a grilling. "Mr. De Quille —"

"Walter, please."

"You formerly taught biology at Washoe
High?"

"Yes. That's how my interest, which trans-
formed into growing concern, started. When
I retired, I knew I'd perish of boredom or my
wife would kill me since I was underfoot so I
threw myself into Washoe Water Rights."

"Have you or anyone involved in the organization ever received threats?"

Walter's large, light blue eyes widened.
"No. Are we in danger?"

"I don't think so, but you may have read in
the papers about the two Silver State Resource Management pumps being blown up.
Because of these incidents we're contacting
people knowledgeable about water issues.
Your organization is at the head of the list."

Walter was not immune to flattery. "Thank
you. Let me be perfectly honest, Silver State
Resource Management is not well thought of
by us. However, wasting water is anathema

to our organization. I hope you find out who is behind this."

"Have you or Washoe Water Rights ever had a confrontation with SSRM?"

"A number of them. Last year we picketed their corporate offices concerning their purchase of water rights as far south as Smith Valley. And we certainly objected to the county's approval for new zoning for Horseshoe Estates. But our actions are always peaceful."

"Did anyone from SSRM come out to talk to you?"

Walter smiled. "No. They avoided any confrontation with us, but the TV stations did air a statement by Craig Locke dismissing us as crackpots — he's the one responsible for buying up water rights."

"Have you ever had direct dealings with anyone in the company?"

"I see them at zoning meetings, but that's it. Let me be clear, they have never threatened us or ever taken out ads against us in the papers. So far it's all been fairly gentlemanly, but then" — he swept his hand outward — "they have so much power and money, they don't see us as a real threat. They can afford to tolerate us."

"But you think this may change in the future?" Pete tried to lean forward only to hear the muffled squeal from the sofa again.

Walter laughed. "Dowser buried his squeaky toy under the cushion."

Hearing his name, Dowser, a boxer, walked out from the tiny kitchen area, blinked, and lay down by the desk.

"Glad it wasn't me." Pete laughed. "A lot of these questions are what you'd expect so let me just get through them, as I'm sure you have a lot to do. Has anyone in your organization ever advocated violence against SSRM?"

"No. Oh, the young people may say something hostile but everyone in Washoe Water Rights recognizes if we become violent we will lose support. We can't afford that. As I said, we are growing as the public is becoming increasingly aware of the problem."

"Yes, I think they are," Pete continued. "Do you work with other environmental groups?"

"Yes, but not enough. Now that I am president, forming viable political liaisons with other environmental groups is number two on my agenda."

"What's number one?" Pete raised his dark brown eyebrows.

"Saving our water from corporate control."

"Do you consider any of your donors to be

competitors of SSRM?"

This surprised Walter. "No. SSRM has no real competition. If the city of Reno wanted, they could extend the city limits to acquire more water and try to make a case for not paying for that water."

"That would be a fight."

"If some brave enough government official tried, I can promise you we'd be at the forefront of that battle. But even if such an initiative succeeded, which is highly doubtful, Reno would still use SSRM to get water to the city."

"Do you think SSRM is a well-managed company?"

"If they were sloppy, our work would be much easier."

"Among other area groups, have you ever had contact with Friends of Sierra County?"

"Just informally. Obviously, we share similar concerns. They are trying to protect their water from Reno, just as we are, but their advantage is they're across the border in California." He held up a forefinger, looking very much like the teacher in the classroom he'd once been. "But who can say what will happen? The economic crisis in California could be a total game-changer. They could nationalize their water. I say nationalize, but you know what I mean. It sounds crazy, but when you think of some of the things that have happened to privacy and the Constitution thanks to the Homeland Security Act, I don't think any mischief is impossible, whether on the federal or state level." He held up his hand as if staving off argument. "I know you all work for the county. I'm not criticizing you."

"Walter, we don't make the laws. We try to enforce them, and I promise you some of them make no sense to Officer Parrish or myself, either." Pete meant this but Walter liked hearing it. "What is the other possibility?"

"The state taking control of water rights would create a tremendous uproar. If California's legislature were smart, they would rescind the law concerning water being sold and diverted to Nevada. The sale of those individual water rights is astronomical. I'm sure you remember the millions paid to ranchers outside of Las Vegas?" Pete nodded he did, so Walter continued. "Many people in Sierra County, pushed to the limit by their state's financial crisis, burdened by increased taxation as well as more hidden taxes, would sell their rights to Silver State Resource Management. California would collect taxes on that private income. A far better way to skin the cat, don't you think?"

"I do." Pete hadn't thought of that tactic. "Do you feel people could become violent over this issue?"

"No doubt about it."

"Let me just throw this out there. Do you have any idea who might be behind these explosions?"

"No. To me, it makes little sense — I mean, if you really care about the environment. I think it's sabotage aimed at SSRM to hurt the company. Then again, it makes people fear for their water supply."

"We've thought of that, too. You said you had some contact with other environmental groups. Have any of them ever used violence as a tactic to inflame the public? Not just about water, but about any of their special interests?"

"No. I try to keep abreast of state groups and national groups for the obvious reason that irresponsible behavior by any group could hurt all of us or really any group concerned with wildlife and the environment. Granted, there are problem groups out there. I don't know if you recall in 2008, I believe an American leader of PETA was in England encouraging people at a conference to kill those physicians engaged in vivisection. He hurt their cause more than helped it. I hasten to add I am bitterly opposed to vivisection. Luckily, most of the public recognized that he was an extremist with little regard for human life. My fear is one of these fanatics will start harming others. There are so many crazy people out there." He took a deep breath. "We've worked so hard to get this far."

"We appear to be breeding crazies." Pete leaned forward, the slight squeaking sound again attending his motion. "Did you know Sam Peruzzi?"

"I did. Terrible thing."

"It was. Did you ever work with him?"

"Yes, at different gatherings with Friends of Sierra County; he was always there — usually in his overalls from the muffler garage. He supported us at the Horseshoe Estates zoning meeting, too. That was the last time I saw him."

"Do you think he might have advocated violence as a tactic?"

"Sam, no, though he was passionate about environment issues. He'd become really angry when he described loss of habitat for an animal, but he never hinted at violence. I'll tell you one thing, Sam was absolutely meticulous in his research. If he was talking about a ground squirrel, he had his facts down cold. Once laptops got lighter, he'd usually have one with him, with graphics and pictures to make his point. He was a very, very nice man."

"How did you find out about his death?"

"President of Friends of Sierra called, Brenda Bocock. Poor woman. Well, we were all shocked. And to be found at the Jolly Roger — we all know what that place is. I suppose you never really know about some-one else, but I never would have thought Sam fooled around. He was too earnest. My wife saw a mention of his death on the eleven o'clock news. Just a terrible shock."

"Did you have the impression he could have been in financial trouble?"

"No. People's mufflers are going to rust out, develop holes, belch smoke. Better to pay Sam than to pay the fine for pollution. California's vehicle inspections are designed to generate income, not keep people safe. One man's opinion."

Pete smiled as he thought the same about most states, but said nothing. He then asked, "Any ideas why someone might have killed Sam?"

"No. Everyone's in shock over this. He truly was one of the nicest guys you could ever meet. He could become a little tedious when he'd harp on his pet projects but he re-ally was a lovely person."

"Well, thank you. I hope you and Dowser

have a Merry Christmas." Pete grabbed the sofa arm to hoist himself up.

After standing, he turned to pull up Lonnie.

"Thanks," Lonnie said.

As they reached the door with Walter and Dowser, Pete turned. "I know you were a biology teacher, but do you have much interest in history?"

"Some," said Walter.

"Ever come across Russian names in your research on water rights?"

"No. Don't come across that many now. Why?"

"Curious."

Back in the car, Lonnie remarked, "Can't get that skeleton out of your mind, can you?"

Pete turned the key. "Nope."

CHAPTER TWENTY

The front office of the towering Silver State Resource Management sparkled with a twenty-foot Douglas fir; all the lights and balls were blue, the icicles silver. Inside, the lobby tastefully celebrated the Christmas season.

On Christmas Eve, the staff worked a half day. Christmas this year fell on Friday. They also had Monday off so it would be a long weekend.

President Darryl Johnson invited George W., Craig Locke, and Elizabeth McCormick, head of public relations, for an informal meeting before noon. These three people, gathered in the twenty-first floor conference room, had Darryl's confidence. George W. could work with his hands and his head, Elizabeth knew how to reach people and how to throw a good party — always useful — and as for Craig, he was tireless in the pursuit of purchasing water rights and identifying parcels where ownership had changed.

"Eggnog?" Darryl pointed to the bar, which had a small silver bowl filled with a potent holiday mix.

"No, thanks." George W. took one of the wing chairs that was set around the massive, expensive coffee table whose top was a slab of black marble with deep green veins.

Craig ladled out a small cup and sipped. "Did you make this?"

"If I made it, it'd be straight scotch." He laughed. "Lolly concocted it. I think it's one of the reasons our Christmas gatherings keep everyone happy."

"Happy?" Craig whistled. "This stuff is lethal."

"Exactly." Darryl smiled slyly.

"Elizabeth, courage up?" Craig held up a cup for her.

"Thank you, no. I have a long drive home. Looks like we'll get flurries, too." She looked out the large glass window at the gray sky.

The three men glanced out.

"Does." George W. agreed.

Once seated, Darryl, as always, steered the conversation. "I'd like a streamlined response to these troubles. Here's what I've come up with and nothing is written in stone. In fact, I hope you can improve on this. First off, Elizabeth, can you develop a series of advertisements, both TV and newspaper, which demonstrate our response to the explosions? The point being, we serve our customers, no matter what. The second series of ads would highlight our development of water resources and our concern for the environment." He stopped. "Our detractors would find the two incompatible. I suppose their answer is to just let people die of thirst because more and more are coming and Reno needs water."

"Does this mean my budget gets a bump?" Elizabeth asked.

"You will have what you need, but I expect you to be prudent as usual. In other words, don't hire Brad Pitt as a spokesman." He laughed and they chuckled with him.

"Rats." Elizabeth appeared crestfallen then brightened. "My suggestion would be to create the explosions ad, for lack of a better term, as reportage. The ads for our future would be more of a narrative. One minute each. Right?"

"Right. Unless you can get a better price, use Crecy's." He named a local ad agency.

"They've been outstanding, really. High quality." Elizabeth nodded.

"George W. You've been the man on the spot and I can't thank you enough for your quick responses. I know you'll help Elizabeth, but my question for you is what is the worst thing this bomber or group of people could do to us? Cause the most damage?"

"Oh, God." George W.'s face registered dismay. "Blow all our pumps at once. But the worst they could do is to contaminate our water supply."

All three listeners sat up straight.

"How could they do that?" Elizabeth asked.

"We have reservoirs. They'd go there first. It would be harder to taint water drawn up from the aquifers, but it's not impossible."

Craig placed his cup in the saucer. "Anyone who would do that once caught would be in jail for the rest of their life. What if people died? I mean, that's pure evil."

"So it is." Darryl exhaled through his nose and looked at George W. "You've given us all something to think about. Darryl, Liz, Craig, I seriously doubt we're up against an individual or individuals who want to actually kill others, but the misguided goal of disrupting service, of calling attention to SSRM's management, seems obvious. It seems to me this is just the beginning. It's not like we have a competitor. We are Reno's water supply."

Craig formed a steeple with his joined fingers, resting his chin on it. "Securing water rights seems more important now than ever."

"The longer we wait, the more expensive it gets." Elizabeth stated the obvious.

"True, but we can't buy what people won't sell. Craig has been masterful at identifying interested parties when land changes hands or when there is a significant change in an owner's situation."

"Thank you," Craig said.

"George W., do you think our repair crews could be in danger, say, if there's another explosion?"

"Not likely. The person, or persons, sets the pipe bomb and slips away without being seen. Our pumps aren't hidden but people driving the roads wouldn't exactly look to them as a thing of beauty." He smiled. "Actually, I think we're all safe because murder is a far worse crime than blowing up a pump. That's why I don't think our water supply is in danger but, Darryl, you asked for the worst-case scenario."

"Worse than I imagined." Darryl rose to pour himself a Coke. The alcohol could wait until the evening.

"Boss" — Liz admired his crisp shirt, tie, pants — "timetable?"

"Forgive me, this is a push. Can you have

the first series of print ads ready for New Year's?"

"Yes."

"The TV ads, ummm, if we can have the first one running by mid-January, that ought to help. I know that takes longer than print, what do you think?"

"I can do it."

"George W." — Darryl liked George W. enormously — "we've got a skeleton crew for the holidays, right?" George W. nodded, so Darryl went on. "If anything does happen, are we prepared?"

George W., voice grave, simply stated, "Two of our flatbeds have pumps and pipes loaded on them, just in case."

"Good." Darryl was pleased. "Craig, before it slips my mind —" This was amusing because nothing slipped Darryl's mind. "Have you encountered hostility lately in your dealings with people or down at the courthouse going over property transfers?"

"No. The recorder of the county and the girls down there are helpful, but even when I call on ranchers, they aren't rude. People simply decline or say, 'I'll think about it.' The only rudeness I ever encounter is, and this is rare, water conservation groups. The last time anyone got in my face was quite a while ago, maybe three years ago. I'm fine."

"Liz, George W., I've thrown this at you and I apologize."

"No apology needed." George W. replied for both of them. "Very unusual circumstances."

"Merry, merry Christmas. You know, I can suffer from tunnel vision, forget to thank the people around me. Thank you, truly. Whatever the New Year brings our team will handle it."

Pete worked an early shift so he was off at sunset. His mother had asked him to deliver to Jeep a mince pie, Rebecca's traditional Christmas present.

Snow swirled on top of the Petersons, a few lazy flakes making their way down to Wings Ranch. The weatherman had predicted snow off and on, no great accumulation. It shouldn't create transportation problems.

Once at Jeep's house, Pete carefully lifted the still-warm pie from the footwell of the Wrangler's passenger side. He took no chances of having the pie slide off. Shutting the vehicle door, he sprinted up the porch steps, grabbed the brass horseshoe, and knocked.

"Just a minute," Mags called out as King and Baxter barked.

Pete heard their claws tapping down the hall as the dogs raced for the door.

Mags opened it and smiled broadly. "Officer Meadows."

"He's a deputy sheriff." Jeep called from her den, emerging. "Pete, how are you?"

"Miss Reed, I mean Jeep, Merry Christmas." He handed her the pie.

"Aunt Jeep, let me take that into the kitchen for you."

"Put it in the oven. Not on the counter. King will steal it if it's not in the oven."

"Not true."

"Can you reach up on the counter and stove, too?" Baxter thought that just wonderful.

"Can," King smugly said.

"Come sit with me for a spell." Jeep took Pete's hand, leading him into the living room. "Sit down and tell me everything you know."

He laughed. "That should take about two minutes."

"If I tell you everything I know, we'll be here for days." She settled in an easy chair opposite him. "The advantage of age."

Mags and Baxter entered the room. Pete stood up. She noticed.

"Deputy, please sit down," Mags said, as she dropped in the other chair across from him.

225

"Please call me Pete."

The living room furniture had been made from the horns of longhorn cattle and their hides. Apart from being comfortable, it looked as western as one could get.

"Can we get you anything to drink?" Jeep asked Pete.

"No, thank you."

"How's the family?"

"All here." Pete laughed. "Kids running all over the house. Mom and Dad love it." He looked around the room. "This place is big enough for a baseball team of kids."

"So it is," Jeep agreed. "Mags, before I forget, Rebecca's gift is under the tree. Remind me to give it to Pete." She turned her warm brown eyes back to him. "We saw you on the news. Hollywood is waiting."

"Sure." He smiled.

"It is strange, isn't it?"

"That it is. We'll track down our bomber. Sometimes you get a lucky break, but I think of this like a mosaic. You collect tiny pieces in all these colors and perhaps a pattern suggests itself. Generally, it's lots of knocking on doors, reading, thinking. It looks glamorous on TV, but mostly my job involves lots of patience." King nuzzled the policeman's leg.

" 'Spect it does," Jeep agreed. "King, leave him alone."

"He likes me." King defended himself, but went and sat with Jeep.

"I called Darryl Johnson today," Jeep said. "Craig Locke shows up here once each season to try to convince me to sell my water rights, which I won't do, of course. But I like Darryl. He's got a big job and one open to criticism from all corners, not unlike law enforcement. Everyone has an opinion, which they are eager to express. Anyway, the *Reno Gazette-Journal* ran a series of articles six years ago about the impending water crisis based on population growth, the water underground, and so forth. You might want to look through it also."

He smiled. "I did."

"Aren't you smart?" Jeep smiled at him. All her teeth were still hers and white, too.

"Not as smart as you."

"Devil." She loved to flirt, especially with a handsome man. "You say that to all the girls."

They all laughed.

Pete sighed. "I'd better get back home to help. It's sure been nice seeing you." He stood up and Mags stood up, too. "You're wearing the dead man's ring."

"Ah, I look at it and wonder about our Russian, you know. Don't forget Rebecca's gift," Jeep said as they walked into the hall.

"Won't."

Baxter trailed the two humans while King stayed with Jeep.

The large tree, now festooned with Victorian ornaments, reposed in the den. The living room may have made more sense, but Jeep spent most of her time in the den when in the house. She loved Christmas and wanted to look at her tree.

Mags knelt down, checked tags, and found Rebecca's huge present. Kneeling, she pulled it out with both hands. She stood, grunting as she lifted it.

Pete placed his hands on the large box to help her. She looked up at him, green eyes filled with light.

"Thanks," he said, hefty box in hand.

"Let me walk you to the door. I've been poking around about our Russian."

"Funny, I have, too."

"We found little bone beads in the grave. I made a bracelet out of them. I grow more and more curious. Haven't found out too much, yet. Aunt Jeep pulled out a visitors' book and Buffalo Bill was here."

"No kidding." Pete imagined the man in buckskin, with long hair and vandyke beard. Then he looked at the bracelet as she lifted her arm to show him.

"Want to make a bet?" she challenged.

"Depends." He liked looking at her.

"Bet you dinner that I find out who he is before you do."

"You're on." Pete smiled. " 'Course, we could both be fifty before we find out. I'll make you a faster bet."

"Here, let me walk that out with you." Mags opened the door for him, a knife edge of cold air sliced in along with flakes. "Jeez."

"Just keeps coming."

"Put on your coat," Baxter chided.

Paying no attention, she hurried out and quickly opened the door to the Wrangler since the box he carried was heavy. He placed it in the footwell, where he'd had the mince pie.

"Cool wheels."

"Thanks. Dad runs the BP station. He found it for me. Fixed it up. Goes through anything."

"Your dad's a mechanic?"

"A good one."

"That's what I want to do," Mags blurted out.

"Fix cars?"

"I really do."

The corners of Pete's mouth turned up. "Stop by and talk to Dad."

"I don't know anything yet. I have to go back to school. Then I will."

"Never met a woman who wanted to fix cars. Sounds like a good idea to me. People sure love their old cars; you'll never be out of work."

"Hope so." She shivered.

"Hey, go on back in. You'll catch cold. Didn't mean to keep you out here."

"You didn't. What's your bet? The quicker bet?"

"This snowfall will accumulate to three inches. The weatherman predicts just flurries."

She held out her hand. "It's a bet."

CHAPTER TWENTY-ONE

Lying on his side, Baxter snored in front of the den fireplace. King, next to him, rested on his back, four feet high in the air. He, too, snored. The dogs, worn out by the Christmas celebrations over at Enrique and Carlotta's, passed out once home.

Jeep believed the fastest way to corrupt children was to give big presents. She provided good quality gifts, but her philosophy was that one had to earn the big stuff. What she would provide was a college education.

"Put your money in your head. No one can steal it from you there." The proclamation was issued from her lips so often that anyone who knew her remembered it.

Mags bought Jeep an early Nevada photo book. It was about all she could afford. Jeep gave her great-niece the new computer that would benefit them both.

Once back from Enrique's, Mags worked at the old computer. As it was a holiday, she wasn't able to set up the new one and transfer the service.

Jeep had stayed back at the little house for a while longer.

Mags tried to get graduate lists from the Nicholas School of Cavalry from various sources without luck. She thought about the number of people who passed through this area thanks to the big silver strike. She searched for information on the old mines of the Comstock Lode — mines like Yellow Jacket, Potosi, Savage, Grosh, Hale, and Norcross — to see if any Russian names appeared. In payroll accounts and accident lists, twenty-one names showed up that were Ukrainian, Georgian, or Polish. No Russians.

Someone from an elite school probably wouldn't be setting charges in the mines with temperatures above 100°F. She'd need to look for buyout offers, visitors from perhaps a Russian company.

It occurred to her that Christmas night might not be the optimum time to do this. But in one last stab, she looked for visiting dignitaries. In the archived *Gazette-Journal* files, she found one cited photo included as he stood in front of William Stewart's law office in Virginia City. Stewart, one of Nevada's first senators, had been an endless

self-promoter. He contrived to have his photograph taken with any and all visitors he deemed sufficiently glamorous. No one ever accused William Stewart of being glamorous so he borrowed it from others. For all his bullying ways, Stewart did advance the water use efforts, promoting new ways to store water for the dry months.

Stewart looked like a dowdy crow next to Colonel Dimitri Saltov of the Chevalier Guard, the Star of Guards on his helmet. The Russian's accomplishments were duly listed, though not his military school if he had attended one. He was on leave from service in Baghdad. Tall, lean, sideburns and moustache, Saltov cut quite the handsome figure. Stewart must have talked him into it or paid him to be in full dress uniform for the photo. It was not a uniform designed for Nevada conditions.

The reporter noted that the colonel spoke excellent English and quoted him as saying, "I've always been curious about the American West, especially Nevada, where men became millionaires overnight."

Delighted that she'd finally found at least one Russian, Mags determined to do more work tomorrow.

The back door opened and closed. King opened one eye, groaned, and rolled over but did not rise.

A few moments later, Jeep ambled into the den. "Two dead dogs."

Mags shut off the computer. "Baxter's never played with children. He didn't really know what to make of the one that just got here in October. So little."

"Amazing, isn't it? Life?" Jeep sank into the sofa. "What are you doing?"

"Looking for Nicholas."

"Ah." Jeep listened as Mags told her about Saltov. "Baghdad. Strange, isn't it, that from the nineteenth century up to today, various powers have been facing off over there? Buying off sultans, being betrayed by the same. Then there was Britain's disastrous time in Afghanistan, mid-nineteenth century, I think. I don't remember the dates, but the British commandeer in Kabul decided the British who were there must withdraw. Women and children trying to leave were ambushed and slaughtered in the Khyber Pass. Now it's our turn."

"So it seems." Mags came to sit beside Jeep. "No one reads history anymore."

"If they do, they don't learn anything. Well, Saltov is a start. Good for you." She smiled broadly, then mused. "What is it about Christmas that makes you remember all your other Christmases?"

235

"I don't know. It's a touchstone, I guess."

"I remember Christmas 1943 like it was yesterday. We were based in Sweetwater, Texas, at Avenger Field. Cold, rainy. We decorated a little tree in the barracks and all of us girls knitted scarves and socks. We gave one another the products. My best friend, Laura, forgave me because my scarf was just awful. We rarely had copilots but on those occasions when we flew the biggies, Laura was my copilot. The scarf I knitted was so awful that everyone laughed themselves silly but Laura wore that damn thing every cold day. What a sense of humor she had, dry. We stayed best friends. Each year we'd have a reunion on the Fourth of July — either in Minneapolis, where she lived with her husband, or here. She died totally unexpectedly in 1972. Heart attack. Boom. Just like that. Here we got through the bloody war and then our bodies betrayed us. How did I get off on that? Morbid."

"Your body hasn't betrayed you. I'm working on mine. I've got to live up to your example." Mags smiled

"Good girl. I have another present for you. It's a loan more than a present. You can't afford to rent that Camaro. Take it back. I have my old Chevy truck, the one with the four-fifty-four engine. Not much by way of amenities, but it's free until you can do better and you will love that engine."

"Thank you, Aunt Jeep." She leaned over to kiss her.

"What are your thoughts at Christmas?" Jeep asked, eyes twinkling.

"Like you, brings back memories. I'm glad to be here. I want to look forward, not back."

"Well, in theory I do, too, but I've got more life behind me than in front of me." She looked down at King. "Do you think dogs ever suffer from insomnia?"

"Not Baxter."

"Must be a marvelous way to live. In the moment. No worrying about the future. No government papers to fill out. All the baggage that burdens us. Maybe in my next life, I'll come back as a dog."

"That's a thought."

"Well, sweetie, I'm tired. Off to bed. Tomorrow is Boxing Day. Big day in England."

"Good night. I'll see you in the morning."

"God willing."

CHAPTER TWENTY-TWO

Little Christmas lights in the shape of chili peppers festooned the topless bar. A silver Christmas tree was wedged in with the liquor bottles behind the bar. Each of the girls hung decorations on it.

The men frequenting Jugs on Christmas night oozed loneliness. A false gaiety filled many of their voices. Old, young, with money, with little, they were all men without women.

The girls, wearing Santa costumes — but topless, of course — acted happier than usual. Sentimentality meant bigger tips.

Lark answered the call of men at the bar, men in the booths.

Nowhere else to go since his family sure as hell didn't want to see him, Teton sat at the end of the bar. Since he was a neighbor, the owner never pressed for him to spend a lot of money nor to drink. He knew of his struggles, as did the regulars. Teton pitched in when help was needed, whether it was helping to throw out an unruly patron or to push one of the girls' ever-faltering cars to give it a jump start. He was a likable guy.

His cell rang. He walked outside to hear, since the Christmas carols playing in the bar were deafening.

"Merry Christmas," Teton answered.

"Did you give Egon my name?"

"It slipped my tongue. He wants to put a lot of money into your next project."

"I could kill you. Never, never give out my name."

"I'm sorry, but he's a good player. He's eager. He loves money."

"That's the American way." The voice on the line lowered. "I'm home. But we'll talk more about this later. You haven't blown my cover to anyone else, I hope?"

"No. Don't worry about it. Egon has a lot to lose if he opens his mouth."

"Like what?"

"Like huge future profit." Teton said.

"Let's hope you're right."

Teton heard the disconnect, then folded the phone and slipped it into his back jeans pocket. "Prick."

Once back in the bar, he hung out until close to closing then gave Lark, quietly, a small wrapped package.

She opened it to find two tasteful, beautiful sapphire earrings flanked with small diamonds.

"Matches your eyes." He smiled.

"Oh my God! They're beautiful." She grabbed him and kissed him.

"Merry Christmas, Lark." Then he blurted out. "I think about you all the time."

"Oh, Teton, you're so sweet."

His reward, once the bar closed, was all he had hoped for and more, though for one wonderful, desperate moment, he'd worried when his face was stuck between her bosoms. He could suffocate.

CHAPTER TWENTY-THREE

Tuesday, December 29, people returned to work. As there'd only be a few days before New Year's, there was a noticeable lack of urgency, regardless of profession. Out of curiosity, Twinkie and Bunny returned to Pump 19.

"Looks good." Bunny lowered himself down.

Twinkie followed. "These new pumps are easier to work with."

"Yep. What do you think about checking out Pump Twenty-two tomorrow?" Bunny ran his fingers over where the blue outtake pipe joined the pump.

"Not a bad idea. We'll see how the seal is holding." He clambered out. "I'd sure like to catch the creep doing this. My hands are still aching from the cold."

They climbed back into an SSRM half-ton truck, their usual mode of transportation. A locked toolbox across the back under the window carried their regular complement of tools. Most jobs required replacing seals, perhaps a damaged pipe. In various spots on their watch, culverts funneled water into small holding tanks. They checked those, too. Given that rainfall was light, catching every drop was vitally important.

Once SSRM secured new water rights, the company set about harvesting water in simple ways. They knew water flow could fluctuate, and the company monitored underground flow for a year before installing expensive equipment like a pump, digging wells, or creating holding tanks.

Born on a ranch, Twinkie believed the color of sagebrush could give you an idea of rainfall, but it wasn't his job to find water. He kept these thoughts to himself.

Back in the half-ton they drove down to Jake Tanner's.

On his Bobcat, Jake saw them turn into his drive. He cut the motor, climbed down, and greeted them.

"Hey." Jake smiled. "Get laid for Christmas?"

"Why would I tell you?" Twinkie shook his head.

"Just the best present, that's all. That's why you want to give your wife something she really wants for Christmas. Bought mine a new stove."

"Then you're both happy," Bunny chimed in.

"Seen anybody up by Pump Nineteen since we put in the new one?" Twinkie asked.

"Nah. Heard you had another blowup south of town. The news did a good job, showed the water in the pump housing. You two looked so pretty." He rolled his eyes. "Same deal?"

"Yeah, looks like. Anyone around here been talking? I mean about the pump," Twinkie quickly added.

"Did when it first happened. Not much now." Jake stroked his long beard. "Some people think it's a way to get back at the politicians who keep bringing up seizing water rights. Others say SSRM is a monopoly and it's about that."

"Hmm. You think anyone around here might pull a stunt like that?"

"Hell, no. Couldn't even set off a cherry bomb."

"Good to see you, Jake. We were checking on the pump and figured we'd better check on you. Never know what you're up to."

"Twinkie, that warms my heart." Jake climbed back up on his white Bobcat. "Oh, hey, there was something. Craig Locke stopped in to visit Howie Norris. Can't hardly see anymore, but he's still kicking. Howie told him to get lost. Guess Craig checks up on people in the upper valley once a year 'round this time."

"Wonder why Howie threw him out? Craig's never rude about it."

"Howie's just getting ornery. Said he doesn't want to see anyone from SSRM, even once a year. Howie's got that big well, you know. A lot of gallons per minute."

"Up there on the northern edge of Wings. Yeah, it must be pretty good."

"Howie, who I called on for Christmas, was just sputtering and stuttering. Said he told Craig as long as Jeep Reed rented his water rights, Craig could bugger off."

"Given that Howie's as old as Jeep, he won't have to deal with anything much longer. The man's probably pickled."

"Ten shots of whiskey a day starting when he opens his eyes. He's still going. I'd be dead. I can knock back a few, but that's it."

"Me too. Good to see you, Jake. Happy New Year."

"You too, boys."

Back in the truck, SSRM logo on the sides, they headed down toward Reno.

"Bunny, let's check Pump Twenty-two now. It's been an easy day. I don't know why, but I keep thinking we're missing something."

Forty minutes later they reached Pump 22. The water had finally drained out of the bottom.

"We should ask George W. for some small sump pumps that can run off a generator. That way if a pump blows we won't be standing in water to put in a new one," Bunny suggested.

"Good idea." Twinkie, at the pump with him, checked the seals. "Looks fine."

"Yep," Bunny agreed. "Don't think we missed anything."

"Yeah."

"You don't sound convinced."

"Just me." Twinkie hoisted himself up and out.

On the way out, Twinkie jammed on the brakes.

"What the hell!" Bunny lurched against his seat belt.

Twinkie was out the door. "Bunny, get out!"

Bunny did. "What?"

"Look down."

Clear tire prints snaked toward the pump.

"Could be one of our guys." Bunny walked up to the pump as did Twinkie.

"Looks like a small car's tire. SSRM

245

doesn't have any small vehicles."

"True, but again, it could be one of our guys in his own car."

Back in the truck, Twinkie dialed George W.

"Christina, will you get me the boss?"

"Sure."

George W. came on and Twinkie asked, "George W., did you send anyone back to Pump Twenty-two?"

"No."

"There are tire tracks here, and not just tracks of someone turning around. Someone drove up to the pump, then came back out."

"I can check. We only have three crews on duty because of the holidays. You stay there. I'll call back."

Within ten minutes, Twinkie's cell rang. "Bosun."

"No one."

"Any ideas?"

"No. I guess the sheriff can send someone out to make casts. I'll see if that's possible. Stay there awhile. I'll call back."

The team showed up two and a half hours later. In the meantime, Twinkie had sent Bunny down to the nearest convenience store for food. He didn't want to leave the site. By the time the people from the Sheriff's Department got there, the two men were full.

It didn't take them long to make a cast.

"Small car?" Twinkie was curious about the process.

"Deep tread. Newer tires. Yeah, small car. Won't be hard to find the tire make, but there has to be thousands of cars with this tire," the man making the cast told them.

"Yeah, but if this shows up again at another pump, that's some help for us." Twinkie felt a rising anger at whoever was doing this.

That evening at seven o'clock, Mags drove her great-aunt back from town in her new F-150. Once out of Reno, darkness settled over them, punctuated by all the headlights coming in the opposite direction. The extended cab allowed the dogs to settle in on the short backseats. A sheepskin throw had been fastened over the leather seats. Baxter, once lifted in, stood on the center console. King curled up. Both dogs loved to ride.

"So much for the white sale." Jeep sighed.

"The four-hundred-thread-count sheets were marked down."

"I'm no good at this stuff," the old lady grumbled. "Dot always did it. You'd think after all this time I'd learn, but I go in those department stores and I'm overwhelmed.

For one thing, there's no windows. I hate stores without windows."

"Me too."

"Don't ever go into Walmart," Jeep said.

"Never been. If there was one in Manhattan, I missed it."

"They're huge and the funny thing is, sound kind of woo-woos. Makes my ears feel like someone covered them with their hands. Here is this enormous big space with no windows. I can't do it. However, millions of Americans can."

"If you make a list of what you want, I'll find it. Sheets and stuff like that."

"Mags, I don't know. I don't notice until they get holes in them. I'm not cut out for this."

"I'm no domestic goddess, but I think I can do better than you." Mags smiled.

"Aren't you a good woman?" Jeep teased her.

"It's been on my mind. So I'll ask you — why did you call the president of Silver State Resource Management to remind him about the series the paper did concerning water? It would seem to me that you and that company are enemies or maybe rivals is a better word. Wouldn't they just kill to get all the water rights you own and those you rent?"

"We both want water rights for different

reasons so we are on opposite sides of the fence. But Silver State owns a tremendous amount, far more than I do. What I control may be critical in the future, but it's not in my best interest to create antagonism."

"Makes life easier, that's for sure."

"Take the long view, Mags. They are the only company capable of supplying Reno. The noise about the city passing a law so they own the water rights is bullshit. It's a way to get people upset and thereby divert them."

"From what are we being diverted?"

Jeep smiled slyly. "You pay attention to national politics, right?"

"It's like watching a train wreck. I can't help it."

"When did the issues of abortion, teaching creationism, and gay marriage surge forward? Well, gay marriage is a latecomer."

"Right around the election, first term of George W. Bush."

"Here it is in a nutshell, where it best belongs: Those issues are fundamentally irrational. I'm not saying they aren't important, but they are so emotional all too often they preclude rational examination. If people are divided, pro and con, on irrational issues it means they aren't paying attention to the store. It was during this time that the controls relaxed on brokerage houses, banks, mortgage lenders. I'll go to my grave believing this latest blatant robbery of the American public was carefully planned and brilliantly executed by diverting the public's attention."

"Oh, Aunt Jeep." Mags felt a flop of her stomach. "That's a terrible thought. I never ever considered that."

"Few have. When I was in the war, I thought I ought to read the classics, you know, von Clausewitz, stuff like that. I learned a lot, but the one phrase that sticks in my mind is from Shu Tzu, the Chinese writer about strategy in his *The Art of War* is, *'Uprising in East, Strike in West!'"*

"What suckers we are."

"It's a tactic that's worked for thousands of years. We aren't suckers, we're just human. And maybe some of our problems are unsolvable. Congressmen who knew what was going on beat the drums for or against abortion or whatever issue would divert the public. That way they didn't have to go home, face their constituency and say 'I don't have an answer to crime, a faltering educational system, the continued rape of our environment, but I am your champion to overturn *Roe versus Wade.*' What's going on in Reno isn't too far from that tactic. Make a big noise, but do more by stealth."

"In what way?"

"Scare people. Maybe folks will sell their water rights if they fear a year down the road they won't get a penny for them if the city declares them public property for the public good. Or if people are all worked up, they might miss the real threat. Strangle the water supply. That will scare them, too."

"So Silver State is behind it?" Mags paused, "Would they blow up their own pumps?"

"Don't know. When there is so much money at stake, I wouldn't rule out anything. Look, it isn't just maintaining what Reno now has, it's the ability to create new subdivisions. Up goes the construction industry, the nursery trade, even interior design. The benefits extend outward. There really is a lot at stake, but to me the primary issue is environmental sustainability. Nevada isn't meant to host large numbers of people demanding services. It is a hostile environment; it's high desert."

"And it's cold."

"Sure is now. You know, this is my home. I can't put up border guards and say to people 'stay out,' but I think the most responsible thing citizens can do, forget the goddamned government, is to honestly assess just how many people Nevada can sustain."

"I can see why you scare them at Silver State."

She laughed. "I've always scared people, even when I was poor. But Mags, you have to cooperate with your enemies to some degree. Again, I shouldn't call Silver State an enemy. I can't deliver the services they can. Their machinery is in place. But what I can do is try to slow down further acquisitions. The whole idea of continued growth, an American faith, is suspect."

"I learned that the hard way but, Aunt Jeep, some people are motivated by lust, some by greed, some by power. Seems to me the ones who are greedy, the ones who want power, win."

"They do, but can they hold on to it once they get it? How long did the Wall Street boom last? Twelve years? Even states with huge internal machines of oppression like the old Soviet system didn't last a century." She paused, then her voice rose. "This is a fight worth fighting. It's a fight not just for the physical space we know as Nevada, it's a fight for the soul of Nevada."

"Do you think people have souls?" Baxter asked King.

"Sure. Most of them forget it, though."

"I think so, too." Baxter stiffened his legs.

"King, there are headlights coming right for us."

Mags, with quick reflexes, dropped a wheel off Red Rock Road, so they teetered on the snowy shoulder.

The SUV just missed swiping them. The driver slammed on the gas and sped away.

"Damn, he was headed right for us!" Mags exploded. "I couldn't see who it was but it was a white SUV."

"Looked like a Toyota 4Runner." Jeep inhaled, grateful they hadn't rolled off the road.

Mags wisely did not turn the wheel sharply to the left. She eased her foot off the gas and kept steering along the road, then gently turned the wheel left until they were fully back on the road.

Mags turned around. "You guys okay?"

"Yep," they replied.

"Drunk!" Mags exclaimed.

"I don't think so, sweetie. That was deliberate."

CHAPTER TWENTY-FOUR

"Anything?" Pete asked Lonnie, who was hunched over a department computer.

"Checked out all the local green groups. Not one of them advocates violence, at least not on their websites. Pretty much what you'd figure."

"What about the list of water rights transfers over the last six months?"

Lonnie pointed to four papers to the right of his computer. "Names, prices — information kindly provided to us by Sam Peruzzi's research."

"Good." Pete scooped them up and read them. "Here's someone in Portland, Oregon, who bought water rights down in what will become Horseshoe Estates." He ran his finger over the list of other names. "Silver State Resource Management. Another one sold to Silver State Resource Management in the soon-to-be development. Here's one sold to a man in Fallon. He must have had megabucks. That price for ten acres was two hundred thousand dollars. Jeep Reed picked up some water rights along Dry Valley Creek. Tomorrow I'll run out and talk with her. She's a deep well, that one. I think she may be able to help us with Sam Peruzzi. She knows everyone."

Lonnie looked as if he were about to break out laughing. "You expect me to believe that?"

"What? That Jeep knows everybody?"

"You want to see Mags." Lonnie smiled slyly.

"Uh." Pete blushed. "I wouldn't mind, but I really do want to talk to Jeep. You can come along."

"No. You can be the big bad cop." Lonnie spoke in a falsetto voice. "Oh, you're so big and strong. Can you shoot that gun?"

Pete pushed him on the back. "Anyone ever tell you you sound good as a girl?"

"You interested?"

Pete shook his head and returned to his desk. He dialed the Portland number and got an answering machine. "Hello, this is Deputy Pete Meadows in Reno. If you'll call me collect, I'd like to ask you some questions about the water rights you bought outside town. We've had an incident in which some pumping equipment was vandalized, and I wanted to ask a few questions relating to your recent purchase."

"Liar."

"Hey, there could be a connection to the pump explosions. No point starting off with murder and by the way, Mr. Ranculli, your name was found on the victim's computer." Pete leaned back in his chair, then sat up straight. "Lonnie, what about Peruzzi's computer? Evans, the officer in Susanville, took it off Peruzzi's computer, right?"

"Right."

"Jesus Christ. Come over here and hit me. I am so bloody stupid." Before Lonnie could reply, Pete dialed the Susanville Sheriff's Department. "Hello, this is Deputy Pete Meadows down in Reno. Could I speak to Sergeant Evans?"

Randall Evans got on the line. After they exchanged greetings, Pete asked, "You combed through Sam Peruzzi's computer?"

"Yes, I did. I think he might've been the only man whose hard drive I've emptied out who did not view porn."

"Is that right?" Pete was amused. "Thank you for making the call on his wife. I'm sure it was tough."

"He was a good guy. Good people. My wife's over there every day. I hope you catch the bastard, then just give me five minutes alone in his cell."

"I'll remember that, Sergeant Evans. What kind of computer did Mr. Peruzzi use?"

"He had a Toshiba in his home office. And another one at the garage."

"Were these laptops?"

"No. Sam traveled with his laptop, his pager, and his BlackBerry. He was the most in-touch person I've ever met. But I didn't see the laptop. His wife thinks he had it with him."

"We didn't find it. Thank you for your time. I promise when we catch the perp, you will be the second person I call."

"Who will be the first?" Sergeant Evans assumed it would be the sheriff of Washoe County.

"His wife." Pete hung up the phone.

"I never thought about the laptop," Lonnie said.

"Walter De Quille mentioned it. It's so damned obvious." Pete slammed his hand on the desk.

"What?"

"We really need to know what's on Sam Peruzzi's laptop."

"Bet the killer has destroyed it by now. Once he got what he needed."

"Maybe. Maybe not. Not everyone is as good with a computer as you are. He may not have cracked all Sam Peruzzi's passwords."

"He can hire a fifth grader to do that." Lonnie, a whiz at computers, couldn't imagine someone who wasn't.

Pete checked the calendar on his desk, right next to his rodeo photos — he loved the rodeo. It was December 30. He dreaded tomorrow. On Christmas, people get overloaded, possibly cranky, but on New Year's Eve they just get drunk.

Lonnie swiveled in his chair to face his partner. "Let's go back to the Jolly Roger. The manager and the maid were so upset at finding the body, maybe they overlooked something. They'll be calmer now."

"Anyone ever tell you you have good ideas?"

"Only the women in my life."

"You wish."

Within a half hour they were sitting in Kyle Kamitsis's cramped motel office. Indeed, he was calmer.

"Mr. Kamitsis, the night Sam Peruzzi died, did you notice any strange cars in your parking lot? I would guess you recognize the vehicles of young, long-term lodgers."

"Everyone who checks in that has a car or truck must register it. So I have the make, model, and license plate numbers."

"Could I have the records for that day?"

"Sure." At the file cabinet, Kyle pulled out the handwritten forms each guest filled out. He bellowed for his assistant, an extremely fat lady wearing a colorful silk scarf.

"Shirley, will you copy these for the deputy?"

"Right." Shirley smiled at the two young men and then disappeared into a tiny room housing a fax, papers, office odds and ends, plus a shelf filled with bags of potato chips.

"Now that things have quieted down, do you recall anything unusual about that night?" Pete continued his questioning.

"It was cold. There's a lot less partying when it's that cold and the weather's bad."

"Is there usually a lot of partying here?"

Kyle shrugged. "Usually it's just couples but a few times it's been a real gang bang."

Pete laughed a little. "I imagine you've seen everything."

"That I have. I've seen guys dressed up looking just as beautiful as the most gorgeous babes you've ever laid eyes on. You can barely tell, although sometimes the hands and feet give 'em away. Bigger."

"Ah." Pete acted as though this had never occurred to him.

"They have electrolysis, the best ones. No hair. A few still have a prominent Adam's apple, but a lot don't. Tell you something, that plastic surgery works miracles."

"If policework ever fails, I suppose I might have a career as a chorus girl." Pete joked, to put Kyle at ease.

"You'd be one big girl." Kyle enjoyed it. "Ah, thanks, Shirl." He took the copies from her as she retreated into her tiny lair. A second later, they heard a game show blare out from a TV. "Here you go." Kyle handed over the copied documents.

"Thanks. You never know when something will turn up. Tiny leads can turn into big ones."

"Any luck so far?"

"We know a great deal more about the deceased. He was a good, well-liked family man."

"You'd be surprised at the number of people who come through here who say they have good marriages and then wind up with the chorus girl or boy." He grinned mischievously.

"I don't think Mr. Peruzzi had time for chorus girls, if he was so inclined. Back to the cars. Anything strike you as odd? Maybe a vehicle that was here for a few moments but not a guest?"

"A Suburban unloaded some people, then left. The other one, I think it was a Toyota

261

SUV, maybe a Lexus. Didn't look too closely, plus by then, the snow was coming down fast." Kyle blinked. "Come to think of it, that driver was a little odd. Couldn't see who it was, male or female, nothing like that. Sometimes the girls meet up here with a trick. But this SUV drove slowly around the lot, then left."

"Might be important." Pete wanted Kyle to focus. "Do you belong to any conservation or environmental groups?"

"Me, no, but I believe in all that stuff." He rolled his fingers, a habit. "We've got to do something."

"I agree. You've been very helpful. Do you think I could talk again to the maid who found Mr. Peruzzi?"

"Sure. Shirley, find Tandy will you?" Kyle called out, then turned to Pete. "I can't pronounce her name so I call her Tandy. A sweet kid."

That she was, and quite a pretty one, too. Pete didn't ask to see her papers. Why cause the girl to panic if she was here illegally, plus that wasn't his task. He actually hated the Board of Immigration.

Pete stood up when Tandy entered the room, quite nervous. Lonnie also stood up.

"Tandy? May I call you Tandy?" he asked, his deep voice reassuring.

She nodded and took a seat where Kyle directed her. "Tandy, don't worry yourself, you're fine. These were the officers who answered the call when you found that man's body."

Pete's voice was gentle. "Tandy, now that you've had some time since your unfortunate discovery, is there anything that comes to mind that you might have overlooked due to the shock?"

"I don't know."

"Little things like was the bathroom a mess? Was he a neat person instead? Did you see a laptop plugged in anywhere?" He turned to Kyle. "Does this place have wireless? Can people get on the Internet?"

"Ah, no. But if they bring their own extension cord, they can get dial-up service. We don't provide it, though."

Pete smiled at Tandy. "Anything?"

"Señor Peruzzi was very neat. He had not taken a shower."

"Did you see him enter the room after he checked in?"

"No, sir."

"If you think of anything, you call me." Pete handed her his card, as did Lonnie. "Oh, one more thing. Tandy, do you believe in conservation, environmental control?"

She looked puzzled, so Shirley hollered out

in Spanish.

Tandy nodded vigorously. "*Sí.* Yes."

Pete smiled again. "I do, too. The reason I'm asking is that the man you found was a hard worker for these causes. We think there may be a connection."

"You do?" Kyle's eyes widened. From the next room, Shirley turned down the sound to her game show. She appeared at the door, leaning against the doorjamb.

Pete looked at the three motel employees intently. "For some industries, there are millions at stake."

"Pigs." Shirley put her hands on her hips. "They're all pigs. I think we should bomb Wall Street."

"The terrorists were damn close," Pete replied. "Mr. Peruzzi cared about wildlife and about sustainable agriculture. He rubbed some people the wrong way. He seems to have been an idealistic and committed man. One liked by many. He would have been glad to know you all care about the environment," Pete said genially.

"Boy, isn't that something?" Shirley replied. "We figured it was the usual, drugs or a heist."

"His wallet had money in it," Kyle said, as he was quite accustomed to Shirley's many opinions.

"But you don't know what else he brought to that room," Shirley fired back. "Something else could have been stolen."

"Ma'am, you've got a point there. It could have been a simple robbery, but we suspect it's much more than that." He smiled at Tandy, who stared into his handsome face with rapt attention. "Every so often, a tiny detail pushes us in the right direction. Well, thank you all. I hope you have a happy and prosperous New Year."

"Prosperous?" Shirley snorted. "Those bastards on Wall Street took all the money."

CHAPTER TWENTY-FIVE

Mags jumped down into the trenches of the dug-out barn. Enrique had at last finished digging. The pipes, neatly stacked against the inside wall, would be laid below the stalls after New Year's.

King hopped down after Mags.

"Come on, little guy." From below, she picked up the wire-haired dachshund and set him down in the large hole. "Let's go over this once more."

"Why are beads so important?" Baxter wondered.

"Think that's what they have to find out," King replied.

Using a bright LED flashlight, Mags slowly paced the area. She'd already sifted the piles of dirt using a four-foot-square sieve that Enrique had built for her. Set on cinder blocks, she would dump dirt on it and go over the pile with a cutoff 2x4. She'd found old halter buckles, bits of horseshoe nails, a brass fitting off a horse collar. The only human detritus that had turned up was a Zippo lighter.

"All right. I guess there's nothing more to be found." She lifted Baxter back out of the dug-out section.

King jumped out. *"Mice in the pipes."*

Baxter dashed after him, scooting right into one of the pipes. King excitedly watched as a mouse and Baxter emerged from the other end. The mouse quickly darted into a hole by the side of the barn.

"Nearly had him!" Baxter exulted.

"Next time I'll know to stand at the other end of the pipe," King said.

They returned to the house to find Jeep and Pete sitting at the kitchen table.

Pete stood up when Mags walked in. "Hello."

"Hi." She looked from Pete to her aunt. "Has he found out?"

"Found out what?" Pete continued standing, looking at Mags inquiringly.

"My Aunt Jeep's a wild woman," Mags replied as she hung up her coat.

"Jeep, is this true?" he asked.

"I hope so," Jeep answered.

"Is this business, or can I join you?" Mags inquired.

"A little bit of business, but sit down, both

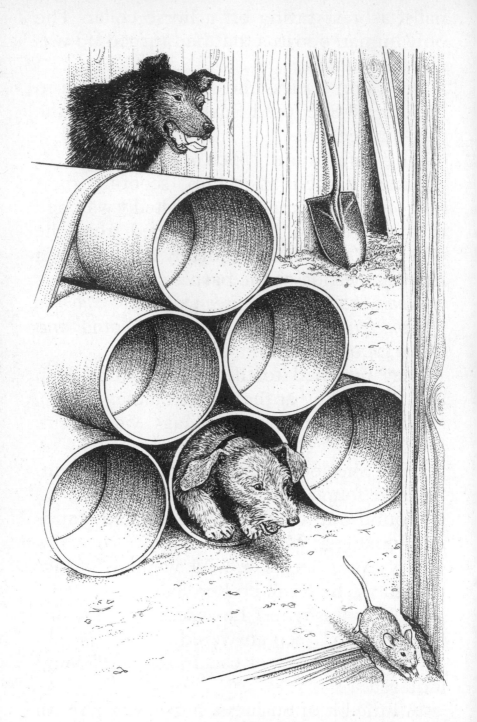

of you," her great-aunt said.

Trying not to look at Mags, it took Pete a moment to remember why he'd come. "I've been chasing down sales of water rights in the last year and saw that you bought the rights to three hundred acres along Dry Valley Creek."

"I did," answered Jeep.

"Did anyone else try to buy these rights that you know about?"

"Craig Locke for Silver State, but the land's owner believes, as many of us do, that we should hold on to our rights for agriculture. He just ran into money problems."

"I can understand that," Pete replied ruefully.

"Aunt Jeep, tell him about getting run off the road last night."

She hesitated, so Mags continued. "We were deliberately run off Red Rock Road last night by I think a Toyota 4Runner. It was dark and we couldn't see the driver."

Pete frowned. "Anyone come to mind?"

"I have my detractors." Jeep raised her eyebrows.

"This was more than a detractor!" Mags said.

"You think it wasn't just a drunk driver?"

Mags shook her head. "My great-aunt has been buying and renting water rights for decades. There are people out there who would sure like to make her sell or surrender them."

"Now, Mags, don't overstate the case. Yes, Silver State has been consistent in asking. Every now and then a politician for environmental control or sustained development cites me as a good example. The other side cites me as a selfish rich bitch."

Pete laughed. "There's always someone out there ready to throw a mudball."

"But —" Mags hesitated, then said, "Pete, given that two pumps have been blown up, I'm a little worried about Aunt Jeep."

"I'm fine," Jeep objected. "Don't forget, I'm a fine shot. I trust my Smith and Wesson. Don't worry."

"But I do worry. I don't know what I'd do without you." Mags meant it.

Jeep shook her head. "You have Enrique, Carlotta, and now the grandchildren. When I cycle off this spinning planet, you'll be just fine."

"Won't be nearly as much fun without you." Pete smiled. "Excuse me for a moment. I just have a few more questions. You knew Sam Peruzzi?"

"Yes, I did. He studied the wildlife here last summer. I didn't know him well but of course his murder was terrible. He was very

270

passionate about the environment."

"It's possible his murder has something to do with that. He had collected quite a lot of information on local water use issues."

"I wonder what he was up to." Jeep had admired the late Sam's efforts. "I had hoped we'd solved the development issue."

"Since Mags didn't know about the initiative in 2008 to link development to water supply, Jeep briefly recapped it for her great-niece. Seventy-three percent of Washoe County voters had approved it.

"Should the population go beyond our water supply," Jeep explained, "the Regional Planning Commission can impose conservation."

"And they can import water if necessary." Pete had voted for the initiative, as had just about everyone. "If all those strategies fail, then we legally would have to limit growth, which would really create a firestorm."

"How many people live in Washoe County?" Mags asked.

"Just about four hundred ten thousand," Pete replied.

Jeep chimed in, "The commission thinks our population growth will reach about six hundred twenty thousand in twenty years. There's no way we can handle that many people. Of course, the developers want growth like that — Silver State, despite what they may say, wants it. More customers equals more money." Jeep paused, then asked a question. "So, in all these recent purchases of water rights, how many were bought up by developers or Silver State? I should know, but I'm behind in my visits to the courthouse."

"Aunt Jeep, just use a computer."

"Mags." Jeep slapped her hand on the table lightly. "People, people, people. You need to talk face-to-face. That's how you find out what's really going on. I know those girls down there and I know the recorder. They'll tell me plenty of things a computer won't."

"Hadn't thought of that."

"Your generation doesn't. For one thing, one simple thing, Mags, how can you possibly know for certain that what comes up on your screen is the truth or backed up by the correct facts? Why you all believe in this technology amuses me, but it frightens me, too. Yes, you can get information in the blink of an eye, but it might be the wrong information. At least if you're looking directly at a person, you can judge their facial expressions, their voice."

Pete said nothing. Like Mags, he'd grown up with computers and had more faith in them than Jeep, but he had to admit the old adage was correct: Garbage in garbage out.

Baxter picked up a rubber dumbbell and carried it to King. He didn't give it to King, but laid it down next to the big dog so if King wanted to take it, he could.

Pete noticed. "Those two are getting along."

"Mutt and Jeff." Jeep laughed, then realized they didn't know what that meant. "An old comic strip. Back to the sales. Most of Red Rock Valley is safe unless, of course, the rights are seized by the government. That might happen if our population explodes as some predict. Right now it seems far-fetched."

"Yes, but what about your personal safety?" Mags was glad Pete was there.

"Don't worry about me. For one thing, I have King, and I swear he can smell an enemy."

"I can." King lifted his head proudly.

"I won't take up more of your time. Thanks." Pete started to get up, then spotted the bone beads on Mags's wrist. "I think they'll bring you luck."

"Hope so."

"I wear the ring, she wears the beads." Jeep held out her hand, ring shining silver, the Star of the Guards quite beautiful.

"I found a Colonel Saltov, a Russian, who came to visit in 1902. His picture was in the paper with Senator William Stewart."

"Think he's your guy?" Pete asked, sitting back down, the interest apparent in his voice.

"No, because I looked him up. Saltov was middle-aged in 1902. Stayed loyal to the czar during the Revolution, and fought with General Deniken for the Whites. He survived by getting out through the Crimea. Saltov wound up in Constantinople, where he died in his early seventies. Not our Russian," said Mags.

"Ah. Well, maybe he knew your man."

"I'll tell you what is odd," said Mags. "My research shows that Colonel Saltov attended every Buffalo Bill show, and he was here when Buffalo Bill visited this ranch. Further, in 1902, Colonel Wavell — he married the Fords' daughter Felicia — also went to all the Buffalo Bill shows in the far West. That sure must have been a terrific show. They saw it in Ogden, Utah, two days in Salt Lake, August 13 and 14, and then on September 3. Both officers were in Sacramento for that show."

Jeep said, "Maybe Saltov was studying how Buffalo Bill managed to move all those people and horses to each location. Remember, at that time no one realized just how mechanized World War One would be. Transporting horses had military significance. The Revolution wasn't until 1917 so when Colonel Saltov was in Reno, he was still an officer of the czar's."

"Hadn't thought of that. If the colonel was on a mission, I'll have to find out." Mags sounded resolute.

Mags walked Pete to the door. She asked him how his Christmas had been.

"Good. My sisters bought me a leather sofa."

"Nice sisters."

"How was yours?"

"Good. Aunt Jeep gave me a cool new computer, even though she complains about them."

Baxter said to King as they stood in the hall. *"Are you hungry?"*

"Yeah. Maybe we can convince Jeep to give us more food." King thought that a wonderful idea.

"Snowed three inches." Pete grinned.

"You win the first bet, but I'm going to win the second."

"Wednesday?" he asked.

"Fine."

"I'll pick you up at six-thirty."

CHAPTER TWENTY-SIX

New Year's Day dawned cold but clear. Mags started the day early, helping Enrique with the cattle and horses.

King and Baxter reposing on the bench seat, Mags cruised the streets of downtown Reno in the old Chevy 454. As it was Friday, people would be in the casinos through Sunday. As many had Monday off, the diehards wouldn't leave until then. Circus Circus, the Sands, the Eldorado, the Nugget shouted their presence with lights. Some even had moving messages, like the famous news crawl in Times Square. Huge light bands around some of the casinos rolled with color. While it dazzled some, Mags thought it was a huge waste of electricity.

Much as she disliked the garishness of it, she thought: If this is what the average resident of Reno tolerates or even wants, then who am I to criticize? She didn't know if she would ever feel part of Reno, but she realized she would never return to New York City nor would she go back to Los Angeles, a place she once loved. Better to move on. She still looked for her mom and dad when in L.A. Whenever anyone swooned about San Francisco, then derided Los Angeles, it irritated the hell out of Mags.

She passed the Jolly Roger, remembering Pete talking about Sam Peruzzi, who'd died there. How awful to die in such a seedy place, and why would anyone meet someone there? Maybe if one had limited funds and that was the only place for a tryst, but otherwise, why even pull into that parking lot with the cracked macadam? Made her shiver.

She cruised over the Truckee River, then turned left on Mountain Ridge Road, which was in a better neighborhood. She wound up on Wells Avenue, the town sliding a bit, then diving straight into seediness as she headed up toward the Livestock Events Center. As with most cities, the money had marched out to the suburbs, where people lived in huge houses with small yards.

"King, if you lived down here I'd have to walk you on a leash."

"I'd hate it."

Baxter, eyes bright, wagged his tail. *"Mom, we don't have to do that anymore."*

"One last errand. Let me run into this supermarket and get milk. I drank the last of it." She parked the truck and checked a note she'd written to herself.

Within twenty minutes she was back at the truck where she put two shopping bags behind the front seat. They squeezed in there.

"Bologna," King said definitively.

"Smells delicious." The little guy inhaled deeply.

Mags fired up the engine but sat a moment as the heater kicked in. Three young people, perhaps in their late twenties, not badly dressed, were rooting through the Dumpster at the side and to the rear of the supermarket.

"I'd forgotten about that," she mumbled, then pulled out into the sparse traffic. "In New York, it's alkies or drug addicts. Here, it's people who have lost all their money in the casinos. Guys, having an obsession must be a frightful way to live, not to be able to control yourself. Makes me sweaty just thinking about it."

Her two companions didn't reply. They could smell alcohol, drugs, and the sweat that accompanies a racing heart. Mags couldn't. She could only see the sad result. Humans could fool one another in ways they couldn't fool dogs. Even someone who appears relaxed and normal will give off the odor of failure if obsessed or addicted.

She drove past the Sheriff's Department. "I can't believe I'm doing this." She laughed at herself for wanting to see where Pete worked, then headed out and up 395. The western side, California, received a bit more rain than the eastern side of the Peterson Range. She went past Red Rock Road and all the way up to the cut through the canyon. As she turned right onto Red Rock Canyon she saw the rock for which the place was named. The canyon was really red. Then she continued south down Red Rock Road and turned left on to Dry Valley Road.

She passed Pump 19 without noticing. Instead, she looked at the ranches, the houses small and not so small out here where most people still ranched.

When Manhattan had overwhelmed her, she'd pull her car out of the garage (that cost six hundred dollars per month to rent), and drive up through Dutchess County, sometimes farther than that, just to be outside a city, to see crops, cattle, horses. Now, she turned on Dixie Lane off Dry Valley Road, drove into Wings, and parked the truck around back in the shed.

Jeep was over at Enrique and Carlotta's so Mags had the house all to herself. She checked her email, many fewer messages than when she had been on a winning streak.

A message from her sister read: "Happy New Year. Love, Cath."

She sent a note back wishing Catherine love and laughter. Then she sent other messages to the friends she'd kept through it all.

Finished, she turned off the computer, stood up and stretched, then walked down the wide, long hall. She studied the drawings and paintings that the highly cultured Dot had carefully acquired over a lifetime. A John Singer Sargent painting hung at the top of the stairs. It was a huge, beautiful society portrait of an elegant lady, but all the rest of the art was of the West. Charles Russell, more Remingtons. A twelve-by-eight drawing, hastily sketched but marvelous, drew her eye. It was a Cossack riding at a full gallop, sword drawn. He was coming straight at her. Signed in the right-hand corner: "Remington."

Turning on her heel, she hurried back to the den, and started searching for the life of Frederic Remington.

Also searching was Mrs. Oliver Hitchens. Karen and her husband were to attend a large New Year's dinner party, but he was two hours late coming home. If he walked through the front door that minute, he'd barely have time to change clothes. It wasn't like him. She couldn't reach him on his cell, which was very unusual. Furious, she called those closest to him, including George W. Ball.

"George, Karen. I know you all didn't work today, but have you by any chance heard from my husband?"

"No."

"He's not home and we need to leave here in twenty minutes to make the Nielsons' party."

"Karen, I haven't heard from him. You know if there was a problem, he'd call."

"Well, he hasn't."

"Maybe he lost his cellphone. It happens."

"I'm sorry to bother you."

"No bother. I'm sorry you're upset. I'll bet he has a good explanation when he walks through the door." He chuckled and thought to himself, *"At least it better be good."*

But Oliver Hitchens didn't walk through the door.

CHAPTER TWENTY-SEVEN

The next morning, a frightened and frantic Karen Hitchens sat in her dining room with George W. Ball, Craig Locke, and Darryl Johnson. The sheriff had already been to the Hitchens home. They were treating this as a disappearance and tried to reassure her that people did show up unharmed. So far they had not found Oliver's Explorer, so there was some hope he might be in it.

Prudently, Karen had sent the kid off to her sister's.

"Strange things happen," Darryl Johnson said. "Karen, he could have suffered a mild stroke and forgotten crucial information." He was looking for any kind of explanation.

Twisting a handkerchief in her hands, she nodded. "The sheriff said that, too."

Craig said, "Has anyone in his family ever had a stroke?"

She shook her head. "No. Cancer runs in his family, though. That wouldn't affect him.

I mean, he just had a physical two months ago and passed with flying colors. He'd call if he could. I know he'd call."

"Not if his mind is affected. People do get amnesia." George W.'s voice was consoling. "Has the Sheriff's Department called hospitals?"

"Yes. No one has shown up who looks like Oliver."

"That doesn't mean he isn't out there hunkered down," Craig suggested. "If you tell us some of his favorite spots, we'll go look. He might gravitate toward familiar places."

"Golf. The country club. We called there."

George W. thought a moment. "He often checked on equipment both on the inventory list and what we had on hand. Thanks to his farsightedness, we were never caught unawares, waiting days for a pump to be shipped to us. I'm going down to check the warehouse. Just in case."

Darryl was relieved at hearing any suggestion. "George, that's a good idea."

"And I'll call the team he's been working closely with, thanks to the blown pumps. Twinkie and Bunny might have some ideas."

"He's been so worried about those blown pumps," Karen said. He went back to check, uh, Twenty-two. Yes, Twenty-two."

George W. inched forward in his seat. "He

did? He didn't tell me."

"Oh, he just wanted to check. Since there wasn't anything wrong, he probably didn't tell you. I tell him when he comes home to leave work outside the door, but he can't. Sometimes I think Oliver is only truly happy when he's fretting about something."

"He's always been conscientious." Darryl praised him.

"You know, before the big storm he actually rented an ATV and drove all over the Bedell Flat right up to the top of the Sand Hills," Karen told him. "Oliver, he could see all of Wings Ranch up there. I told him he was crazy to drive one of those things in cold weather. The one he rented went up to seventy miles an hour."

Craig smiled. "Maybe he was switching from golf to off-road running."

"He said going out there had to do with work."

All three men stared blankly at her, then Darryl spoke, "Karen, Silver State doesn't have any business over there. No one does."

"That's funny. Oliver said he felt there would be future problems with Bedell Flat."

Stumped, but not wishing to argue or push, Darryl stood up. "As I said, he was far-sighted so perhaps he was thinking decades down the road. If you hear anything, anything at all, please call me."

"Karen, call any one of us if you need to." George W. took her hand and held it for a moment, then turned to Darryl. "If you hear anything, let me know."

Craig also offered his support. When the three men stepped outside, for a moment no one spoke.

"I'm going down to the warehouse," George W. remarked, feeling deeply uneasy.

Before he moved toward his car, Craig said, "What was Karen talking about — Bedell Flat? We have no interest there."

"I don't know, but Oliver wouldn't be scouting that area if he didn't think something was brewing." Darryl folded his arms over his chest, then asked Craig, "Have you ever investigated water rights over there?"

"In a cursory manner. I discounted it because it would be fantastically expensive to get the water to Reno from there. The Sand Hills are an effective barrier."

George W. surprised them. "Not necessarily. If you came down through Whitney Spring and Juniper Spring, it would be possible to lay pipe underground and tap into that aquifer."

Craig answered, voice rising. "George W., those rights are tied up. We couldn't get them if we offered triple-digit millions. Jeep

Reed bought most of them back in 1962."

George W. knew that. "Right, all I'm saying is Bedell Flat isn't unthinkable. One could also put holding tanks on top of the Sand Hills. It could be done."

Darryl, listening hard, stepped toward George W. "I suppose it could. It would make more sense to tap into Antelope Valley and swing around Freds Mountain." He named another towering barrier between Antelope Valley and Reno.

"Guys, if you want the water rights in Antelope Valley, better tap into the U.S. Treasury first." Craig shrugged.

Darryl looked down at his shoes. "I tell you it makes no sense, but Oliver wasn't given to flights of imagination. If he was out there, he knew something, or he thought he knew something. Damn, I hope he shows back up."

Craig softly added, "Alive."

Clipboard in hand, George W. double-checked every pump in the warehouse. He wanted to know if any of them had been taken or even moved. They had not. In fact, the warehouse was a testimony to order, cleanliness, and Oliver's amazing capacity for detail. He hung up the clipboard on the pegboard, putting his initials in the right-hand column with the time and the date.

Back in his truck, George W. called Twinkie at home, giving him the news.

"Jesus." Twinkie walked to his living room window, where reception on his cell was better. "And you say Oliver drove over to Pump Twenty-two?"

"That's what his wife said."

"Checking up on my work," Twinkie grumbled. "I know everyone is worried, but my God, what a son of a bitch to work with. 'Course he never thought you worked *with* him, only *for* him."

"I know. I know. But he's valuable to the company and —"

"He kisses your ass." Twinkie interrupted. "Sorry."

"It's true. If anything was amiss with Pump Twenty-two, Oliver would have told me. I just wonder why he went down to Holcomb Ranch Lane.

"The repairs there will hold until spring or longer. This whole thing with the blown-up pumps has all of us jumpy," said Twinkie. "Too jumpy, I guess." A long pause followed. "Maybe he figured out who was dropping pipe bombs."

"Maybe, but I think he would have told me that right away."

"Not unless he was sure. Oliver likes to

have his ducks in a row."

"That's true. But blowing up two pumps isn't the same as murder, if that's what you're suggesting."

Another long pause followed.

"Twinkie, did Oliver ever mention Bedell Flat to you, especially in connection to water rights?"

"No. It's a big wasteland, pretty much." He reconsidered that statement. "Well, there is Bedell Spring tucked on the eastern side of the Dogskins."

"Too far away to be useful," said George W. "But I just wondered if Oliver had ever expressed any interest in Bedell Flat."

"No."

"All right then. I'm sorry to disturb you on a Saturday. I'm going to call Bunny."

"Sure. If anything comes up, let me know. I mean, I can't stand the guy but I don't wish him any harm."

George W. ended the call and called Bunny, whose replies were close to Twinkie's. Bunny was upset that Oliver hadn't told any of them he went back to the pumps. He wondered if it had been Oliver's car they'd made track casts of.

Back in his office, George W. wanted quiet time to think. He didn't want to burden his family on the holiday weekend. He studied

the maps on the wall of new housing developments, none of which were in the Red
Rock area. He had no answers, but he sure
had some big questions.

CHAPTER TWENTY-EIGHT

Oliver Hitchens's mysterious disappearance made the front page of Monday's *Reno Gazette-Journal*. The story ran in the right-hand column with a mention of SSRM's recent troubles with sabotaged equipment.

Jeep sat at the kitchen table reading the *Gazette-Journal*. When she was younger, the *Gazette* was the morning paper and the *Journal* was the evening paper, each with a distinct point of view. Most cities had at least two newspapers back then, and she never believed in watching the TV news. Reading an article took time. A three-minute report with pictures on television wasn't the same. She feared anyone under forty had no patience to seek out the different sides of any particular issue.

Mags walked in, surprised to see Jeep. "You're up bright and early."

Baxter tagged behind his human.

Jeep glanced up at the wall clock, a big

round brass one with long black hands ending in arrow points. "Six. Okay, a half hour early. Couldn't sleep. Start of a new year, the business year. I like Mondays. I know many don't. Coffee's ready."

"You make the best coffee."

"Thank you, dear. Starts with the water." As Mags went to the coffee pot, Jeep told her the news. "A Silver State Resource Management person has gone missing. He was second in command of equipment maintenance and purchase. Very odd."

"Did you know him?"

"No. If I were the treasurer of SSRM, I'd be poring over the books right now. Hell of a way to start the new year."

Baxter spoke loudly to Mags, *"You aren't going to drink that coffee without feeding me first, are you?"*

King had slept in the room with Jeep, and bragged, *"Already had mine."*

Looking down at Baxter's handsome face, Mags sighed. *"All right."*

She opened a can of food, mixed it in with kibble, and placed it on the floor. When she sat down, her great-aunt pushed the paper toward her.

After reading the article, she handed the paper back. "Oliver Hitchens would have had opportunities to steal, wouldn't he?"

"Padding purchase orders is tried and true."

"Ever have it happen to you?" Mags wondered.

"In small ways. Someone would order hay and behind my back have made a deal with the supplier. I never let anyone write checks other than Dot and me. It's relatively easy to steal from busy people because we don't have the time to go over details. But when I get down to it, I leave no stone unturned."

"Or tern unstoned."

Jeep smiled. "Quite right. Once Enrique came back from college and took over the day-to-day management of the ranch, my life got a lot easier. Someone who works at a corporation where large pieces of equipment are bought — that could be a real gravy train. And it wouldn't be that hard to hide your trail for a while, especially if one is doing business with places like China. For one thing, you can juggle currency rates."

"That's a thought." Mags took a deep, grateful sip. "What kind of coffee is this?"

"Jamaican. I learned to make coffee when I was stationed in Sweetwater. Took my hard-earned pay and bought a coffee grinder. Hand grinders then, and I began to sample different kinds of beans. The girls loved it. Then when I was mustered out —"

She looked up again from the paper. "One day we were flying and the next day we weren't. It was badly done, I can tell you. Some of the girls were flown home but others had to take a bus. We were shabbily treated. That's when I decided I was going to be my own goddamned boss." She folded the paper and snapped it on the table, which made King bark.

Baxter, mouth full of food, prudently did not open it.

"There've been some books about the women pilots."

"Guess I should read them. I try not to look back too much. I was so angry and let down at the time. Mags, I don't wish war upon you and I know I've belabored this, but I loved flying. I still love flying on those rare times when I get to do it. But being with others who loved it, who had a purpose, God, it was glorious." She picked up the paper again, then put it back down. "What in the hell is going on at SSRM?"

"Maybe when they find Oliver, we'll find out."

"If he was stealing, they may cover it up. Banks routinely do that or the teller or officer commits suicide and nothing is said about why."

"Even now?"

293

"Even now. But since this story has made the front page I expect a good reporter at the *RGJ* won't let it slide." She used initials for the *Reno Gazette-Journal,* which most folks did. "Mags, has anyone from SSRM ever approached you about selling water rights once I go to my reward?"

"You mean, when I was in New York? Never. Why bother?"

"Because the profits would be astronomical. You're only a phone call or email away in New York and it's no secret that you and Enrique will inherit."

"Friends know, but not necessarily SSRM," Mags responded.

"Reno is a small town in many ways. Word gets around. I think that's why your sister's porn movies sell so well at the local sex shop. At least, that's what I've heard. Maybe it was that gossip and the subsequent sales that finally got her out of debt." Jeep laughed.

"That's one way to do it, though Catherine will likely be in debt again. She's a spendaholic." Mags grabbed the sports section. "Play-offs."

"Sometimes the conference title games are better than the Super Bowl. How are you doing on your Frederic Remington research? I've passed that drawing on the wall so many times I forgot it was of a Cossack — if I even knew in the first place. I tend to concentrate on the horse. Another one of Dot's finds."

"I found out that Remington also loved Buffalo Bill's shows. There's a wealth of material to research. I have to dig deeper. It's pretty exciting."

"Yes, it is." Jeep looked at the paper and read some more. "Mmm, revenues are down from gambling. Too bad they don't report prostitution revenues. I still want to know what that gal did for eight thousand dollars, the one who served your former governor."

"My fear is that I've done the same for free."

They laughed.

A half hour later, Enrique popped his head in the door. "Any special orders today?"

"No. Say, has anyone from Silver State Resource Management ever discussed the selling of water rights with you — you know, when I die?"

He entered the kitchen and closed the door. "Oh, maybe three years ago, Craig Locke brought it up. I said I would do as you have always done."

"Did he come here to the ranch?"

"No, I ran into him at Big R," he said, mentioning a ranch supply store.

She waved the paper at him. Taking it from her, Enrique read the article about Hitchens and handed it back. "Money is sticking to someone's fingers."

"I think so, too," Jeep agreed.

The first thing Darryl Johnson did when he came to work that Monday was to ask the treasurer to go over every single purchase or repair of equipment signed off by Oliver Hitchens. This took until lunchtime because the treasurer downloaded five years' worth of materials from the computer.

Calling George W. into his office, Darryl handed him the stack. "Go over this. If you can do it today, I'd appreciate it. If it takes longer, tell me."

George W. knew what Darryl was looking for so he said, "I'll call suppliers to confirm that all the billings are on the up and up."

"What makes you think they'll be telling the truth?"

"I don't know, but it's a start. I can't imagine Oliver doing anything crooked."

"That's what people always say in a situation like this."

"Right, but to just leave Karen" — he shook his head — "I'll get right on it."

George W. called suppliers and, with Christina, went over each unit. They found nothing. At six in the evening, for everyone worked late that day, he was back in Darryl's office.

"Oliver's squeaky clean."

Darryl sighed. "I'm glad to hear that and I'm not." George W.'s quizzical look elicited the following from the president: "Now I fear the worst."

CHAPTER TWENTY-NINE

"Look at this." Pete set a topo map in front of Lonnie. The maps had a sort of plasticized coating so one could work with them outside and wipe them off none the worse for wear. Made them harder to tear, too.

The two had stopped at a convenience store for a Coke. A low pressure system had snuck up on them, making them tired. Gray skies added to the feeling.

Lonnie put his Coke in the cup holder.

"What am I looking at? I see a bunch of little squares."

"Sam Peruzzi's notes." Pete pointed to the area. "This is Horseshoe Estates, the development that won its zoning. In blue are the parcels where SSRM or Wade Properties owns the water rights. The small red ones — ten of them in Sam's notes — were bought up by individuals. I need to go down and check the transfers at the court-house; some are small. Everything was purchased in the last year."

"By the samc person?"

"No. Ranculli, the fellow in Portland who bought one, called back to say he thought it was a good investment. Not much for divulging information, Ranculli."

"You thinking what I'm thinking?"

"All you ever think about is sex." Pete fired back.

"And you don't?"

"I just don't talk about it." Pete awarded him a superior smile, then laughed. "Okay, let's see if we are thinking the same thing. What is a guy in Portland doing buying water rights to a half acre in Washoe County? How did he know to buy there?"

Lonnie nodded in agreement. "It's not like it was advertised. Prices would have skyrocketed if people knew what they were up to."

"Yes and no. By law the county has to send every resident in the area a letter whenever a zoning appeal is made. This they did, but the zoning appeal came at the end of this year of purchase."

"Didn't make the papers."

"A zoning appeal isn't big news unless it's a Walmart, something like that. The newspaper did carry a notice of the filing. Nevada newspapers make about ten thousand dollars each year because of the published notices. But it wasn't treated as hard news until after the zoning meeting."

"Maybe after the Steamboat Hills idea got shot down, the paper figured Horseshoe Estates would be, too — so why waste space until after the fact?"

"They sent a reporter to the meeting." Pete again pointed with his forefinger to the squares. "Apart from Ranculli, the other purchasers were within Nevada. One from Las Vegas, a doctor; one from Carson City; one from Virginia City; the other six are from Washoe County."

"How did they know to buy there?"

"To find that out, we are personally calling on the locals who bought. We'll go up to Virginia City and Carson City eventually. Everything points to prior knowledge on the part of the purchasers."

"Doesn't mean they're going to tell us."

"Come on, you're a cop. By now you should know when people are lying."

Their first stop was south of town, at the Shear Delight beauty parlor. Housed in a pleasant, small strip mall, the outside was painted black, a sign affixed to the wall. Black with gold lettering edged in red, it spelled out the name with a large pair of scissors underneath.

As they entered this hive of activity, the receptionist looked up and saw they were in uniform. In her mid-thirties, Tiffany Kinder had long lacquered nails and pink hair. She could have been seen from a satellite. She smiled. "You two need haircuts."

Lonnie, hat off, ran his hand over his sandy hair. "You think?"

"I think." She smiled again, twirling a long pencil with a tiny figurine of Elvis Presley on the end. "What can I do for you?"

"Is there a Mattie Billingsley here?"

"She owns the place. She's on the floor. If you gentlemen wait right here, I'll get her. Did she forget to renew her license plates? She'd forget her head if it weren't attached to her body." She said the last sentence in a whisper. "But she's a good boss and a lot of fun."

Protected from street view by a beautiful frosted etched glass divider with a scene of wild horses galloping across the sagebrush, the clients could be heard laughing amid the noise of hand-held hair dryers.

In a black smock with the Shear Delight logo embroidered on it, Mattie Billingsley swung around the divider. A slightly portly woman with flair, although not quite as much as the receptionist, the shop's owner walked over.

The men got to their feet as Pete made introductions.

"What did I do now?" she asked. "I'm sure my business license is current. I think my driver's license is, too." Uncertainty crossed her attractive face.

"Actually, Miss Billingsley we'd just like to ask you a few questions. You're not under any suspicion. We've been investigating the two pumps of Silver State Resource Management that were blown up."

"Please sit down." She sat with them.

"SSRM has been targeted, but we don't know who has done this or why. You bought property with water rights to a quarter of an acre where Wade Properties now plans to create a thousand-home subdivision."

She beamed. "Yes, I did. What luck."

"As you probably know, SSRM will supply the water."

"I read about that in the paper."

"Can you tell me why you selected that quarter acre?"

"Sure. Good roads. Close to town. My husband and I thought we might build out there someday. Plus it was cheap."

"How did you find it?"

"Online. Our realtor has a website where you can look at properties before you go in person. Saves a lot of dead-end visits. Saves time."

"Who is your realtor?"

"Benjamin Realty. They're very good. Jake and I had been looking for two years. The places we liked we couldn't afford. The places we didn't, we could — until we found this." She beamed again. "Given what Wade Properties has paid us, we might be able to afford one of their homes." She paused. "Too ritzy, though. Affording it is one thing, maintaining it is another."

"So now you're looking again?" He glanced over at Lonnie, busy scribbling away.

"We are."

Pete stood up. "Mrs. Billingsley, thank you for your time."

"No problem."

Back in the squad car, the corner of Lonnie's mouth turned up. "Can you imagine going to bed with a woman with Day-Glo pink hair? I mean what if that receptionist was Day-Glo everywhere?"

Pete winced. "You'd need sunglasses."

The second stop was Teton Benson's walk-up on Fourth Street in downtown Reno. Knocking on the residence's door produced no result.

"Got a work address?" Lonnie asked.

"No. We'll come back later."

"I'd look in the bar, but it's too early."

"Never too early." Lonnie laughed.

The third call was at Larkin Surveyors. As it happened, Jonas Larkin was in the office, having just returned from a job. He glanced up from his computer, not happy to see who just walked in the door.

"Is Mr. Jonas Larkin here?"

"I am Jonas Larkin." He rose from his desk and walked over to them.

The small office had two desks side by side. No receptionist or secretary was in evidence. Larkin Surveyors appeared to be a two-man show.

After introductions, Jonas did not ask them to sit.

Sensing the man's wariness, Pete got right to the point. "Mr. Larkin, you bought an acre of property where Horseshoe Estates will be developed. Why did you buy there?"

"Wherever I survey, I look around. Wade Properties has their own team of surveyors. Last year I was on the other side of the road on a small job and I spotted their team. I found out what was available over there and bought an acre. Wade never surveys in vain. Actually, I own a fair amount of land. Sometimes I ask for payment in parcels of land." He quickly added, "I keep expenses down, as you can see. Rent on fancy offices, secretaries, and all that are passed on to the client. I keep it lean and mean."

"Wise," Pete replied simply. "Has Wade Properties offered to buy your acre?"

"They have." He smirked. "I'm holding out. I'm going to walk away with a lot of money on this one."

"Do you ever run into Silver State Resource Management people in your work?"

"Sometimes. They have in-house surveyors, too, hydrographers. It's a big company. I pay attention to all of it."

"Do you know anyone in the company, apart from the surveyors?"

"Not really."

Back in the car, a mile down the road, Lonnie said, "He's hiding something."

"I know."

A half hour later they were in a condominium building with a doorman who smiled as though two police officers were the very people he wanted to see.

"Does Anthony Diamond live here?"

"He does, sir."

"Can you buzz him for me?" Pete meant for the doorman to call up to announce his presence.

"Mr. Diamond is in California. He works in Sacramento."

"Lives here to avoid California taxes, does he?" Pete asked. Many Californians kept addresses in the high-rise condominiums, claiming that as their primary residence. It saved thousands upon thousands of dollars.

"I wouldn't know that, sir." The doorman replied smoothly.

"When he returns, give him my card, will you? He may be able to help us concerning an investigation."

The doorman took the card in his gloved hand and Pete slipped him a five dollar bill folded under it. Dealing with doormen was a necessity in this town. Before doing so, Pete always attached a fiver to his card with a paper clip. He slipped this in his pants pocket before questioning any doorman.

Doormen can be crucial points of information.

"Thank you, sir."

The fifth call was to High Rollers Casino. The chef there had bought two acres. Chefs at the big casinos are highly paid, their work being crucial to the success of the enterprise. Most casinos rented space for special occasions, meetings. None of this involved gambling, but at most such functions, the people feeling well-off — which a full stomach produces, plus being a bit lubricated — invariably find their way to the casino tables after the function.

Pete and Lonnie waited fifteen minutes for

the chef. The casino manager was visibly upset at having to pull him away from supervising the kitchen, but did so, allowing them use of a meeting room near his office.

Egon Utrecht swished in, his large hat on his head, his whites impeccable. Imperious, not gay but very swishy, he looked down at the two officers from six foot four inches. Wide, too; he clearly enjoyed his own cooking.

"I am in complete compliance with every city and county health ordinance," he bellowed.

"We're not here about that, Mr. Utrecht."

This somewhat mollified him. "Well, why are you here?"

"This won't take long. We know how busy you are." Pete smiled. "You're Reno's most famous celebrity chef."

Visibly pleased, Egon pulled a chair away from the table and sat. Given his bulk he had to sit sideways, so Pete did the same while Lonnie dutifully used the table to write, a small pleasure for him.

Pete ran through his preamble about Horseshoe Estates.

"I did buy two acres. I buy land all over this county and Churchill County, too. I am what you might call a land speculator."

"Sure beats the stock market."

Egon pursed his lips. "People get what they ask for. I have never put money in the market and I never will."

"I'm sure a lot of people wished they had made your choices. Can you tell me why you bought land there?"

"I liked what I saw."

"Which is?"

"Far enough away from Reno to be private, but close enough that even in rush hour traffic you should be able to get to your office in a half hour."

"Did you know this area was to be developed?"

"I figured it would be sooner or later."

Back in the car, the two checked out the address for the sixth purchaser in Washoe County. Neither said anything about the chef.

Kylie Prentiss, a young nurse at a small neighborhood clinic, was uncomfortable and kept it almost to monosyllables. She had no explanation for why she'd purchased a quarter of an acre. She kept repeating that she thought it was a good idea. She'd been saving for something.

Back in the car, Pete said, "I need another Coke. I can barely hold my head up. There must be another storm coming in. See if you can get a weather report."

Lonnie flipped out his cellphone, which had every feature known to man. He punched in the website. "Light snow starting at seven tonight. Ends in the morning, then clear skies, forty degrees Fahrenheit."

"Let's head over to Benjamin Realty. As for Kylie Prentiss, she's either a highly nervous person or another one hiding something."

"I vote for the second choice."

Benjamin Realty was located in another strip mall. Attractive, the interior of the place invited clients to relax and look at offerings on the large screen before hitting the road and driving to them. It served a middle-class market, one concerned with good schools and low crime, people wanting a neighborhood that provided community.

Warmly greeted by the receptionist, they asked if the realtor who sold Mattie Billingsley her property was in.

Hearing this from her desk, a well-groomed middle-aged woman stood. "I did. Isn't that the best story you've heard all day?" She launched right into the client's good fortune as she approached the men.

Pete introduced himself and Lonnie. He told her about the pumps and so forth.

"Isn't that the damnedest thing? Why would someone want to blow up pumps?" Babs Gallagher shrugged.

"Ma'am, did you know that Wade Properties was going to develop out there?"

"I'm good, but not that good." She smiled. "Sometimes you can figure out what they're up to; you know, you see people show up sometimes too many times for it to be random, but that wasn't the case this time. However, I am thrilled at the way this has turned out. Mattie and Jake are the sweetest people in Reno. If anyone ever deserved to hit the jackpot, it's them."

As they drove away, Pete said, "I think Mattie and Babs are the only people who have told us the whole story."

"Seems like it." Lonnie watched another strip mall pass by. "I noticed you didn't mention Sam Peruzzi to anyone."

"I will if I go back again. No point in scaring people."

"How about Oliver Hitchens?"

"No point in mentioning him, either. I'll check in with Finny to see if they've found anything." Fergus Fincastle was the officer in charge of that case.

Pete checked the time on the dash clock. "Almost quittin' time. I want to talk to the people in Carson City and Virginia City in person but, you know, I've been thinking about the budget crunch. I'll phone them. If it seems promising, then we can justify burning Washoe County gas to go."

"Right. Isn't your date tomorrow night?"

"Is. You're not invited."

"She's hot."

"That's why you're not invited."

CHAPTER THIRTY

Mags liked physical labor. It proved an antidote to her former life. Each morning she rose, ate breakfast, then went outside to do whatever chores presented themselves. A pair of extra hands on a ranch is always useful. Baxter tagged along. She was amazed at how quickly the little guy learned the boundaries of the ranch. He already knew every ground squirrel within a mile of the house and barns.

His head in the hole, his tail wagging, he'd dig with fury. King would watch while offering no comment; he had herding blood. Didn't mean the larger dog couldn't chase varmints, but digging them out wasn't his forte.

Throwing hay, picking stalls, and checking on the laying of the pipe in the old barn took three to four hours each morning. After, Mags would troop back into the house famished, since breakfast was light.

Carlotta cooked her an early lunch. Jeep would join her, then both would disappear to other chores while Carlotta planned supper. Carlotta loved pleasing people at the table. Given her skills, this was easy.

January 6, Wednesday — Epiphany — found Jeep and Mags in the old barn observing the last of the pipe being laid. The eight-inch drain covers stood straight up on the waste pipes, also eight inches wide. The liquids would eventually, thanks to the grade, go outside the barn to a 3,000-gallon buried holding tank. Jeep loved construction of any sort. Her return from the barn found her buoyant.

The chill had gotten to them. Once inside they drank hot chocolate.

"I have good news," Mags said to her great-aunt.

"I'm always ready for good news."

"Buffalo Bill had Cossacks in his show."

Jeep straightened up, her hands warmed now by the mug of hot chocolate. "Really?"

"He called his show 'Congress of the Rough Riders of the World' and employed Mexicans, Filipinos, Indians, Cossacks, German cavalry officers, and English cavalry officers. He had chiefs, braves, squaws, and one papoose named Willie White Bird. He paid Arabs, Cubans, and Hawaiians, as well as cowboys. They would set up quarters in the winter. They were like a small army."

"Imagine his payroll."

"Had to be huge, but so were the profits. Buffalo Bill's European tours took years. I don't know when he first went abroad, I'm still working on that, but he did a European tour in 1891. What struck me about that was he had brought with him survivors of the Charge of the Light Brigade. Can you imagine?"

"Must have been very emotional."

"He was in Europe again from 1903 to 1906. In each country he'd stage a cross-country race. If they were in Germany, a Prussian *uhlan* would win — that's one of their cavalry types. If they were in England, a foxhunter would win. When they were here, a cowboy won. And Frederic Remington sketched all of this. You know, Aunt Jeep, it must have been one of the most fascinating shows in history, just like some of the events in the Roman Coliseum throughout history. It's almost unimaginable: the planning, then the execution. Funny what survives."

"A good time best remembered." Jeep smiled. "So, Cossacks?"

"Bill's Cossacks were led by Prince Ivan Macheradze. I suppose the personnel

changed over the years, but I found a program printed in a book, *Buffalo Bill and the
Wild West* by Henry Blackman Sell and Vic-
tor Weybright."

"I'm glad I bought you that new computer,
though I'm also amazed at how much you
remember. 'Course you always had a good
memory, even when a little thing."

"I have the names of the Cossacks. I'll go
get them for you." Mags returned with a
computer printout of the page from the
book. "Here."

Nine names were highlighted with a yellow
marker.

Mags continued. "I also found the name of
four women riders as Cossacks. They rode as
women in Cossack attire. They must have
been fabulous. Of course, over time some
went back to Georgia, others stayed in
America. Pretty fascinating. Now what I
have to do is find out about each of these
people."

"Like the one who didn't go home?" Aunt
Jeep said. "That doesn't mean that would be
our fellow." She looked at the ring. "But then
again, maybe. This is exciting."

That evening, at dinner, Mags told Pete
her news. He didn't tell her what his day had
been like. Tracking down more people who
had bought land in what was to become

Horseshoe Estates wasn't as fascinating to him, anyway, as her story.

However, Mags, after her explosion of excitement, asked, "How was your day?"

"I interviewed one person today, a fellow from California: facelift, Patek Philippe watch, expensive shoes. You get the picture."

"He lives here?"

"A lot of Californians do. Reno is their main address so they escape state taxes over there."

"Ah. Makes sense."

"You'd be amazed at how few people actually live full-time in those expensive high-rises downtown. And right now, few are buying the new ones."

"I guess that's everywhere. So what about Mr. Facelift?"

"Evasive."

"Think he committed a crime?"

"I doubt it, but he might lead me to someone who did."

"Your work sounds either exciting or tedious, one or the other."

He smiled. "You're right. Okay, now for the really important question." He leaned forward to look right into her eyes. "You like baseball, right? Who is your favorite team?"

"The Dodgers."

He groaned.

"Who's yours?"

"Giants. They aren't doing much, but just wait."

"I used to live in L.A., so the Dodgers makes sense, but the Giants?"

"Closest major league team to Reno. But we've got our own team now. It's minor league, but fun. The Aces. I go to every game I can. I play in the summer leagues in the park, too."

They chattered on over dinner, never running out of things to discuss.

Pete dropped her off at Jeep's, walked her to the door.

Mags kissed him on the cheek. "Thank you for a lovely evening."

He drove back home, thinking how much he liked her. It's one thing to lust after a woman, it's another to find her desirable and also truly like her.

He was looking forward to their next date.

Before that could happen, though, all hell broke loose.

CHAPTER THIRTY-ONE

By mid-morning on Thursday, the mercury had climbed to 40°F which, given the last few weeks, felt warm. Ranchers checked their cattle, people drove to the office, all feeling relief from winter's bite.

Having tagged along for the chores, King and Baxter became distracted by a coyote moving southward.

"Let's chase him," King said gleefully.

Baxter happily complied and the two rushed after the gray animal who stayed far enough ahead of them to keep them interested. Coyotes rarely work harder than is necessary and this fellow knew he could smoke those two domesticated twits any time he wished.

He ran more or less parallel to Dry Valley Road where a creek bed also ran more or less parallel. The gently sloped banks were four to six feet high, steep in places. In a few spots the drop was precipitous, sheer on every cut-back into the soil with an overhang. Once at the bottom, the creek bed was wide, water trickled along — always a welcome sight to have running water. Brush dotted the edges. Come spring, the shrubs would green up. In spots, a small ledge offered protection for varmits.

After a mile of running, Baxter, not in as good shape as King, began to trot.

The coyote dropped over the bank, ran through the creek, then *poof,* disappeared.

Piles of rocks dotted the landscape higher up, fewer marked the other side of the creek. The rock piles seemed to increase with the height almost as if they'd been laid there by giant hands. No doubt the coyote had a den in an outcropping. King loved to chase things, but he wasn't going to confront a coyote in his den, assuming he could even find it. A clever coyote would mark various dens to throw off an enemy. Usually more than one coyote lived in each den. Better not to find oneself outnumbered.

King stopped as Baxter caught up. *"Time to go back."*

Baxter lifted his head, sniffed deeply. *"Something's in the creek bed."*

King followed, flared his nostrils. He'd been so intent on his coyote, he hadn't paid too much attention to competing scents. To him, this one smelled sweet, alluring.

The dogs dipped over the bank and moved southward along the creek bed, stopping at a small overhang on the west side. Dry Valley Road was thirty yards away.

King splashed across the water to the overhang. Baxter did also, getting his tummy wet.

Transfixed, the two animals stared at the human corpse stashed there. One wouldn't see it from the road. Coyotes had eaten some of the best parts — including the nose and lips — but since it froze at night what wasn't chewed was well enough preserved. If the mercury rose more, the heady fragrance would announce a jackpot of carrion to the local critters. By then, even the humans would get a whiff.

"He's not far from dinner." King stayed focused on his coyote.

"We never see anything like this in New York." Baxter was excited. *"Do people just stick their dead anywhere here in Nevada?"*

"Not unless there's a problem. They bury everything mostly so no one can get to them." King sniffed the corpse. *"Let's see if we can pull an arm off and take it home."*

"Do you think they will want it?" Baxter didn't think humans liked this sort of thing.

"Probably not, but what a prize!" King

grabbed what was left of the hand and pulled.

Baxter did his best to help. Being short, he had to stand on his hind legs, so he couldn't pull as hard as King. Finally, two fingers dislodged, but the wrist bones stubbornly would not yield.

Disappointed, King looked at the mangled fingers. *"Well, it's better than nothing."*

On the phone in her office, Jeep heard Carlotta's screams. Running to the kitchen, Jeep, like her daughter-in-law, was horrified to see two discolored human fingers on the floor. King proudly stood over them, wagging his tail frantically.

Baxter, also thrilled, stood on the other side of the treasure.

King reached down to pick them up again.

"No," Jeep said firmly. "Carlotta, put a pan over these, will you?"

With distaste, Carlotta did just that.

The dogs guarded the pan as Jeep called the sheriff's office. Then she called Enrique. Mags, with Enrique at the time, hurried home with him.

Once in the house, Enrique carefully picked up the overturned pot, his lips curled up. King made an attempt to grab the fingers.

"No," Jeep again commanded.

"They're mine!" King protested.

"I helped." Baxter wasn't to be cheated of this increasingly pungent treasure.

Within a half hour, Pete and Lonnie also viewed the grisly find. Pete put on thin rubber gloves and gingerly dropped the fingers in a bag.

"Could I have a Ziploc filled with ice? Let me put this in that."

Carlotta quickly fixed him one. She wanted the damned fingers out of the house. "The dogs came through the door and just dropped them," Carlotta informed them as she handed over the large bag of ice cubes.

"Lonnie, let's go outside and look," Pete said.

He dropped the ice bag in the back of the squad car, then called HQ. After, he and Lonnie started walking around the buildings as did Jeep, Mags, and Enrique.

"If a body was this close to the house, we'd have found it," Enrique said.

"No doubt," Pete replied, "but we'd still better check."

The two agitated dogs kept barking and heading southward, then coming back.

"We should follow the dogs," Jeep suggested.

"At last, someone with sense." King

gloated. *"She is the smartest of the lot."*

Pete hesitated, so Mags said, "Aunt Jeep, why don't you and I follow them on the ATVs? Pete and Lonnie can keep looking here."

Five minutes later, the two women sped after the dogs. Swerving to avoid isolated rocks and large sagebrush, they kept the creek bed to their right. They stopped when the dogs jumped down into the bed. Following, the grisly sight shocked Mags. Jeep didn't much like it, either.

Mags called Pete from her cell. He showed up ten minutes later, seeing them parked on the side of Dry Valley Road.

Carefully, he and Lonnie dropped down into the creek bed.

"Think they'll give us any of this?" Baxter wondered.

"No," King replied with some regret.

"It's Oliver Hitchens, isn't it?" Mags asked.

"Yes," Pete replied simply.

CHAPTER THIRTY-TWO

Murder raises issues most people would rather not consider. The first being why, the second being that most of us have somewhere within us the capacity to kill. Some admit it, some don't.

Best not to jump to conclusions about anything, not even identifying the body. The Sheriff's Department scrambled to reach the next of kin before the news was blasted across TV screens. The minute Pete called in to HQ, a female officer was dispatched to Karen Hitchens, another male officer to Darryl Johnson. The Hitchens's son, away at college, was later called by his mother. Oliver's daughter, at high school, was picked up by her aunt, who, thank God, lived in Reno. Even with the mutilation of the corpse, Pete knew it was Oliver before he confirmed it because he found his wallet and ID inside his coat pocket.

▪ ▪ ▪ ▪

Darryl Johnson called a meeting of upper management the moment the police officer left his office. Those who had seen the uniformed presence suspected it had to do with Oliver Hitchens's disappearance but still the news of his death came as a shock.

After providing some details and withholding the most gruesome ones, Darryl said to the employees gathered around the conference table, "Our first priority is Karen and the kids. George W., you know the family better than any of us, I think. We should stop by to express our condolences right after work, all of us, unless you feel otherwise."

"No, no, that's the right thing to do."

"We should bring food." Elizabeth McCormick suggested quietly.

"Lolly and I will take care of that." Darryl folded his hands on the table. The president, like all such leaders, had expected to solve many problems during his tenure. He'd never expected this.

For a moment, nothing was said. Outside the closed doors, phones could be heard ringing incessantly.

Elizabeth advised quietly, "Our first ad appeared in the paper today. I think we should pull the rest of them until February."

"It's a good ad" — Darryl inclined his head toward her — "but you're right. SSRM is going to receive a lot of media scrutiny and I'd advise all of you to say as little as possible. Any stray comment could be misconstrued or, worse, impede the search for Oliver's killer. Is that understood?"

All said, "Yes."

"Good. Go back and inform people in your respective departments. Elizabeth, stay back a moment."

Craig Locke, moving toward the conference room exit, stopped a moment, started to say something, then thought better of it.

George W. put his hand on Craig's shoulder as they walked out the door into the hallway.

Craig asked, "Anyone know how he was killed?"

"Not yet, or if they do, they aren't telling us."

"This all started with Pump Nineteen." Craig's voice was bitter.

"Craig, at this moment I don't know anything except that Karen and the kids will need all our support." George W. reached the elevator bank and pushed the down button. He'd head to the warehouse now, along the way calling his crews on the road.

Back in the conference room, Darryl asked Elizabeth, "Help me prepare a statement to the press, will you?"

"Of course."

They worked diligently as the phones reverberated throughout the building. By the time they had finished, a mobile TV crew had pulled up in front of the SSRM corporate offices, shooting the outside.

Late in the afternoon, after Oliver Hitchens's body had finally been removed, Pete and Lonnie drove back to Jecp.

Having returned with Mags hours ago, she was already curious for an update. Seeing them coming down the long drive, she opened the door. "Come on in," she said from the porch. "Can I get you anything?"

"No. Thank you for your help and I'm sorry you had to see that," Pete said kindly.

Mags came down the hallway and stood behind her great-aunt. "It was awful."

"Pete, whoever put him there was someone who knows the land out here, someone who must have walked it a time or two, and right on the southern edge of my ranch."

"More than likely. Either that or the killer had blind luck finding that crevice. But I think you're right."

Jake Tanner, out on his Bobcat, saw the swirling lights.

Unless there's a range, one can see for

miles in this part of the world. When he spotted a sheriff's vehicle coming down Red Rock Road from the north, Jake knew something big was happening. He hopped in his old truck and cruised slowly down Red Rock Road. Then, despite wanting to know what was happening, he decided if he showed up in the middle of everything he might just be in the way. So he turned and drove up to Pump 19. From there, he'd have a good view below.

Oliver's car sat in the parking area. You wouldn't see it from Red Rock unless you craned your neck upward. Then you might possibly catch sight of the Explorer's taillight.

From his cell, he immediately called the Sheriff's Department.

Just as Pete and Lonnie were leaving Jeep's they got the call.

Lights flashing, going fifty on the twisty road, they managed to meet Jake within twelve minutes.

"It's Oliver's," Jake decreed simply. "I checked the registration." Jake pointed inside the car to a long, smooth notebook wedged in the glove compartment.

Pete put his gloves on. "Damn! Now it has your fingerprints." He retrieved the notebook from the car and flipped it open.

"What's going on down there?" Jake couldn't contain his curiosity.

"Jeep's dog found Oliver's body. Someone stuffed him into a crevice of the creek bed, on the road side so no one would see him as they drove by."

Jake's eyes grew large. "Jesus Christ."

Pete looked around inside the Explorer. He noticed a six-inch by eight-inch notebook, covered in red ripstop cloth. The SSRM logo in blue was embroidered in the right-hand bottom corner. Opening the notebook, he saw just three words scribbled on the lined papers: "Drainage basin. Bedell." Nothing else. Pete checked other pages, but they were blank. He returned to the glove compartment. Halls lozenges, small packets of Kleenex, and a couple of ballpoint pens filled it, along with the vehicle manual.

"I bet I've driven by here every day since Oliver went missing," said Jake. "Never looked up."

"Jake, you did good." Pete shut the door to the Explorer.

"Know what I think?" Jake was about to tell them, whether they wanted to hear it or not. "I think someone is sitting on a pile of money."

CHAPTER THIRTY-THREE

Back at Washoe Water Rights, Pete was questioning Walter De Quille, who was doing his best to make complex issues understandable.

"Let's go back to the beginning for a moment. I'll make it brief." The older fellow smiled. "We became a state in 1864 and we knew even then we'd have water problems. For those of us in this part of Nevada, the Truckee River is our lifeline."

"What about the aquifers?"

"To get into those underground stores, you have to dig down deep. It depends on the soil. And those aquifers depend on what little rain we get, plus the snowpack runoff. In drought years, the snowpack can be easily depleted. We've had five drought years up until now."

"Why don't we build more reservoirs?"

Hunched at a table, Lonnie scribbled away, listening intently.

Walter dropped his hand on Dowser's head as the boxer settled beside him. "In the current economic climate, the expense is out of the question. We have some small reservoirs, but the headwaters of the Truckee are in California. In the nineteenth century there was endless squabbling over Lake Tahoe, drawing water from it for here. This flares up every time we have prolonged droughts. California, then and now, refuses Nevada access to the Truckee's bounty on their side of the state line. This is understandable but they have more water than we do. Remember that. The political uproar for a project as huge as a new reservoir would paralyze the state. I really believe that."

"Could folks bring in water from another part of Washoe County?" Pete asked.

Walter stroked his chin, a thin white stubble showing. "Well" — a pause followed — "what you're talking about is an interbasin transfer. The first one occurred in 1873. Water from the Hobart Reservoir was sent to Virginia City, then in the big boom of its existence" — He twisted in his chair, sweeping his hand toward the bookshelves that covered a wall of the storefront. Low file cabinets were interspersed in other locations — "everything on those shelves or in those file cabinets refers to our history: legal proceedings, reports from the state engineer." He paused. "I still don't know it all, but I think I know where to find it."

"What about going online?"

"Better to have primary sources in hand. You'd be surprised at how many inaccuracies are online. I use the web, don't misunderstand me, but I can get up and pull out the information on that first interbasin transfer with comments written in the margins by prior researchers. If I had three lifetimes, I would not know it all."

"Can developers tap into Pyramid Lake?"

"Now there's a hot potato." Walter relished the thought. "The Paiutes live there and the Truckee empties into it. That would start a shooting war."

"And as I recall you don't think the projections of our ability to sustain, ultimately, some six hundred thousand are accurate?"

"No. It would be a disaster to keep emptying out the aquifers and to use more of the Truckee. Let me put this in perspective. You and I look at a creek or a river running and we feel all is well. But even in a nondrought year, we cruise into July, August and many of those have dried up, especially the feeder creeks. The underground water is held in various types of sediment, and some are in a recharge area that is quite saturated. It's what you can't see that really keeps us going in many ways. The largest aquifer in the world is right here in the United States, the Ogalalla Aquifer, which undergirds most of the western states. The recharge area for the Ogalallas are the western mountain ranges. Most of that vast aquifer accumulated over tens of thousands of years. It's falling three-point-two feet a year but the recharge rate is one thirty-second of an inch."

"What happens to the ground?"

"It compacts. No water can get back in once enough is drawn out. In some cases, the earth simply sinks. Phoenix, Tucson, and Albuquerque sit over depleting aquifers. Right now in Reno we're holding our own, but for how long?"

Pete crossed one leg over the other. "When I was online last night I pulled up the Hydrographic Area Summary for Red Rock Valley."

"Right now, Red Rock is stable. But its proximity to Reno makes it worth watching. Pump Nineteen serves Lemmon Valley" — Walter named a small community — "but one could send water up to Reno once all the pipes were laid."

"But are there other areas more vulnerable?"

"Yes. They don't have Jeep Reed. The obvious one being Horseshoe Estates, land south of Reno."

"It occurred to me while I was researching on the computer that all our attention has been focused on water being sent to Reno."

"That's the obvious destination."

"But isn't it possible to take water from, say, the small springs around Winnemucca and develop over there? It's on the back side of the Dogskin Mountains. There has to be some runoff and there is a good road."

"In theory — that is, if you could get the water rights — yes. But it's too difficult to be a commuter community to Reno. The geography would make building good roads outrageously expensive right now. There aren't enough roads over there. Put the point of a compass in Reno and draw a circle that represents a half-hour commute. Then draw one representing forty-five minutes and, lastly, one hour. Those are the hot zones, closer the better, obviously."

"What about on the California side?"

"If it's within shouting distance of Reno, it's vulnerable. I believe Sam Peruzzi foresaw that vulnerability and feared that, sooner or later, the California legislature would sell out Sierra County for the phenomenal tax revenues that water rights sale would generate. And this would kill the wildlife Sam

335

loved — again, sooner or later."

"Did you know Oliver Hitchens?" asked Pete.

"No. Terrible thing. The news hasn't said how he was killed."

"He hadn't been examined yet by forensics, but it looked like a blow to the back of the head."

"The papers said he was in the equipment and repair division. He wasn't the fellow out there buying up rights? Curious. But then again the pumps are blown. Still, the blown pumps and murder can't be about equipment."

"Right." Pete straightened his leg. He'd run that morning after working out in the gym and for some reason his leg ached.

"Deputy Meadows, when you were searching about on your computer, you came across the Orr Ditch Decree from 1944?"

"The law that says all old claims are recognized. Nothing can change regarding them."

"Right, except that those same rights can be converted from agricultural to municipal. That's the reason, the whole force behind picking up water rights. To convert them."

"One could just sit on them and wait for the right time."

"You'd have to be prophetic to know where the next development will be. If it were that easy, everyone would be doing it."

"Do you think you know?"

"No. For example, I know the area where Horseshoe Estates will be built, but I wouldn't have thought of the exact location. I would have put it a bit farther west because the developer wouldn't have to build such a long access road. Of course, with the prices they'll be charging for the homes, I expect they'll get it."

"That they will. Mr. De Quille —"

"Walter." He looked down. "Walter and Dowser. Do you know, Deputy Meadows, that animals, buffalo, antelope, even Dowser here can smell water from miles away? I read that Jeep's dog and a little wire-haired dachshund found Hitchens. Of course, that's a different odor."

"But it was cold. Those dog noses are incredible."

Walter affectionately stroked Dowser's head. "They know when someone is going to have a heart attack, an epileptic fit. I think they even know when you've got cancer. They know so much and they live within nature, they live within their personal limits. We don't."

"I expect we have a lot to learn from dogs."

CHAPTER THIRTY-FOUR

After seeing Walter De Quille, Pete pulled the police vehicle into the parking lot at Subway. Fishing in his pants pocket for money, he handed over fifteen dollars. "The usual. Lunch's on me. And hot water."

"All right." Lonnie stepped out of the car, cold air hitting him. "I hate winter."

"Me too." Pete took his personal cellphone from the door pocket and called Mags. "I'm sorry I couldn't get back to you again yesterday, but it was a nonstop day. Are you all right?"

"I'm okay," she said. "I guess you see stuff like that all the time."

"Never quite like that, though. You stayed calm."

She thought a moment. "There's nothing pretty about death, but there's not exactly anything you can do about it, either."

"Not for the dead, true, but you can work for the living. Oliver Hitchens left a wife and two children. That offends me."

"I think I understand. Am I allowed to ask you about the case?"

"Sure. I don't know if I have answers."

"Whatever is at stake must be something close, it must be pressing. What do you think?"

"Yes." He didn't tell her that he thought Sam Peruzzi's death was also connected. "Too many things in a compressed time period."

"Would that mean that the killer is under threat?"

"Mmm, not necessarily. He may now feel he's removed the threat."

"Meaning Oliver had dangerous knowledge." She changed the subject. "If you come by after work, I'll cook you a meal. Me, not Carlotta — which means you take your chances."

"If you gave me potato chips, I'd be happy." His voice lifted.

"I'll try and do better than that. When can you come by?"

"Six-thirty."

Just as he was hanging up, Lonnie opened the passenger door and set down the cardboard tray. "What's up?" Then he grinned. "Should I look the other way?"

"Shut up." Pete grabbed his half of a foot-long sandwich.

"You're in a better mood than when I left."

"Feel like I won the lottery." He took the change Lonnie handed him, stuffing it in his pocket. "Close that door." He lifted the cardboard tray so Lonnie could slide in.

"Colder than this morning. Okay, what's up?"

"Mags asked me to dinner tonight after work. She said she'd cook."

"Buddy, you're one step from the bedroom unless you blow it."

Pete sipped his tea. "I'm not hurrying anything. I like her too much."

Lonnie, for all his focus on sex, knew what Pete meant. "You going to bring her flowers?"

"I was thinking about a book."

"Flowers."

Pete grinned. "Both."

"I'd have a hard time knowing what book to buy a woman." Lonnie shoved his sandwich in his mouth.

"If you'd read more, you wouldn't. You find out a lot about people by what they read or if they read."

"I get the fidgets. I start out just great, then I want to get up and do something." Lonnie didn't much like all the time he sat in the squad car, either.

Pete changed the subject. "Mags brought up something, that the killer might be under pressure, under threat."

Lonnie polished off his sandwich. "Of course, given Oliver's personality, maybe his killer thought he was doing the world a favor."

"I think it's an inside job. You know when we opened Oliver's car, the notebook?"

"Yeah."

"The cloth looked like the bits of cloth we'd found at the blown pumps. Now I'm sure it can't be that hard to find similar notebooks, but still."

"Let's go to Staples, Office Depot. If it's easy to find, it will be there. It's not much, but it's something."

After finishing a quick lunch they pulled into Staples. There were all kinds of notebooks but none covered in ripstop cloth. Office Depot yielded similar results.

"One last try." Pete headed toward the most expensive shopping center in Reno. Inside was a stationery store.

The owner looked up as they entered. "May I help you?"

"Do you have notebooks covered in ripstop cloth?" Pete asked.

"No," she replied. "We have some lovely leather ones though from Smythson of London. Bond Street."

A table with the Cerulean Collection of notebooks arranged in concentric circles were beautiful and expensive. The blue covers jumped out at you.

"Sorry to bother you. They are unique." Pete picked up one and saw the price of $850. "You might help us with a case we're working on. We've found pieces of a notebook, white lined paper with a red ripstop cover."

Pencil behind her ear, the lady put up her forefinger. "Hold on one minute." She went behind the counter, pulled out two large catalogs. "I have a few catalogs from companies we don't carry. Now let me look." She thumbed through one from New York. "Here you go."

Pete and Lonnie stared down as she turned the book toward them. "That's close."

"Here, let me grab their largest competitor's catalog. Companies will order glasses with their logo on them, fleece blankets, all kinds of things. Calendars are always big and they offer low prices based on volume." She thumbed to the correct pages. "Here you go."

"That's it." Pete checked the available colors.

"Would you like the catalog?" she offered.

"Ma'am, that would be helpful. And thank you."

Back in the car, Lonnie asked, "Why didn't you just call the president's secretary at SSRM?"

"Because, like I told you, I think this is an inside job. Why let anyone in the company know we're considering that?"

"Right. It's not much to go on." He flipped through the catalog. "Hey, I can buy trolls and put your name on them."

"You're too good to me."

"Too bad we can't examine bank accounts." Lonnie fiddled with the window button. "Can't do that without a blizzard of subpoenas and crap."

"Something tells me whoever is behind all this is too smart to put their eggs in one basket."

"He could have put the money in an offshore account, have Wade Properties or whoever is kicking back send it direct," Lonnie suggested.

"That's not as safe as it once was and it would mean a bunch of people would have to be in on it."

"Don't the presidents of companies have discretionary funds?"

"They still have to report them to accounting."

Lonnie thought a moment. "I still think Oliver just pissed someone off. Why are we going north on three ninety-five?"

"To look over at Sierra County and to turn right onto Red Rock Road, come back down from the north."

"Some nice ranches over here," Lonnie noted. "More water."

The difference in terrain and moisture was obvious.

"Yep."

When they turned right and headed down Red Rock Road, the Peterson range was now on their right.

"We know this," Lonnie remarked, looking at the landscape.

"Doesn't hurt to be reminded."

That evening, Pete brought Mags a dozen pink roses and a DVD of a PBS show called "Fly Girls."

Jeep clapped her hands together. "I can't wait."

"Aunt Jeep, we'll watch it together."

Mags had made pork chops with apple-sauce and a big salad. Carlotta had made crème brûlée with a delicious topping of raspberry sauce to help Mags since she wasn't too good at making desserts.

"I hope she remembers to give us the

344

bones." Baxter loved the odor of pork.

King sat at Jeep's feet, looking up at her adoringly. *"Try this."*

At the end of the main meal, the dogs got their pork chop bones.

After dessert, Jeep excused herself and King followed. Mags, Pete, and Baxter repaired to the living room.

"Would you like an after-dinner drink?" Mags asked.

He looked over at her. "I'm pretty much a beer guy and then I wait until summer."

"That's smart." She sat across from him as he settled in the comfortable sofa. "What a wonderful gift, 'Fly Girls.' I've never seen it. The flowers are beautiful, too."

"Every time I drive under the gate and look up at that propeller, I imagine what it must be like to fly one of those old planes."

"Aunt Jeep loved it."

"Can you shoot a gun?"

"I can pull the trigger, but if you're asking me about my marksmanship skills, I don't have any."

"Will you allow me to take you to the shooting range and teach you? There's paperwork to fill out. I know Jeep has guns. Maybe she'd let you use one and then we could put it in your name."

"Are you worried about me?"

"Every woman should know how to use a gun. And, well, yes, I am a little worried. Pump Nineteen isn't that far up Red Rock Road and a murder victim was found at the southern edge of your aunt's property."

"I'll protect her." Baxter spoke quite clearly.

Mags reached down to put him in her lap. "Actually, the shooting range sounds like something I'd enjoy."

"If you're free Saturday, I'll pick you up. If you find you like it, there are things like shooting clays, stuff like that. For some people it's a real passion. Takes good hand–eye coordination."

"I'd rather shoot clays than birds."

"Me too. I don't really want to kill anything."

She curled her feet up under, having kicked off her shoes. "I'm still on the trail of Nicholas. I have the names of all the Russians who rode for Buffalo Bill. One curious thing: An English officer who was part of the show was a friend of Colonel Wavell, the rich baron who married the Fords' daughter. It seems Felicia's husband attended every show he could and the ones in England, too. Colonel Wavell was an officer in the elite Household Cavalry. I don't know to what unit the officer in Buffalo Bill's show belonged."

"That's more than you knew yesterday."

She laughed. "Progress comes in little steps, for the most part."

Later, he checked his watch. "It's ten-thirty. I had no idea. Why didn't you throw me out?"

"I didn't know what time it was, either. We haven't yet run out of things to talk about."

She walked him to the door and gave him a hug and big good-night kiss. He returned it and didn't want to let her go.

She watched his taillights as he drove down the road.

Baxter watched, too.

CHAPTER THIRTY-FIVE

January 14, Thursday, was the Festival of the Ass, much celebrated in Europe during the Middle Ages. Back then every village mounted a theatrical representation of the holy family's flight into Egypt. The part of Mary, always hotly contested among local beauties, was usually awarded to the one who pleased the priest the most or the one attached to the most powerful man in the community — say, a count's daughter. The part of the ass was never hotly contested.

Since 1955, Jeep had rented a casino banquet hall to celebrate this festival. On the bottom of the printed invitation was a quote, "We are celebrating a different kind of ass."

Jeep had long ago realized that in the dispirited season after Christmas, with cloudy skies and the bills rolling in, everyone needed a pick-me-up this time of year. Any veteran of World War II in Washoe County was invited. Some years past, when so many

World War II vets were still alive, the party cost her close to $200,000. These days, the gathering was still large, but smaller nevertheless, the men as old, some older, than herself. The bulk of the partiers were friends, family, those with whom Jeep did business — neighbors like Jake Tanner, whose big appetite was more than satisfied by the bountiful menu.

A band with the big band sound always played, for that was Jeep's favorite music. When they'd take a break, as a concession to youth in attendance, another more au courant band would fill in with the latest music.

As Mags put on her mascara, looking in the mirror above her bedroom dresser, her cell rang. At the foot of her bed, Baxter barked in response, as if alarmed.

"Mags." Catherine's voice sounded crisp and clear. "Are you aware that the Nevada Supreme Court is going to reconsider a decision from 2007 that could affect water rights back to 1947?"

"Well, that's a warm and welcome greeting," said Mags. "But to answer your question, yes. Aunt Jeep was talking about that. She said it might take a year."

"All the way back to 1947!" Catherine exclaimed.

"But Jeep's rights go back to 1880," Mags argued, suddenly suspicious about the subject of this conversation.

"Not purchase of land whose water rights don't fall back that far. Jeep might have to refile on Wings. She bought it in the fifties."

"Catherine, I'm getting ready to go to a party. Get to the point." Mags's distrust rose.

"If she refiles, put some of those properties in my name."

"Even if I wanted to — which I don't — I can't do that! I'd have to go through her battalion of lawyers."

"Jeep loves you. She might do it for you if you asked. I'm owed part of that estate."

"I won't do it."

"Fuck you!" Catherine slammed down the phone.

Mags shut off her cell. "Baxter, that is the most selfish bitch God has ever put on earth."

"I'm sorry."

She kissed his head, then returned to the mascara.

Six hundred guests came to this year's party. The veterans who could still fit into them wore their uniforms. Jeep wore her dark blue uniform and looked fabulous. The fitted jacket had notched lapels. On each top lapel was a gold-tone pair of wings sprouting from what looked like a vertical propeller. On the bottom notched lapels, in bold metal letters was "WASP." She stood at the door greeting everyone, King by her side. Even though the casino had a no pets policy, it was waived for Jeep's annual party. Wives at their side, men who'd fought Zeroes over the South Pacific, men who'd survived the Battle of the Bulge, sat in chairs with poodles, Yorkies, and mutts in their laps. Every wife received a corsage with ribbons in the colors of her husband's branch of the service.

A special potty area was roped off for the dogs and Jeep paid handsomely for a casino employee to scoop up the results. The dogs had bones and treats. The humans gorged on delicacies. Chef Egon Utrecht made sure no one would ever forget this menu and the casino. As a tribute to the veterans, he had an ice sculpture made in the shape of an un-furled flag. This greeted everyone in the main lobby, even those nonguests who were headed for the gambling areas. The casino also did a great job of decorating, placing over the party room's entrance a propeller with a sprig of evergreen behind it.

Most folks in attendance who had not done military service wore jeans and shirts

— belt buckles being an indicator of status, as well as fancy boots, which always drew comments of approval. Some men sported monstrous horseshoe rings, most were a bit more conservative. The ladies, regardless of age, wore jeans or long, brightly colored skirts with cowboy boots also in bright colors. Jewelry ranged from turquoise necklaces to Cartier. One thing was for sure: When you stepped into this room, you knew you were in Nevada.

Apart from Jeep, three other women wore uniforms. Pauline Winters, Navy, rolled around in a wheelchair with a little horn on the arm.

Pete attended with his parents. Lonnie at his side, too, was slack-jawed at the attendees, the band, and some very hot women. He thought he'd died and gone to heaven.

In the receiving line, Mags stood next to Jeep. Enrique was on her other side with Carlotta. With all the jewelry she wore, Carlotta had to have weighed ten more pounds. As always, she carried it off. Enrique wore a tux coat with jeans, his boots were peanut brittle–colored ostrich. Baxter and King sat by their humans, overwhelmed by the food smells and suspicious of other dogs until those animals lowered their eyes. King could be very commanding.

Despite their clashing ideas about Reno's future, Jeep had invited the upper management of SSRM, as she did other corporate leaders. She also invited Twinkie and Bunny because she liked them, and Jake especially liked them. She wanted to keep her neighbor happy. Reno in particular, Nevada in general, was a great place to do business — all thanks to no taxes and a climate conducive to business. Big national companies like John Deere were in Reno. Four thousand eight hundred and sixty-two businesses in Washoe County were women-owned, which made Jeep proud; back in the day, when she had just returned from the war, you could count them on your fingers.

Darryl Johnson and Lolly attended, as did Craig Locke and his wife. George W. and his wife also were there and were warmly welcomed in the receiving line.

Jeep was glad to see SSRM's president. "Thank you so much for coming, Darryl, I know this has been a difficult time. Perhaps tonight will raise some spirits."

"Thank you, Jeep. Lolly and I wouldn't miss this. It's a great way to start the year."

Lolly enthused, "You look wonderful in your uniform. Must have driven the men wild in the day."

"Still do." Jeep laughed. "But now they run

353

away in fear because they don't want to be corralled by a mean old woman."

As the SSRM people went down the line, some partiers noticed. Many expressed their sympathy to Oliver Hitchens's colleagues, others were just nosy.

Guiding Lonnie toward one of his high school classmates, Pete paused a moment, nodding in the direction of the SSRM people. As he did, a photographer from the *Reno Gazette-Journal* and the *Reno News & Review*, the weekly paper, snapped photos. Within seconds all three of the SSRM employees were cornered by curious reporters from those papers.

Lonnie noticed, but his attention was drawn to Amelia Owen, Pete's classmate. Buxom and brunette, with a curvaceous body, she attracted both admiring and envious glances from many of the guests.

"Pete Meadows." Amelia threw her arms around him, kissing his cheek. "How are you?"

"Good. I'd like to introduce you to Lonnie Parrish. He's not half bad. We work together."

She appraised Lonnie, who exuded boyish appeal.

"Pleased to meet you," he said.

"How's business?" Pete asked, then informed his partner. "Amelia owns her own construction business."

"Hard work," Lonnie said.

"It is, but I love it," gushed Amelia. "Just love it. I can't sit behind a desk and you know, Mr. Parrish —"

"Lonnie."

Pete smiled. "That's what you should call him now. God knows what you'll call him later."

Amelia laughed. "Lonnie, the best part of my work is finishing the job and knowing someone will make a home in it. I just love it and" — her voice became even more animated — "I don't have to answer to anybody else."

"I'll leave you two to get acquainted," said Pete. I'm going to see if Mags needs a drink. She's been standing in that line for over an hour. Jeep, too. Woman's tougher than nails."

Amelia touched Lonnie's forearm and her voice softened. "Not one bank would give me a loan when I wanted to start my own company. They didn't say because I was a single woman, but I knew. I tried every bank in this town. Then my grandmother suggested I talk to Jeep. Do you know she bankrolled me at two percent interest and gave me twenty years to repay the loan? That's extraordinary. I paid it off this Christmas. Tell you what, there isn't anything I wouldn't do for that woman. The best part was when she handed me the check" — Amelia looked slyly at Lonnie — "Jeep said, 'there's an old boys' network. To succeed we need an old girls' network. Some future day, help another woman.'"

Lonnie's eyes fell to her ample bosom during this story and he really was listening but he couldn't help himself, which made Amelia laugh all the louder.

Pete put his forefinger to his temple, by way of salute, and walked across the crowded room to the receiving line. "Could I get anyone a drink?" He looked down. "Baxter, King?"

"God, yes." Jeep fanned herself for a moment. "Scotch on the rocks. Tell the bartender it's for me."

"Mags?"

"Just tonic water, I think. Lime."

Enrique nodded. "Corona Extra." He looked to Carlotta. She nodded. "Two. Perhaps a glass for my bride."

"Water," the dogs barked.

Pete found a waiter and told him to bring a table to put behind the receiving line so the folks there could put their drinks down. Then Pete asked him to bring two bowls of water for Baxter and King. After, he strode over to the bar and gave his order, handing over five dollars for a tip.

Just then Egon Utrecht burst from the kitchen, bellowing orders to someone who had forgotten a bowl of sauce. Egon, sweating profusely, saw Pete and nodded. The famous chef was nervous, shouting at staff, a real whirlwind. As he walked by, a pair of guests handed him glasses of champagne, which he downed in a gulp.

Given Jeep's status, Egon had cause to be nervous. He wanted the guests to be talking about the food until next year when he'd try to outdo this year.

Within five minutes, Pete returned to the receiving line with drinks, a waiter in tow to help carry them through the crowd. He also brought napkins.

"Thank you." Jeep reached for her scotch. "I'm parched."

The dogs wagged their tails as they drank.

"How much longer will you all stand here?" Pete asked. "I can bring chairs. It's a long time to be on your feet."

Jeep looked down her small receiving line. Nearly all the guests had arrived. "How about another ten minutes and then let's eat?"

Before Pete left, Mags said, "I liked meeting your parents."

"Thanks. I was lucky. I got a good pair."

People sat at the various tables, the head table had a small model of a P-47 on it. Once Jeep and her family finally sat down, they could barely eat as people kept stopping by to talk. Every time Carlotta threw her arms up to hug someone for the third, fourth, or fifth time, her bracelets jingled a happy tune.

Mags looked out over the room and thought what a tribute to her great-aunt. Sure, she had more money than Midas, but she had done so much good with it. Mags knew she could never match her great-aunt that way, but she hoped she, too, would wind up making a good life, one that reached out to help others, one filled with friends and laughter, one filled with real people.

Jeep nodded to the band, now filing onto the dais. Soon the tables would empty and the dance floor would fill with people. The bandleader tapped his baton, the trumpeter stood and blew a few merry notes.

Escorted onto the stage by Enrique, Jeep acknowledged the crowd's cheers. After wishing everyone a booming happy New Year, she cited by name those few veterans in the crowd. The room applauded thunder-ously. The women guests cheered especially for the three female veterans.

Jeep spoke in her characteristically clear, pleasant voice. "Folks, don't listen to the naysayers, the crybabies, the special interests. Sure, times are hard but believe me and those of us in this room over seventy when we tell you, we've seen harder times than this. Forget Washington," Jeep continued in her inspired oratory. "That's the problem, not the answer." At this, her speech was interrupted by people whistling and cheering. "We'll pull through. Leave it to the people. I'll do my part and I expect you'll do yours. Forward!"

The cheers roared and men stomped the floor with their heavy boots.

She held up her hands for quiet. "Egon Utrecht, please come out here."

It took a moment for a casino employee to fetch Egon from the kitchen. Emerging through the door, he looked around, then smiled as if by afterthought. He moved through the crowd.

Jeep extended her arm in his direction. "Our compliments to the chef." Cheers followed.

He stopped and bowed to the hostess, put up his right hand like Mussolini used to when driving through the crowds, and bowed to the assembled guests before returning to the kitchen. He was again handed champagne glasses as he passed tables.

Jeep wrapped up her speechifying. "All right. This is Reno. Let's party!"

At that, the band struck up "Boogie Woogie Bugle Boy" and the dance floor was flooded with enthusiastic couples, and a few singles.

Having eaten whatever was given them (or had fallen) from the table, Baxter and King watched. Mags put the dachshund on her lap. Pete asked Jeep to dance. He was a good dancer, whirling her by his mother and father, who were also dancing. For the next song, he asked Mags.

When the band had started, Darryl Johnson and Craig Locke walked into the kitchen.

"Egon," Darryl called to the surprised large man holding a ladle. "This is a triumph. If we can get a room here, would you be willing to oversee our annual company dinner?"

Egon, eyes nervously darting, calmed himself. "Of course." A champagne glass, half full, sat by a pot.

"This really is the best banquet meal I've ever had." Craig complimented him.

"Thank you." Egon set down his ladle beside the large boiling pot.

"We'll be in touch." Darryl left, Craig in

his wake.

One hour later, the party had reached a crescendo. The various dogs either ran around the room or had fallen asleep under their masters' chairs.

Pete made sure to dance with his mother. Then he danced with ex-classmate Amelia, who pumped him about Lonnie, who was six years younger than they were. Next, he asked to dance with the three women veterans. Pauline Winters he wheeled onto the floor, and she waved her hands to the music. The other dancers came by, one by one, to seize her hand or kiss her on the cheek.

Mags watched Pete's every move.

Jeep observed her great-niece. "Ever notice, sweetie, how a real man never has to advertise?"

"Aunt Jeep, I've met so few."

This elicited a deep laugh, then Jeep said, "We've got 'em by the squadrons here in Nevada."

At one point, Pete took Lonnie by the elbow, whispered a few words, then Lonnie also asked to dance with the lady veterans, as well as a few of the widows in the room. Somehow that's when one minds being a widow the most, at a dance when you need a drink from the bar. If another man doesn't notice, a polite older lady is out of luck.

Then, too, so many husbands and wives of the older generation loved to dance. With her partner gone, many a widow sat. But not at Jeep's party.

Having a strong mother and two independent sisters, Pete had learned early. He understood a woman's need for attention — not the obvious sexual kind, but the small courtesies that made a woman feel wanted and special.

After a break filled with live rock music, the big band was up again, playing "The White Cliffs of Dover." This sentimental song from the war could reduce anyone from the British Isles to tears and not a few Americans as well. After making his way back to Mags, Pete held her tight, but not too tight, as they glided around the dance floor.

"Did I tell you that you are the most beautiful woman in the room and the most fascinating?"

"Now I know you're fibbing. Aunt Jeep is the most fascinating."

"She'll have to share that honor with you." He put his cheek next to hers.

A scream from the kitchen stopped him short. Pete pulled away for a moment and saw one of the chef's assistants run out from the back in a panic. Dr. Carl Detweiler, sitting this dance out, stood as the assistant

reached him and gestured wildly. They both ran to the kitchen.

"Mags, I'll be back."

The band played on. Lonnie excused himself to Amelia and hurried behind Pete.

Baxter and King reached the kitchen first. Any scream will alert a dog, and now all the dogs in the place were barking.

Egon rolled on the kitchen's spotless tile floor, his white chef's topper a few feet away. In obvious pain, he foamed at the mouth.

Just inside the door, Baxter put his head down, did not touch the suffering man. *"Bitter. Bitter smell."*

"He's dying," King said matter-of-factly.

Egon's eyes rolled back, violent tremors shook his body, then the massive frame lay still.

CHAPTER THIRTY-SIX

Friday's *Reno Gazette-Journal* ran a well-written article about the collapse and suspected poisoning of celebrity chef Egon Utrecht. As the reporter actually had been at the party to cover it, the details proved accurate. The quotes from shocked eyewitnesses jumped off the page.

Egon's assistant chef, Lisa Giogionides, said, "He clutched his throat, made a strangling sound, and collapsed." A waiter who wished not to be identified reported, "Egon had been knocking back champagne most of the night. He had one temper tantrum after another." What the reporter didn't include was, "I hated the son of a bitch." Jeep Reed was quoted: "What an enormous talent and sorrow to die so young. Our hearts go out to his family."

Dr. Carl Detweiler, the pulmonary specialist on the scene, was quoted as saying, "His death is deeply suspicious. I do not think it was natural but, of course, we all await the autopsy report."

The coroner's slate was full after a rash of street deaths. In the latest bout of cold weather, some of the local homeless had frozen to death. The coroner's report on Egon's death would be issued at the earliest by Friday night or Saturday morning.

A smaller article buried deeper in the first section of the paper outlined the difficulties authorities faced in trying to locate and house the homeless in shelters. Many refused to go to the Salvation Army, as they emphatically did not wish to hear about salvation in any form. They preferred hunger to prayer. Other shelters were full up. These days, whole families were destitute and homeless.

Not too many people paid attention to that story since the possible murder of a celebrity chef commanded more attention, especially coming on the heels of the killing of Oliver Hitchens. Tongues were wagging.

This was big news.

From the passenger seat, Lonnie read the paper aloud as Pete cruised down dilapidated Fourth Street to Teton Benson's apartment. They'd yet to find the mysterious man who'd bought two acres in what would become Horseshoe Estates.

After parking next to the curb, Pete knocked on Benson's shabby door, then tried the knob to see if the door was unlocked. No luck.

This was the officers' first visit when Jugs was open. The two policemen walked into the neighboring topless bar.

A thin young man — the bartender — with an equally thin beard, glanced up to see the men in uniform. "Hi."

Behind him women paraded, none of them exhibiting their natural breasts. Every single woman had had surgical enhancements.

"Do you know Teton Benson, lives next door?" Pete asked.

"Yeah. He in trouble?"

"No. We're hoping we can save him from trouble," Pete replied genially.

The young fellow kept polishing a glass. "He's not using. Tets is clean."

"That's good to hear. Do you have any idea where he is? We really need to find him."

"Last week I saw him leave with his duffel bag, and the mail's been piling up. Didn't see him get in his car, but he usually parked it on the street."

Although usually quiet, Lonnie spoke. "Did Mr. Benson ever talk to you about land investments?"

The fellow laughed loudly. "Tets? Hell, he could barely pay his rent. I'm hoping now that he's clean he can hold a job. Maybe it makes sense to move on from here. Too many people know his rep, you know?"

"Did you ever see anyone unusual go into his apartment? By that I mean if they looked, say, a little better off than Tets."

"No. Even though he had family in town. He embarrassed them. I never saw anyone stop by for a visit."

"Did he talk about his family?"

"It's not like we were best friends." The slight fellow stopped a moment. "All he ever said was he'd had every advantage and had blown it, and that his family was sick of him."

"Well, thank you very much."

Back in the squad car, Pete said to Lonnie, "We're going to have to track down other Bensons in Washoe County." They headed to the other side of town.

"Let's be glad his last name isn't Smith." Lonnie scribbled Benson in his notebook. "Jeep sure took masterful control of that mess last night, didn't she?"

Jeep had stopped the band once she knew what had happened to Egon Utrecht. Requesting her guests to remain seated temporarily, she'd asked Pete if he needed to question everyone. With six hundred guests, Pete let them all head home. He had all their names on Jeep's invitation list.

"Jeep Reed can handle just about anything," said Pete. "You ever see the planes she used to fly? Pilots actually flew them, controlled them. No computer chips. They had to have physical strength. Impresses the hell out of me. Anyway, I'm glad we questioned the staff before their stories got cloudy. As it was, some were scared and others were glad he was dead."

"Lisa Giogionides seemed close to Utrecht," said Lonnie. "I guess she was his apprentice, but he never mentioned anything to her about land purchases. Maybe that's not so weird, but most people can't resist bragging about a good investment. Still, one thing I thought interesting in her statement was when she said Utrecht had been increasingly irritable and worried for the last week. She thought it had to do with Ms. Reed's upcoming party. He was hoping to make all the gourmet magazines or whatever. I think there's more to it." Lonnie fell silent as Pete pulled into a parking lot. "Ah, Jonas Larkin." Lonnie looked at the small wooden sign by the front door. "Office is closed."

"Dammit."

"Probably working."

"We'll come back later. Leave a message on his answering machine, will you, Lonnie? Just say we'd like to chat again, slippery creep. Don't say that."

As Lonnie was dialing the number, Pete again crossed the bridge over the Truckee, the water running strong now. He parked the SUV in front of Anthony Diamond's high-rise.

The doorman greeted Pete with his ever-present smile. "Deputy Meadows."

"Hi, Chaz. Is Mr. Diamond here?"

"No. He left last week. Said he was going to Maui for two weeks. Lucky devil."

Pete smiled, palmed him five, and climbed back in the car. "Another one gone. Diamond went to Hawaii."

The last person Pete and Lonnie called upon was the nurse, Kylie Prentiss. She looked like she'd eaten a prune when she saw them. Again, her responses to their questions were terse.

As they drove back to HQ, Lonnie asked, "Do you think it's us she's afraid of, or someone else?"

"She wasn't all that happy on our first visit," said Pete.

Back at their desks, Pete and Lonnie phoned the remaining three purchasers of land.

The doctor in Las Vegas seemed calm. This was the first time Pete had spoken to him.

Lonnie reached the elderly lady in Carson City who bitched him out for bothering her again. However, he did manage to wrangle out of her who it had been that advised her to buy the property at Horseshoe Estates.

"My grandson."

"And what is his name, ma'am?" Lonnie asked.

"Jonas Larkin."

"Slippery, our Jonas, like I said," Pete replied when Lonnie told him.

Their last stop of the day was at a Virginia City clothing shop. Again, its owner swore the real estate purchase was just dumb luck. She sounded about as convincing as a congressman who has just switched votes on a highly public issue.

After, the two men sat silently in the car.

"If I were a smoker, this would be the ideal time for a cigarette." Pete blew out his cheeks, then changed the subject. "Amelia's something, isn't she?"

"Got a date with her tomorrow night."

"And you waited this long to tell me?"

"Lot going on."

"Ain't that the truth? Lonnie, nervous people make other people nervous, don't you think?"

"I'm not nervous. I know she's pretty unusual, owning a construction company, but she's hot." He put his finger to his thigh and made a hissing sound.

"I'm not talking about that kind of nervous. I mean Egon Utrecht kind of nervous."

"Oh, yeah. Good chance that Teton Benson took off because he's scared, or smart in some way we don't yet know. As for Anthony Diamond, you know he's pretty smart. He drives a Bentley." Lonnie had checked his records.

"That's over the top." Pete grimaced.

"I want a Dodge Ram half-ton. No extended cab or that crap. A real truck. Black with a gold pinstripe and a mascot, a bucking bronc. Leather interior. Great sound system. Bentley's are for old rich men. And if I have an air mattress I can use the eight-foot bed for" — he paused, looked heavenward — "those intimate moments."

"I'd wait until spring." Pete laughed but thought it was a pretty good idea. "Okay, let's find Teton's family."

Turned out there were eighteen people with the surname Benson in Washoe County. From the car, Pete and Lonnie started making calls.

Ten minutes later, Pete got out of the car and stretched. "All we do is sit on our asses in this squad car here. Drives me crazy."

He took a five-minute walk, came back, and started calling more Bensons. He also phoned Mags.

"Sorry to leave you last night."

"You saw us to the car," Mags said. "How long did you stay?"

"Until one."

"Utrecht was poisoned, wasn't he?"

"Looks like. Ready for the shooting range tomorrow?"

"I am. Pete, isn't someone taking a terrible chance killing Egon like that, at a big party?"

"Yes, but there's also safety in numbers. No doubt our man is under pressure. You were right."

"I guess it'd be pretty easy to hand Egon a bad drink."

"With everyone pouring champagne into his glass or handing him glasses, it would be hard to pick out anyone in particular. One thing, nothing toxic was in a bottle, or there'd be more dead people."

"I guess we can be grateful for that."

CHAPTER THIRTY-SEVEN

Saturday morning at seven-thirty, darkness still enveloped Dixie Lane and Wings Ranch. Jeep and Mags walked from the house to the old barn. Mags had already gotten in her morning three-mile run so she felt terrific.

"You'd think after all these years I would get used to the loss of light," Jeep mused.

"So many people get depressed. There was this one woman in my old office who used to sit and bake below an ultraviolet light during the winters."

"Did it do any good?"

"Not that I could tell." Mags watched as Baxter raced ahead of King. "Out here less light means it's harder to get your chores done."

"True, but it's also a great time to attack those inside jobs. Dot's major redecorating fits always took place late in winter." She pushed open the barn door.

Baxter and King had slipped in through

the back animal door so they awaited the humans, their lot in life. Humans did everything so slowly, including the way they ate. Took forever.

Jeep hefted the heavy door closed after Mags stepped in.

"I could have done that," the younger woman said.

"I'd rather wear out than rust out. Would you look at this?" She swept her hand away from her. The pipes had been laid, the various layers of drainage over the pipes had been tamped down. Two large drains, slightly recessed, shone in the center aisles and each stall also had a recessed drain.

"Great job."

"See, winter is good for the inside stuff. Now I've got to put PaveSafe down." That soft surface that interlocked, resembling bricks, would cost Jeep a pretty penny. "If I don't install PaveSafe, then the soil and fine sand will get into the drains. All this work would be for nothing. I wish I could find a way to make the PaveSafe look old, you know, like the original surface, but I can't."

"It's nice to walk on."

"It is. That's one thing I notice as I age. If I'm on my feet a long time, they hurt." She looked around. "King, you're alert."

"Mice."

"I can kill them but they are hiding," Baxter bragged.

"Those two have become good friends." Jeep smiled. "You know, Mags, if dogs as different as that can get along, what's wrong with us?"

"I don't know, Aunt Jeep. Maybe the human animal was born to dominate and kill anything that competes for the same food. Ever notice how animals who eat different things rarely fight? Why would a woodpecker and a cow fight? Sometimes I harbor dark thoughts about us, especially after what I saw on Wall Street. People acted with absolute compelling disregard for other people, lying and ruining lives." She shook her head. "Maybe we aren't a very nice animal."

"But then think of people diving into a river to save others, sometimes even strangers. I'm older than dirt and I just have no idea why we are the way we are, but I'm starting to think what we call due process of law just allows criminals to flourish. Take the bastards swindling the little guy out and shoot them. Catch a man molesting a child, take out the son of a bitch. Wouldn't the ACLU have a field day with me?"

Mags put her arm around her great-aunt's waist. "I have a field day with you."

"Liberal, are you?"

"More than you." Mags changed the subject. "What's next after the PaveSafe?"

"Put the stalls back up, natural wood, of course. Oak. Should be oak. Lasts forever, but Christ, it's heavy. And expensive. Anyone who could, used oak. Well, it's still the best. But given the expense, most people use pressure-treated pine. I love doing this the way Dot loved colors and fabrics." She paused. "I don't suppose you have gifts in that direction."

"Decorating? Well, I'm better than you." Mags laughed.

"That's not saying much." Jeep walked to the other end of the barn, Mags with her. She slid open those doors a crack, the view was toward the southeast. "Pink. Why is the sunrise so exciting?"

"Hope."

Jeep then pointed in the other direction toward the Petersons. "Can you see Dixie Lane?"

"Barely."

Jeep moved her arm toward the left. "Connects to Dry Valley Road. If we had been working outside, we might have seen the headlights of Oliver Hitchens's killer. But, of course, it's winter. I'm starting to take these murders personally. One man is dumped at the edge of my property and another killed

378

at my party."

"It's too close for comfort. I'm glad Pete is taking me to the shooting range. I think if I practice, I'll be a pretty good shot."

"Poor guy, comes to my party and winds up working late. And Lonnie" — she laughed — "he was affixed to Amelia's apron strings."

"Actually, Aunt Jeep, I don't think that's where he was affixed."

They laughed, then Jeep said, "What a success story Amelia is. Which reminds me. Are you going to car school or whatever you call it?"

"I've been looking into it. I'm definitely doing it. Then I'll be able to help around here by doing more than repairing barbed-wire fences."

"Good. Ever think about tractor repair, as well?"

"No."

"It's different because you pull the motor apart vertically. You might consider it. There's quite a need, especially for someone willing to travel to the ranches. Just a thought. Ah, look at that now. Isn't that beautiful?" She'd turned to the eastern sky, awash in crimson and pink.

Then she looked back toward the Petersons. They showed pink except for the folds in the range, which stood out as charcoal or Prussian blue streaks.

As they closed both sets of doors and walked back to the house, Baxter, next to King, asked, *"Are we friends? I know you didn't want me here when we first met."*

"You're okay," King replied. *"But you're so low to the ground."*

With that, they took off running.

That afternoon Pete stood next to Mags at the firing range. Once she was under way, he practiced, too. Shooting, like any other skill, demands lots of practice.

When finished, they removed their ear protectors and left the range.

"Should I clean my gun?" she asked.

"Wait a bit. The metal is warmer than you think." He sat at a table in the clean room. "Would you like a drink?"

"Coke."

He returned with a Coke and a plastic cup of ice. "You looked like you were having fun."

"I like that I can do it myself. Other sports you need an opponent. Once it gets warm, we can try clays."

"Sure." He took off his Aces ball cap. "How's Jeep?"

"Herself."

"She handled those people like a pro. Calm. Gave clear orders. So many people would have panicked or you'd have heard the strain in their voices. You stayed calm, too."

"Doesn't do any good to scream and holler. Pete, what's going on, really?"

He lowered his voice. "Ten people bought land where Horseshoe Estates will be developed. Land with water rights. With the exception of one individual who I actually think just got lucky, I'm pretty sure all these people were tipped off by someone in SSRM or Wade Properties."

"Egon was one of them?"

"He bought two acres and made out like a bandit."

"And Oliver Hitchens?"

Pete shook his head. "Nothing. I think maybe he smelled a rat." He put his hand over hers. "There's a great deal of money at stake. The other people who bought land are uncooperative, nervous, or scared. One left town and we haven't found him yet. I know I'm on the right track."

"I'm glad Jeep didn't buy anything in that area."

"No, thank God. She sticks to the northern part of the county." He finished his Coke. "If I can figure out what the payoff is, I'll be that much closer to closing in. And what do these nine people have in common?"

"Wish I had some idea." She turned her hand up to squeeze his, her makeshift bracelet of the colored bones showing. "But let me show you what I've found."

Back at the house at Wings Ranch, Mags led him into the den. "Look at this."

"David Cadjaia, Dimetri Mgaloblichvily, Toma Baramidzi, Miron Tschonia, Ivan Baramidzi, Emile Antadzi, Loucas Tschartishvily, Michael Antadzi, Vladimir Jacutahvi, and Sergei Makharadze." He read the list of names she gave him. "Who are they?"

"Remember I showed you Buffalo Bill's signature? 1902, September?"

"Right."

"Well, when researching his show I discovered this program listing the Cossacks riding. Now I don't know if any of these men actually came out here with him to Wings because all he signed in the visitors' book was 'Buffalo Bill and the Boys.' But if I can find later programs, and one of these names is missing, then I might be onto something. I already know some of these men returned to Georgia. They were really Georgians, not Russians."

"So was Stalin. Not much of a recommendation." He smiled. "You're really on this, aren't you?"

She held up her left wrist making the beads slide. "I'm going to find out. I swear it. These guys were stars, well all of them were, the Vaqueros, the English cavalry officers, the Arabs, Cubans, Hawaiians, German cavalry officers, Filipinos, Indians. They had followings. I found drawings of some of the riders, sketches by Frederic Remington. Doing something like this is when I love a computer. Aren't the drawings fabulous? I know there are more that I haven't found yet."

"They're dynamic. If a name isn't on the program and you can't find a record of him going home, you think that's your Russian?"

"Maybe. There aren't any other candidates at the moment. One thing that's curious is that Felicia Ford married a colonel in the British Cavalry, the Household Cavalry, at that. He seemed kind of obsessed with Buffalo Bill's shows." She paused for a moment. "I've never been much of a student of history but I've recently learned that Great Britain and Russia weren't exactly enemies the last half of the nineteenth century, the early part of the twentieth, but they had competing interests that both felt imperiled their nation's security, so they placed spies everywhere — in one another's embassies, military units for field maneuvers, even actresses and ballerinas. You name it."

Pete put his hands on her shoulders. "Exactly how did they endanger each other? England and Russia, I mean."

"The Brits thought Russia wanted India. I mean we're taught that England was the center of the industrial revolution, hence the great wealth, but at least part of all that money flowed out of colonial India. What a cornucopia."

"Mags, I'm not following."

"The Russians had, I guess you'd call them client states. They paid the rulers of the countries we now call Iran and Iraq, plus they edged into the eastern borders of Afghanistan. Well, what's on the other end? The Khyber Pass and India. England's imperial ambitions were clear. Russia's were becoming more clear. They were headed for a clash, which I guess World War One averted."

"Isn't that something? Here's Afghanistan, one of the most inhospitable geographical places in the world and it was a hot spot back then, too."

"If you were the British Prime Minister or the Secretary of Foreign Relations in Russia, I don't know the correct title, wouldn't you want to know what the other side was doing and wouldn't you want to know what the

United States was up to? We were the colossus on the other side of the Atlantic."

"Okay." He sounded a little confused.

"Pete, after 1815 we've always been allied with Great Britain. So if you're Russian you want to keep an eye on us or, the coup of coups, pry us from England and make us an ally. What I'm getting at is that I think Buffalo Bill's Wild West Show was full of spies."

He leaned down and kissed her on the cheek. "Anyone ever tell you you're smart?"

They talked, laughed, ate a late lunch, then Mags took him for a ride on the ATV up to the Sand Hills to look down on Bedell Flat. The dogs joyously ran along and Jeep watched from the kitchen window as they took off.

On top of the Sand Hills Mags pointed down to Wings and told Pete her great-aunt's dream.

"She's eighty-five and she wants to start this new big enterprise. God, I hope I'm like that."

He stepped off the back of the ATV to look down. King put his head under his hand while Baxter whined to be lifted up. Pete picked up the little guy and kissed his head.

"I hope we're both like that."

Pete stayed for dinner. He and Mags played cards with Jeep.

For the heck of it, Mags dealt Baxter a hand, as he was sitting in a chair, then she played it for him.

"He won?"

"Of course." The wire-haired dachshund loved the attention.

Later, after Pete left, Jeep said, "My bed-room is at the other end of the hall. You're a grown woman. Do as you wish."

Mags kissed her. "Thanks. I'm working up to it." She touched the Nicholas Cavalry School ring on her great-aunt's finger. "Think I'm getting close."

"Good. While you work on that I'm going to stick my nose into all this commotion around here. Like I said this morning, I'm starting to take this personally."

Old as she was, Jeep's ego was large and strong. It provoked her onward. Ego can get a person in trouble.

CHAPTER THIRTY-EIGHT

"Why aren't you in church?" Jeep asked Jake Tanner when he greeted her outside his ranch house.

"Could ask the same of you." He put his hands in the pockets of his insulated Carhartt overalls.

"I worship in the Church of the Blue Dome." Standing next to her truck, she pointed to the sky, amazingly blue on this Sunday, January 17. "But to hedge my bets I went to the early service at Trinity."

"Chicken."

"You know, Jake" — she placed her gloved hands on the hood of her F-150 because it was warm — "I think about these things. Afterlife. God or gods. If there is only one God, then who has him? Jews? Christians? Muslims? Monotheism presents an unsolvable problem. Seems to me hatred, unrest, and ultimately war follows. History bears me out."

King's hearing was so sharp he could hear outside with the windows up. He turned to Baxter, his paws on the dash, eagerly watching. *"Why do they worry about those things?"* King asked.

"It's not like they don't have enough else to worry about."

King shifted his weight. *"They believe God looks like them. Vanity."*

Baxter half laughed, half snuffled. *"I hope not. Have you really looked at humans? Some are okay-looking, apart from stumbling around on two legs, but so many of them, best to close your eyes."*

Jeep, hearing what sounded like barking, tapped the driver's window. "You two behave."

Jake walked over and stood next to her. "You think about more things than I do. My wife reads the Good Book. I do sometimes. I don't know, Jeep, why worry about something I can't see, prove, or understand?"

"You've got a point. Jake, walk with me a minute."

She headed east across scrubby land. Jake's ranch rested two miles north of Pump 19. He ran cattle, scratched out a living, and did odd jobs with his equipment. The state sold used equipment, as do all states. Jake had friends in the various agencies, but especially among the road crews. He knew what bulldozers, Bobcats, backhoes, and Ditch Witches were in good order and which ones would cost a fortune to repair. Over the years he'd made wise purchases.

"That was some great party, except for the end. You'll never top that."

She blew air out of her nose forcefully. "Goddamned mess." She stopped, pointing east. "Your spread goes up to August Spring on the west, then you go right on up to the base of Porcupine Mountain. You can be sure you've got good water running deep under there because on the other side of Porcupine Mountain is Renner Well."

"Don't you own some of those wells?" He knew she owned the southernmost ones.

"I do."

Jeep's ranch consisted of ten thousand contiguous acres, but she owned acreage throughout this part of Washoe County. She also owned acreage in other parts of Nevada. Given what the land had yielded to her, she believed there were few investments as wise as raw land. She also owned a few thousand acres in Elko, some in eastern Montana toward North Dakota, and even a sliver along the Wyoming–Montana border. That was grassland.

Jake puffed up. "When I was young I figured there was water on the other side of Porcupine and over there in Lees Flat, why not on this side?"

"You're a smart man. That's why I'm here."

He loved hearing that. "Well, sometimes I am and sometimes I'm not."

"Have you been thinking about the murders?"

"Hard not to, especially Oliver's. He was a first-class prick, excuse me." He bowed his head slightly. No cowboy wishes to swear in front of a lady, but sometimes he can't help it.

She tapped his forearm. "Jake Tanner, you've heard me say much worse."

He laughed. "Oliver always irritated me. When Pump Nineteen was blown there he was useless, wouldn't get his hands dirty, but in charge. You know the type."

"Do."

"The funny thing was — about the pump, I mean — the bomb was set so we couldn't repair the pump. I mean, Twinkie and Bunny couldn't. An entirely new pump had to be put in. That's not cheap. SSRM uses two types of pumps, a vertical turbine, now that baby costs big, big bucks and it's set above the ground. Blasts out a high volume of water. Pump Nineteen is the old kind of pump and it's right for the volume used in Red Rock. It's in a casing below the ground. Well, you know, you've seen it."

"Actually, Jake, I haven't. I've passed the site, looked up, but I don't know anything about it. My water comes out of a well. Don't have that kind of equipment."

"The submersibles are the most common kind used by SSRM. They aren't cheap, but nothing like the turbos. Whoever set the bomb knew the equipment."

"That could be anyone who works with water, even a water surveyor might know."

Jake stroked his beard. "Twinkie and Bunny showed me where they thought the bomb was wedged. Actually, they slipped the piece of pipe to Pete. They didn't want Oliver to see it."

This surprised Jeep. "Why?"

"Figured he'd take credit for it. He was like that. They also took pictures with their cellphones and sent them back to George W. They wanted to protect themselves. I mean, it wasn't below Hitchens to blame them if more had gone wrong."

"I had no idea."

"George W. knew, but I reckon Oliver had some worth to the company or he wouldn't have been tolerated."

"I guess. Did Twinkie and Bunny talk to you about the other pump that was destroyed?"

"The one down south of here, they did. Same deal."

"Do you think Oliver set the bombs? Sometimes people do things like that to look like a hero."

Jake shook his head. "No. He wouldn't have done that."

"You wouldn't have wanted to see him dead."

"Coyotes eat him?"

"Something nibbled off his lips and chewed his extremities." She looked him in the eyes, then pointed toward Porcupine Mountain. "There's so much talk about getting water to Reno, but what if we're all looking in the wrong direction?"

"What do you mean?"

"Send the water into Bedell Flat or north up to Dry Valley, which — as the crow flies — isn't that far from Reno. Think about it, especially Dry Valley. If that were developed, all people who lived there would need to do is drive out to three ninety-five, close, and come to work in Reno."

"Never thought about it."

"I didn't, either, until I started studying the maps, the aquifers, and the population growth. I don't know if all this is related to that, but SSRM sure seems to be in the middle of it."

"Seems so." Jake jammed his hands back into his pockets.

They walked back to the truck. Prancing around on the door controls, King had locked her out of the truck.

"Got your keys?"

"I do. I learned that the hard way about twenty years ago when King's mother locked me out of my old Ford. Remember that truck? I took the muffler off. You could hear me for miles. This is one thing that drives me crazy. America builds the best trucks in the world. So why can't the geniuses figure out how to build a truck your dogs can't lock you out of?"

"Maybe they don't have dogs."

"That's an awful thought." She smiled and hit the unlock icon on the key fob to open the door. You need to learn to unlock it if you lock it." She pointed her gloved finger at King.

"Too much trouble." King sighed. He had heard the lock when he locked the truck, but wasn't sure how to hit the unlock button.

She climbed in and started the motor to get the heat going. "Jake, anyone come around and try to buy your water rights?"

"You rent them."

"Yeah, but everyone might not know that."

"Only Craig Locke, once a year. Sometimes twice. Guess he has to say he's tried."

She nodded. "Anyone ever tell you you look like an Old Testament prophet with that beard? If it gets any longer, you won't even need clothes, Jake, just wrap it around you."

"You're just jealous because you can't grow one." He waved as she pulled out.

A mile south she pulled under a gate, smaller than hers, a wagon wheel on either side of the support posts. The one-story house, once painted peach, now peeling, bore testament to the occupant being home. A furl of smoke escaped from the chimney, tried to rise then flattened, keeping close to the ground. Jeep cut the motor, pocketed her keys, got out, and looked west. A weather system was coming in. A thin layer of clouds was now overhead, with darker clouds piling up behind the Petersons.

She knocked on the door.

"Who in the hell is it?"

"Venus, the goddess of love."

A shuffle was heard and the door opened wide. Howie Norris beamed. "Why didn't you say so? Come on in, beautiful."

Howie, perhaps four years younger than Jeep, couldn't keep his place up, but he did his best by himself. If he could have afforded help, the ranch wouldn't take much to come back up. Doing all the work himself kept him in shape.

"Coffee?" he asked.

"No, thank you."

"Sit down. Isn't often I'm visited by a goddess. May I take your coat?"

"Sure." She slipped out of the old sheepskin jacket, like the one she'd given Mags years ago.

"How you been?"

"Mad as hell."

"Me too."

"And why are you mad?" she asked.

"Dunno. Old age. Every time I turn around it's some new law, some new bullshit. My truck's on its last legs and even if I had the money I wouldn't buy a new one. All I want to do is put the key in, turn it, and have the motor turn over. I want a dial to turn up the volume of the radio and a dial to tune it. I'd like heat and maybe air-conditioning but I can live without that. You can't buy a truck like that nowadays."

"Everything's run by computer. Have a new truck out there. Rides like a dream, but I turn the key, pop it in Drive, and the doors automatically lock. Drives me crazy, I know just what you mean."

"Is that what's got you riled?"

"No. The chef was poisoned at my Festival of the Ass party. Where were you?"

"Ah, Jeepie, I don't want to go out. I feel out of place. Hell, I'm usually the oldest person in the room."

"Not if I'm there." She smiled at him.

That picked up his spirits. "Women are stronger than men about a lot of things. When Dot and Dan died, you went down, but you came back. I don't know, Jeepie, I can't seem to pull myself up since Ronnie's gone." He named his late wife.

"It's a hard, hard blow. You two were made for each other. It's been four years. You've let the place slide a little and I know money's tight, but you need to get out. How long have we known each other, Howie?"

"Fifties."

"Then I'll tell it to you straight. Ronnie would never want you to give up. She loved you and she wants you to enjoy what's left of your days. She's up there looking down, cussing a blue streak."

He smiled, voice soft. "That woman could cuss."

"I'll send the boys over. We can fix your shed in a hurry, do whatever you need to do. 'Course, you got to come out and work, too."

"Ah, Jeep, don't do that. I can never make

it up to you."

"Over fifty years of being a good neighbor more than makes it up. But you've got to snap out of this. And you know, if you found someone to keep company with" — she used the old term — "Ronnie would be happy. You're too good a man to sit here like a ground squirrel in its hole."

That perked him up. "Well, maybe." He wiggled to the edge of his chair. "Sure I can't get you anything?"

"No, but you can help me."

"Anything."

"Has anyone come 'round and tried to buy your water rights? I know, I know, I rent them, but someone might not know that or they could offer more."

"They can get their fat ass off my ranch, too. The only person is Craig Locke, once a year. This year I didn't want to hear his bullshit. I threw him out."

"Have you noticed anyone else poking around?"

"No. Every now and then I see Jake down the road. That's about it. You worried because of finding that body? I mean, worried the killer's hanging around? I am. I don't even go out to the mailbox without my gun."

"I am a little worried. Look, if you see anything or anyone, or something occurs to you, call me. I'll send the boys over on Wednesday." She stood up. "Do me another favor, if you're out on your ATV or just being nosy with your binoculars, let me know if you see anyone around Renner Well."

"Be glad to." He handed her her coat. "You think what happened in Las Vegas can happen here?"

"You mean driving a pipeline three hundred miles away to siphon our water south? In time, yes, it could happen if we aren't vigilant."

"Maybe, maybe not. They had that big setback." Howie referred to the Nevada Supreme Court issuing a ruling invalidating the awards to Pat Mulroy and those involved with her for the pipeline.

"It will drag on. What interested me was the charge that the state engineer exaggerated water yields in his earlier decisions to award water to Mulroy. If ranchers hadn't brought suit, that pipeline would be being dug right now."

He nodded, "Seventy-nine million dollars they spent buying out some of the ranchers. Seventy-nine million."

"There's a lot at stake — not just here, Howie, throughout the West. Failure now could mean catastrophe later. I understand how cities like Las Vegas, Phoenix, Tucson, and Albuquerque bring in lots of tax dollars to their states, which allows for new schools, all manner of improvements. But the ultimate price really could mean death for many animals and plants and ultimately, us, too. You can't live without water."

"You're right there. But when people throw millions of dollars around —" He whistled.

"Seems like a lot until you consider the developments, the shopping centers, the *billions* and billions of dollars. Hey, what's the life of a cow or ground squirrel compared to that? Look how many creatures we've destroyed over the centuries, to say nothing of one another. Well, it's Sunday, didn't mean to preach a sermon."

"You're preaching to the choir." He kissed her on the cheek as she left.

The dogs adored riding around, noticing other dogs, other animals. If Jeep would have opened the windows, had there been a hint of scent, they would have commented on that, too. A few flakes lazed down. She dropped in on other neighbors and finally pulled into Wings at about four that afternoon. Pete's vehicle was parked out front.

She pulled the truck into the back shed next to the old Chevy 454. Not wishing to disturb Pete and Mags, Jeep tiptoed into the kitchen, but the dogs roared through the house to greet her.

"We're in the den!" Mags called out.

Pete, sitting next to Mags as she worked on the computer, stood up as Jeep walked in.

"Sunday afternoon and you two are sitting in front of that machine. I could think of a few better things to do," she teased.

"I'm getting closer to finding our Russian or at least finding who he isn't. Pete's helping."

Jeep started to leave when Pete said, "You might be able to help me if you're willing."

He told Jeep everything he knew about the case. He mentioned Sam Peruzzi, Walter De Quille, the people who had bought land in the soon-to-be Horseshoe Estates.

"And Egon was one?" She dropped her chin in her hand.

"He was. And I know he lied to me." Pete shrugged. "People usually do, but I think whatever he knew or was worried about was what led to his death."

"And one of the other purchasers is missing?"

She lifted her head. "All of those people have to be connected in some way, even though they cover the gamut in terms of class and accomplishment. Why don't you see if any of them went to school with anyone at SSRM or Wade Properties? The center of it all seems to be SSRM. Or maybe these folks are related to someone? There must be a connection."

And indeed, there was.

CHAPTER THIRTY-NINE

Teton Benson's 1985 Ford truck was parked in Beatty, Nevada, on the edge of the Mojave Desert, found after an alert had been sent out across the state. A 2003 Trailblazer had also been stolen from the town. Pete and Lonnie figured there was a connection. Perhaps Tets was on the move.

"I hope he's still alive," Lonnie muttered.

"If we could get our hands on him, we'd find out why he's making himself scarce. Might take a bit of persuading." Pete pulled down a dirt road, parking to the side.

Jonas Larkin and a young woman were surveying land fifteen miles from downtown Reno in sparsely populated Washoe Valley. The temperature that day had surprised everyone by climbing into the low fifties. After the weekend's snow flurries, the change felt wonderful, but Nevada being Nevada it could plunge to twenty tomorrow. Enjoy it while you can.

Jonas looked up. His assistant held the rod thirty yards distant. Seeing the two young officers, his lips puckered and a low curse followed.

"Mr. Larkin." Pete touched his hat with his forefinger.

Jonas yelled, "Becca, be a minute." He turned to Pete. "It must be important because you've driven way out here to find me."

"You didn't return my call." When Jonas remained silent, Pete continued, "A man was killed Thursday night and another man has disappeared. Both of them purchased land in Horseshoe Estates."

Jonas's face stayed impassive — too impassive. "Could be coincidence."

"We don't think so. Everyone who purchased land in that development with water rights may be in danger."

A slight twitch at Jonas's mouth was his only facial response. "I'm not worried."

"Let me ask you something. Did you go to school or college with anyone from Wade Properties or SSRM?"

"No."

"Do you have friends in either company?"

"I know a few people. I wouldn't call them friends."

"Who?"

"Roger Malmed, Wade Props. I've seen Darryl Johnson a few times, but I can't say I know him. That's about it."

"What about George W. Ball?" When Jonas shook his head, Pete asked, "Craig Locke?"

"Yes — again not well, but he's all over the map, looking at land."

"Elizabeth McCormick?"

"No."

"Teton Benson?"

A long pause followed this. "Knew Tets in the old days, right after he changed his name."

"Mr. Benson wasn't exactly living high on the hog. Do you know where he came by the land? Anything you can tell me about him may save his life."

Jonas scuffed the loam. "He was a drug dealer back when I knew him. Had good stuff. We were all wild." He stared up at Pete. "Long gone, those days."

"Given that it's illegal, that's a good thing."

"Hell, Deputy Meadows, you can't stop drugs in America and if you think you can, you're smoking opium. And you know it."

Pete did, so he didn't respond to that. "Is there a chance Teton sold to or partied with someone at Wade Properties or SSRM?"

"I wouldn't know. Like any good dealer, Tets never spoke of his other clients. I know he had a lot of rich ones; there's easy money in Reno. But I expect they've all gotten older. I heard he did the rehab number."

"Word is, he's clean," said Pete.

"Can you think of anyone who might have lent him money?" Lonnie piped up.

"For all I know, he stashed what he made in the old days."

"Seems strange he'd live on Fourth Street," Pete said.

"Not if you know Tets. He's a rebel."

"Did you ever talk to him about Horseshoe Estates?"

A wrenching pause followed. "Yes. He called me and told me to buy out there."

"Who tipped him off?"

"He didn't say."

"Mr. Larkin, you weren't honest with me during our first interview. Why should I believe you now?"

"I didn't outright lie." He sounded surly. "And thanks to my work, I do see places that I think will eventually be developed. Once you know what to look for, it's obvious: how close to a major highway, school district, surrounding area, population density, and, of course, water. Carson City has the road plan for the next ten years and even beyond. All you have to do is go down to the department and see what roads are planned. Same with the state engineer. His department must give you maps of aquifers, wells. You pay a small amount for them. The information's there for the asking if you know where to look."

"An insider tip is even better."

"You'd have to ask Tets that one."

Driving back to Reno, Lonnie tapped the notebook in his chest pocket. "Larkin wouldn't put his money down on the word of an ex-dealer who he says he hasn't seen in a long time."

"He's lying about that as well. Damn, we can't get it out of him. Son of a bitch."

"He thinks he's safe, so maybe he is." Lonnie shrugged.

"Maybe he's closer to whoever is behind this," Pete said.

"Hey, you know what else is in Beatty?"

"I have no idea."

"Shady Lady."

"Oh, yeah, prostitution place."

"Well, they've got a male prostitute, a gigolo who was a porn star and is an ex-Marine."

"You're kidding."

"No. He gave an interview in *Details* magazine. Maybe you and I are in the wrong line of work."

"I'll pass." Pete thought a minute. "Can you imagine what the women have to service? Fat guys, ugly ones, ones who can't get along with anyone, including their dog if they have one. Jesus, it must be revolting."

"You against prostitution?" Lonnie asked.

"No. It's a good way for someone to make money and if you're smart you get out in time. I just don't know how they do it. I expect that ex-Marine will have to do his duty and service some unappealing types. It's easier for a woman."

"Maybe he has secrets. Or he closes his eyes."

"I guess." Pete pulled into a gas station. "We're low."

"Why shouldn't a woman pay? Beats pretending you want to know someone. Sometimes all you want is relief."

"But all a woman has to do is wait," said Pete. "Sit on a bar stool or go to a party, there's almost always a man who's ready and willing. Why pay?" He thought a minute. "Then again, you're right, why pretend you want a relationship when all you want is sex? Maybe there should be more men in that line of work."

"Plenty of gay ones."

"Yep." He unhooked the seat belt and the annoying beep began.

"I'll pump." Lonnie opened the door as

Pete cut the motor.

"I know you will." Pete smiled.

"Hey, no one's complained yet."

"Well, that's the point of the male prostitute, isn't it? Women don't complain and I guess there's a bunch of us who aren't very good at making them happy in bed. So whoever this guy is in Beatty, he must know his stuff."

Lonnie shut the door and thought about what Pete had said. Once tanked up, he took out the receipt as it came out of the slot on the gas pump, and climbed back in. He put it in the zippered bag they kept for receipts.

"You read *Men's Health,*" Lonnie said. "They have tips in there about how to drive women crazy in bed."

"Right."

They drove in silence until Lonnie piped up. "If she doesn't tell you, how do you know?"

"Beats me." Pete sighed. "When I was married, I thought everything was terrific. Then Lorraine leaves me and tells all her friends, who, of course, told all my friends, how rotten I was in the sack."

"They all do that when it's over. And they always say you have a little dick. Do we say they have shrunken breasts?"

"Nope." Pete sighed. "My magic member

has never failed me but it failed Lorraine."

"Women make sex too complicated."

"It is for them. I can't imagine it."

"I don't want to."

"At some point, buddy, you've got to think like they think. We can't feel what they feel, but we can learn what works. Pretty much it's physiological, but it's emotional, too. What's the best sex you ever had — with someone you cared about, right?"

Lonnie thought about this. "If I'm in bed, I care."

"Liar."

"No, really. I can't get it up if I don't like her. Sure she has to be hot, but you've known hot women who were poison."

Pete blinked. "Strychnine."

"That's what you should call Lorraine behind her back."

"It's been a couple of years. I'd just as soon forget it. Strychnine killed Egon. You can't buy it over the counter, but if someone has friends or knowledge it's not that hard to make. Let's check that out."

"Rat poison's sure easy."

"Yeah, the rats love it," Pete said sarcastically. "Back to work. All the buyers that are out of town, while not cooperative, don't appear to be afraid."

"Haven't reached Diamond yet," Lonnie

said. "But I called the place in Maui. He's there."

"He'll call back at some point. Cocky."

"Rich people usually are, in one way or another. Even Jeep. Maybe especially Jeep."

"She's been powerful for a long time. Hey, Mags thinks the dead Russian may have something to do with Afghanistan."

"No shit?"

"She's a bulldog. Won't let it go. It is fascinating, though, what she's learned about politics at that time. 1902. She's pretty sure that's the year he was killed."

"She sure held it together when they found Oliver," said Lonnie.

"She did. When's your next date with Amelia?"

"Friday night. Second date. I'm praying the third one is the charm."

"Depends on your charm."

"Hey, I'm full of it. I overflow with charm."

"I wouldn't put it that way."

"You wouldn't. Hey, where are we going?"

"Horseshoe Estates."

Within twenty minutes, they pulled onto the dirt road, stopped, and got out.

"Damn, this weather feels good. After a while, I get tired of winter."

"Yeah. I keep my spirits up in the gym, and following the teams in winter camp in

Florida. Okay, bearing in mind what Jonas said, how far are we from a two-lane paved highway?"

"Mile. If that."

Pete squinted. "How far from three ninety-five?"

"Five, six miles."

"Ultimately, the two-lane highway may need widening. Not yet. One thousand homes, all of them over a half a million dollars. Some way over that. Can you see it?"

"All I see is sagebrush."

"And the water is underground." Pete walked over the broken ground, which sloped off to the east. "A little creek — it'll be dry four to five months out of the year. More if there's a drought." He turned to his partner. "How did they know?"

"Tipoff," said Lonnie.

"Payoff. Whoever tipped them off didn't do so out of the goodness of his heart. Kickback. Probably more than half."

"Yeah, but why hasn't this happened before? SSRM works with developers."

"Because this is the most upscale development Reno has ever had. The payment for the land will be much higher. Think about it. Wade Properties has bought eight hundred acres. If they want the rest, they'll have to pay whatever it takes."

"Maybe Teton took his share and didn't want to give any back."

"Or maybe he's trying to stay alive."

"Or both," Lonnie offered.

Pete's cell rang. "Hello." His face brightened upon hearing Mags's voice. "How are you?"

"Great," Mags said. "Aunt Jeep thinks she's found some connections among those people who bought at Horseshoe. She doesn't know if it connects everyone. She wants you to come on out as soon as you can."

CHAPTER FORTY

"SSRM's founder, Darryl Johnson's grandfather, realized long before anyone else that Reno's continual growth would require a consistent water supply. This was 1956, which I believe was the year Elvis Presley recorded 'You Ain't Nothing but a Hound Dog.'" Jeep paused and folded her hands around her knee. "Funny how one remembers things. Anyway, Archie Johnson studied hydrology at the University of Montana right after the war. Navy man. Guess he'd seen enough water. He was a strong man, survived the kamikaze attack on the aircraft carrier *Enterprise*. Like most of us, once the war was over he wanted to come home to Reno. By 1956, our population was edging up toward forty thousand. Archie believed Reno would bloom. He formulated a simple, clear plan: buy up water rights, especially on the eastern side of the mountains. He rounded up funding from individuals, who were then named to his Board of Directors. There was a recession right after the war so it was tough finding investors. People sold cheap, though, so he bought a lot of water rights. That was the beginning."

Lonnie shifted in his seat, writing in his notebook as fast as he could.

Mags and Carlotta brought in hot tea and hot chocolate plus some cookies. Both women left, Carlotta because she couldn't sit still longer than ten minutes and Mags because she'd heard all this already. She figured she'd pop in twenty minutes from now and then she might join them.

Jeep continued. "Archie Johnson's biggest backer was Tim Benson, who made his money in dry goods. There was always a Benson on the board."

"Why not now?" Pete inquired respectfully.

"I'm getting to that. Took me a while to piece this together. While I know these people, I'm not close. Anyway, Archie's son, Frank, took over. And Tim Benson's son, when he stepped down, was put on the board. As I recall, Tim Benson sired three children, the oldest I think lives in Texas, teaches there. The middle one is the one you call Teton, real name Robert. And the youngest was a beautiful girl, Reno rodeo queen actually, Margaret. She married Frank Johnson's son, Darryl. That's Lolly. Robert, alias Teton, is her brother. That's all I know."

"That's a lot." Pete thanked her. "If you'll excuse me, we'd better get over to Lolly Johnson's right now. Teton has disappeared."

Jeep sat upright, dropping her hands from her knee. "Not another one."

"We don't know. He left his apartment, drove his truck to Beatty, Nevada, and he may have stolen a 2003 Trailblazer there. He was smart enough to know we'd put out a call for the truck. 'Course now he's in a stolen vehicle, I think. But he'll just keep swapping vehicles. He may have enough money to buy one, but I don't think he'll risk it until he crosses a state line."

"Dear God."

"You've been a great help." Pete said.

"Hold on a minute. Mags will surely fuss at me if I let you go without telling her." Jeep rose and walked down the hall.

Within minutes she and her niece came back to the living room.

"Done?" Mags asked.

"Maybe just beginning. I hope so. Jeep has been wonderful."

Lonnie nodded. "What a memory. Wish mine were that good."

"Mind's a muscle, use it. Your memory will stay sharp," Jeep advised. "Well, good luck, gentlemen, and I truly hope Robert Benson or whatever his name is doesn't show up dead."

"We do, too, ma'am," said Lonnie. "Tets knows something."

An hour later, no thanks to traffic, Pete and Lonnie pulled into the drive to the Johnson home, an impressive manse. Lonnie called ahead, had gotten Lolly on the phone, so she was expecting them.

She opened the grand front door before they'd even knocked. "It's not Darryl, is it? I know you'd never tell me that on the phone. Please tell me he's safe."

"Mrs. Johnson, your husband's fine but we need your help."

"Please, please come in. I am so relieved." She shut the door behind them and walked them into her sunken living room, much more modern than Jeep's.

Lolly must have kept decorators happy. Her home was as immaculate as she was. Now in her mid-forties, she may have given in to some "work," but a woman in her position must literally keep up appearances. For all their money the house still exuded homely warmth. So many don't. Lolly had warmth and charm, too.

"Oh, do sit down." She perched on a chair, so they sat, too. "Now what can I do?"

Pete tried to approach carefully. "Mrs. Johnson, this may be sensitive but you may be able to save lives."

Not knowing what to expect, she tensed. "Go ahead."

"Your brother."

"Not again." Her hand flew to her face.

"Ma'am?" Pete asked.

"He hasn't been picked up again, has he? He can't stay straight. He tries. He's been to rehab a few times." She paused, a look of concern swept her lovely features. "Oh, God, he's not dead, is he?"

Pete said consolingly, "No. We think he's alive." On seeing the distress on her face, he continued, "We're sorry to trouble you, but I believe Teton, as he calls himself, knows we're looking for him and he's doing his best to steer clear of us. When was the last time you saw him?"

"Four months ago. Don't tell Darryl, please. My husband is finished with Robert. Look, he has a problem, he can't get a handle on it. I just don't understand it at all. He blazed through a lot of Mom and Dad's money until they gave up on him. Then Darryl, at my urging, lent him ten thousand dollars to go to a fancy rehab. After that, Robert stayed clean for maybe a year, then he went right back on. Darryl can usually keep his temper in check, but that sent him right over the edge." She paused. "We have money, that's obvious, but no one wants to lose ten thousand dollars to a relapsed drug addict. I'm sorry to say it, but that's what he is. Darryl swore we should have given the money to a charity. We might as well have burned it and, of course, I felt just awful. Guilty, you know? Still feel that way even though my husband is good about it. He said, 'It's got to be hell to turn your back on your own brother,' which I did up to a point. But four months ago I — I don't know — I had to see him."

"Where did you see him?"

"I went to his apartment. Fourth Street isn't my favorite and I was even reluctant to leave my car parked there. His apartment, while very basic, was spotless. Robert was clean, too. You know how people take on a gray pallor when they do drugs? He looked in the pink, as they say."

"Did he ask for money?"

This surprised her. "No. He knew I was taking a chance to see him, that Darryl would be angry. Robert told me he was working on something to make a nice little nest egg. I'd heard that before, but I let him rattle on."

"Did he say what it was?"

"You know, Officer, I didn't ask. I'd heard so many cock-and-bull stories I couldn't stomach another. I was just glad to see him and I didn't know when I would see him again. I hope he's alive. He has struggled so much, and he has made a hash of his life. He's weak, I guess. Maybe we all are in some ways. His way is just obvious."

"Would you say that your husband and Robert will never talk again?"

"If they do, it will be a few words, foul ones most likely." She half smiled. "Darryl was tolerant for years. He said we have to practice tough love. He's probably right so, really, in my way, I'm weak. I don't want to give up on Robert. My sister in Texas got stung, too. She lent him the money for his last rehab stint. They are sort of locked up for one month. The place was here in Reno." She named an upscale rehab center.

"Did your brother know Egon Utrecht?"

"I didn't know his friends. How would he know a celebrity chef?" She paused. "Well, it is Reno. Anything's possible."

"What about Oliver Hitchens?"

She shook her head. "Oliver would never have even spoken to my brother." She clasped her hands. "I don't wish to speak ill of the dead, but Oliver was very ambitious. He would never have done anything to offend my husband."

"So you think Mr. Johnson was aware of how Oliver played up to him?"

"Yes. Darryl knows how to get the best out of people for SSRM. He is a company man, it's in the blood. Actually, and again I shouldn't speak ill of the dead, he thought Oliver a toady, but one who was excellent at his job. Oliver wanted George W.'s job when he retired."

"Can you think of anyone who would want to kill Oliver?"

She half smiled, as so many loathed Oliver, then her voice rose slightly. "You don't think Robert killed him, do you? I mean, he had no reason."

"No, we don't, but we do think your brother knows a great deal about what is going on. That's why we must find him. Let me ask you something else: Was Robert angry with Darryl?"

"Can't stand my husband. As the years passed and Robert spiraled downward, that's when the hostility came out. Darryl, never one to mince words, used to berate Robert before he hit the bottom, telling him to snap out if it. Pick himself up. Others have done it. Robert, who can be self-involved, really resented it."

"Do you think your brother would want to get even with your husband, say, through SSRM?"

This stopped her cold. She thought, then struggled to answer. "When Robert is at his worst, yes, I don't put it past him."

"Was there anyone else in the company with whom he was friendly?"

"I don't believe so. It would be hard to imagine, because if Darryl got wind of it they'd be in hot water, excuse the pun."

"But those who had been with SSRM know who Robert is?"

She nodded. "As time went on, he didn't come to our parties. They knew him from the summer picnic at Lake Tahoe, events like that."

"Can you think of anyone who might be in contact with him, either from SSRM or from his former life?"

"No."

"Did he know anyone from Wade Properties?"

This also surprised her. "I don't think so. That's a fairly new company. Robert was already sliding by the time they started up."

"Do you know any of his current friends or associates?"

"Not personally, but he has a few. His last stint in rehab, he made friends. He mentioned a nurse, Kelly, Carrie? I don't recall, but he said another ex-addict is the only person who truly understands."

"We've taken up so much of your time. Thank you very much." Pete stood up. "When we find your brother, we'll call you."

"Please, if the news is bad, let me break it to Mom and Dad."

"I'll do what I can."

"Thank you, Officer." She also stood. "I pray he's alive."

"So do I." Pete meant it, but for different reasons.

She walked them both to the door. As she opened it, she said to Pete, "That was a wonderful thing you did Thursday night, taking Pauline Winters out on the dance floor. That horn on her wheelchair just cracks me up. She was a beautiful woman. Jeep was a looker, too. Both of you danced with our lady vets and then other men did, too. You won every woman's heart that night."

Pete blushed and Lonnie did, too — unusual for him.

"Thank you, ma'am," he stammered.

CHAPTER FORTY-ONE

Kylie Prentiss's face curdled when Pete and Lonnie walked through the door of the small medical center where she worked. Fishing out a color-coded file from behind the desk, she stopped, hand in midair.

"Miss Prentiss, if you'd give us a few minutes. It's extremely important," Pete said quietly but forcefully.

Kylie nodded and pressed a button on the phone, "Jennifer, can you take a file back to Dr. Zacharis for me?"

Jennifer appeared from down the hall within seconds, took the file from Kylie's hands, looked at the two officers, then said to Kylie, "I'll cover for you."

"Could we step outside?" Kylie asked.

"Sure."

She grabbed her coat. Pete and Lonnie flanked her in case she decided to bolt.

Once outside on the sidewalk, Pete said, "Three people have been killed. Teton Benson has disappeared. We don't know whether he's alive or dead. We think you may be able to help us find Mr. Benson. He's in danger."

She took a deep breath. "Okay."

"You know Teton Benson?"

"Yes. We were in rehab together."

"Was he the person who told you to buy land in Horseshoe Estates?"

"Yes."

"Did he tell you why?"

She put her hands in her coat pockets. "He told me that Wade Properties was going to buy up a couple of hundred acres there to develop. He said there were small parcels that we could pick up now before Wade moved forward. I bought a quarter of an acre, which you know."

"You had enough money?"

She took a deep breath. "It was twenty-five thousand dollars. I only had five saved so he advanced me the rest. He was right. A year later, the zoning cleared for the development. Wade Properties had bought up all that they could buy, but my little quarter of an acre and Teton's two acres, they had to pay a lot for them."

"And you repaid the twenty thousand dollars?"

"The deal was once Wade bought me out, I'd give back seventy percent. That included

425

the loan. I made forty thousand dollars —
well, subtract the five I put up, thirty-five."

"That's a sweet deal."

"Teton was a good friend to me. He knew
I was struggling. When I went into rehab I
resigned my job at the hospital. If I hadn't,
they probably would have fired me. Luckily,
nurses are hard to come by, so I was able to
get this job when I got out. But I barely had
enough to get an apartment. Rehab is expensive." She looked up at them. "But it was
worth it."

"I'm sure it was," Pete said. "Did Teton
ever tell you how he knew about the future
development site?"

"He had a friend in SSRM."

"Did he tell you his or her name?"

"He said it would be better if I didn't
know."

"Lonnie, can you read off the list of
names?"

Lonnie flipped open his notebook and
read the names they'd gathered of property
investors.

"Ranculli, Larkin, Haverstock, Utrecht —
they were in rehab with me. Not everyone
for the full month. Dr. Thomas referred people from Las Vegas, people who didn't want
to go to a center where they lived. I don't
know, people find out sooner or later. An-

thony Diamond used to buy coke from Teton back when he was dealing. According to Teton, Anthony went into rehab in California." She paused. "I heard about Egon Utrecht being poisoned. Teton told me Egon had bought two acres, so that scared me." She added, "Egon was at the center on an outpatient basis. He worked at night so during the day he'd sit in on sessions."

"Did Teton tell all these people about this investment opportunity?"

"I think so. I mean, he didn't tell me everything he did or said but he used to say that those of us who had been through 'the process,' as he called it — I called it 'the grinder' — needed to help one another. Outsiders don't trust us."

"I know this has been hard for you." Pete opened the door for her to go back in.

"You won't say anything to my boss, will you?"

"Not if you've told me the truth."

"I swear I have. If you find Teton, tell him I'm praying for him."

"I will."

As they headed for the car, Lonnie raised his eyebrows. "Larkin next?"

"He's worthless. We won't get anything out of him. I think if we find Teton's SSRM contact we find our murderer, and I'll bet you

Oliver Hitchens was onto him."

"And Sam Peruzzi?"

"Possibly. Our perp must have creamed a couple of million off this. People kill for less. Sam was some kind of a threat."

It was turning into a long day. They managed to find Ann Haverstock in her shop in Virginia City. Like Kylie, she was wary, but Teton's disappearance made her worried. Her version of events paralleled Kylie's. Teton had advised her to buy her acreage.

As they drove down the steep mountain back into Reno, Sergeant Perez called on the radio.

"Found the 2003 Blazer in Indio, California. Benson switched plates. The original owner of the plates didn't notice until he got pulled over, thanks to the plates off the stolen car."

"He's not stupid, Teton."

"Nope."

After signing off, Lonnie said, "Looks like he's alive."

"Yep."

Pete called Lolly Johnson who was still terribly worried about her brother.

As he slowed down for the sharp curves on the Geiger Grade — the views unfolded for miles — Pete said, "It might be better for Teton if he gave himself up. He'd be safe in jail."

"Ever notice that sometimes when people are carrying an object and they start to fall they still don't let go of that object?"

Pete glanced at Lonnie. "So what's Teton holding on to?"

"The money."

CHAPTER FORTY-TWO

Late in the afternoon on Tuesday Mags peered intently at the computer screen. She'd found various Frederic Remington sketches tucked away in museums all over America. Of course, Cody, Wyoming, had some, as well as the Bradford-Brinton Museum in Big Horn, Wyoming. Dallas, Texas, Kansas City — many museums had one or two.

She'd found an entire series of beautiful Remington drawings scattered throughout America, detailed sketches of the various riders in Buffalo Bill's show. She called up and enlarged each of the Cossacks. Then she enlarged the British officers. One, Major James Plunket, looked stunning in his tunic and helmet.

"Wait a minute."

Baxter raised his head off his paws.

Mags clapped her hands, which made the tough little guy bark. "Sorry, Baxter, but if only you could see this. The Dragoon has a square-beaded bracelet peeking out from under his sleeve." She left the computer on, threw on her coat, and ran out to the old barn.

"What's up?" Jeep noticed her niece's flushed face.

"She's pretty excited," Baxter stated.

King walked over to Baxter to touch noses.

"Aunt Jeep, I've found something important. I think I've found something that will lead us to our killer. If I only knew why." She stopped before saying more. "Mr. Locke, I'm sorry. I was so excited, I didn't see you there. Excuse me."

"Hey, sounds pretty exciting."

Jeep smiled at Mags. "I'll be up later. Enrique and I were just talking to Craig about the water rights issue now being considered by the Nevada Supreme Court."

"I dropped by. Wanted to hear what your aunt thinks. She's usually ahead of the rest of us, plus I can always try to buy her water rights. Reno will need a lot more water. It's right under our feet here at Wings Ranch.

Enrique smiled slightly. "Craig, Mom is not going to sell a drop, nor will I."

"Aunt Jeep, sorry, I'll see you later." Mags apologized.

After she left, Craig returned to his take on

this. "A ruling in their favor would be a big victory for environmental groups, but it will only exacerbate our water problems."

"Who could have imagined that this would happen?" Enrique knew a long, expensive fight would ensue and as a matter of protection, people would have to refile water rights back to 1947.

"The state engineer's office charges three hundred dollars per application. Some people aren't going to be able to afford this." Craig pressed his case. "That means their rights are imperiled no matter what the ruling might be. 'Course, that means SSRM can buy them up."

"Craig, I don't see it that way," said Jeep. "Groups like Washoe Water Rights and Friends of Sierra will file suit to prevent the indigent from losing their rights if the ruling goes the wrong way. The right way for you" — she half smiled — "wrong way for others, but I think this issue might turn the tide on squandering our resources."

"SSRM doesn't squander water."

"You may not, but this state can't afford increased irresponsible draws on our water. You know as well as I do that in 1989 the Las Vegas Valley Water Department, the old name, filed applications and they were approved to draw eight hundred thousand acre feet of water a year from parts of rural Nevada. Eight hundred thousand! Sailed right through. But the sleight of hand that allowed the 2007 request for forty thousand acre feet of water to be siphoned off of Spring Valley in eastern Nevada was the straw that broke the camel's back. That may be the wrong metaphor." She frowned for a second.

"I think the 2007 request was at fault over a technicality. The Supreme Court will look at the case in its most narrow form. Those forty thousand acre feet may now be denied, rolled back, but I just don't see water rights being at issue all the way back to 1947 because of this." Craig persisted.

"People are furious, Craig. Furious at big government, furious at higher taxes, lower services, furious at anyone who is an elected official and an appointed one, too. I think this battle that's brewing is going to be one of the biggest blowouts in Nevada's history and it will trigger similar lawsuits in other western states. For all I know, it might even provoke eastern states to take a careful look at their water tables."

He remained silent for a long time. "It's possible, but then what happens? Do we lose population? Does our economy stall?"

"We've heard that argument before. I'm deeply opposed to compromising rural water to feed cities. And, if I might pontificate, if this state is smart and keeps away from personal income tax and other forms of theft, which we have always done, business will stay. We're the best deal in the United States. We have the lowest per capita state spending in the U.S. Some people, big-government types, see that as a negative. I see it as the old Nevada way. Take care of yourself. We really are the best deal in America."

"But can business expand if we freeze — forgive the pun — our water supply? We can't cut back."

"We can and we must. All this yap about modern technology. Well, let's see all those brains work on ways to recapture water instead of emptying our underground basins."

"All right, I tried." He turned to Enrique and motioned at the barn's restoration work. "You're doing a beautiful job here."

"I'll give you credit, Craig, you never miss any new angle to enlarge SSRM's bank of rights."

"That's my job." He walked to the barn door, Jeep accompanying him. "I'm sorry you and Mags found Oliver."

"We did," the two dogs said in unison.

"It was most upsetting. Mags handled it fine, but it's funny the way things affect people. She loves her twilight run and her dawn run. She won't run that way down to Dry Valley Road now."

As he drove away, Jeep went up to the house. "Where are you?" she called out.

"In the den," Mags answered. "Come look."

Jeep hurried down the hall, the heels of her cowboy boots slightly reverberating. "What?"

"Look." Mags pointed to the drawing that she'd enlarged, the bracelet around the Major James Plunket's wrist.

"The beads!"

"We can't prove he's our killer but he worked every day with our Russian. I've tracked down all but two of the Cossacks. Those who returned and those who stayed. I'm getting close."

"I think you are."

King lifted his head off his paws, he'd been dozing in front of the fire. *"Someone just turned onto our ranch road."*

Baxter, also snoozing, scrambled up. *"I'll take care of it."*

By the time the vehicle stopped in front, Jeep and Mags had heard it as well.

Jeep looked out the window, the rough-hewn rocking chairs on the porch moving slightly in the wind. "Two ladies on a mission."

"I'll go to the door." Mags rose, arriving at the front door just as they knocked. "Hello."

A skinny lady, bundled up, her brown curls showing under her cap, said, "I'm Mrs. Armor Miller and this is Miss Shelley Pietrzak. We're from the Department of Social Services."

Jeep walked out to join the group. "Come in, ladies. Let me take your coats."

The dogs eyed the two women who Jeep shepherded into the living room.

"We're here to investigate a case of elder abuse." Mrs. Miller whipped out her notebook. "I assume you are Magdalene Reed?" she asked Jeep.

"I am and this is my great-niece, Magdalene Rogers."

"We must respond to every complaint. I hope you understand that. And we received a call informing us that your great-niece may be abusing you. Naturally she'll have to leave the room. We need to speak with you alone."

Mags exploded, "Catherine! I'll kill her."

"Mags, that's enough. Go out and help Enrique."

Red-faced, Mags stomped out of the room, yanked her coat off the hook, and left, Baxter on her heels.

"I'll bite them. I'll drive them off," the little guy offered.

Mags was so furious she didn't notice.

Back in the house, Mrs. Miller and Miss Pietrzak asked many questions. Then they asked if Jeep would roll up her sleeves.

She did. "Not a mark." Then she added, "As you can see, I am in possession of all my wits. I'm not battered and bruised and more to the point, my great-niece does what I tell her to do, not vice versa."

"As I said, we must, by law, investigate each and every complaint. I'm glad this is a false alarm." Mrs. Miller cooed.

"What do you do with the report?"

"We file it. It's not public record."

"I see."

Once Jeep politely ushered them out the door, she leaned against it. "I told Mags to take a stiletto when she had lunch with Catherine. Maybe next time she will!"

CHAPTER FORTY-THREE

Even in summer the high-desert dawn is crisp. In winter, it's bone chilling. Since she didn't have the money for a gym membership, Mags hoped the farm chores supplanted those workouts. Sure felt like it. If anything, those chores proved a better workout. She was using muscles she didn't know she had. But once one got into a routine, it felt better to keep at it, so she continued her jogging, running between two and three miles at dawn and sometimes another run at sunset.

This morning she ran to the end of the driveway, Baxter keeping right up, as did King. Sometimes King ran along and other times he stayed back. He found he liked being with someone young, someone who could run, jump, and even skip rope.

Mags started to feel that fabulous lift just as she turned right under the P-47 propeller blade. Way down Dixie Lane she saw a parked 4Runner. She wondered what the vehicle was doing there but she stupidly kept running.

As she approached, the driver's door flew open. A man wearing a ski mask stepped in front of her. Heart racing, she swerved. She was faster than he anticipated. He lunged like a linebacker, managed to grab her left ankle, and pull her to the ground.

"Get him!" Baxter barked.

The man lifted a knife. King smelled the acrid odor of combat and fear on him. Leaping upward, the German shepherd mix grabbed his wrist in his powerful jaws.

Mags twisted as the man released his grip. Getting to her feet, she kicked him as hard as she could in his groin.

The man pulled in his knee defensively, King attacked again, as did Baxter. The wire-haired dachshund may have been small, but his teeth were damned sharp. He sank them into the man's throat.

Mags kicked him again. The knife flew out of his right hand. She bent to pick it up, prepared to stab him.

King pinned the attacker down. *"Bite his arm. Leave his throat to me."*

Baxter did just that. King threw his weight on the struggling man. As his larger jaws closed around the exposed throat, Baxter's

puncture wounds oozed blood. With a savage clasp and shake, King ripped out the man's throat.

A shot of blood arced upward, then spilled over the front of his zipped jacket. His right hand, badly mauled, went to his throat. Mags stood over him ready to finish the job. A gurgle told her it was done.

Far too angry to be frightened at this point, she let out a yell of victory and relief.

"He tried to kill my person! Baxter growled, still hyped up.

King, satisfied the killer was dead, said simply, *"We took care of that!"*

Mags turned and ran back to the ranch, her adrenaline so high she barely felt her feet touch the ground.

Bursting through the door she hollered, "Aunt Jeep! Aunt Jeep!"

In her robe, Jeep hurried to the top of the stairs. "What?"

"Someone tried to kill me. The dogs killed him. He's lying down on Dixie Lane."

"I'll be right there. Call the sheriff. I'll call Enrique."

Within ten minutes, Jeep, Mags, and Enrique were wide awake, dressed, and in the truck. Enrique pulled up to the 4Runner, the door hanging open. The three got out of the car.

"You can see the bastard's windpipe." Enrique reached down to pull off the ski mask.

The dogs, who'd hopped into the truck, already knew who it was, thanks to scent.

"Craig Locke!" Jeep's hand went to her forehead.

Mags's legs felt a little shaky. Enrique put his arm around her waist.

Two hours later, Pete and Lonnie sat in the living room with Mags, who had mostly recovered. She patiently and accurately recounted the attack.

Pete sat next to her, Lonnie across from her. Jeep was in one of the longhorn chairs.

"Why didn't he use a gun?" Mags wondered.

"The noise would have carried all the way to the Old Ross Ranch. He knew that," Pete said.

"I think I know what happened," Jeep said quietly.

Enrique came into the room, having checked on the cattle, and sat down. "Sorry to be late."

"Craig called on Enrique and me yesterday," Jeep continued, "trying once again to pry loose some of my water rights." She shrugged. "Anyway, in the middle of this, Mags bursts in and says she's close to finding the killer. She meant our Russian's killer, but Craig must have thought she meant Oliver Hitchens's killer. That's why he tried to kill Mags."

"Thank God for the dogs," Mags said.

The next day, Teton Benson turned himself in at the Sheriff's Department. He'd driven up from Indio, California, in a brand-new Mustang.

The sheriff immediately called in Pete and Lonnie to question him, down at the department's interrogation room. Teton admitted to stealing the Blazer. He said he did nothing else wrong.

"We need to know how you became involved with Craig Locke," said Pete.

"I knew him through my sister. I knew most of the SSRM people until I got so bad my brother-in-law told me not to come to any of their functions. As I began to slide, Craig noticed. At first he offered help. He actually drove me to the rehab clinic. Once I was out, he said we could make money together."

"He pointed you to the small parcels of land?"

"He also gave me the money. I know he'd done this before. He had a large cash reserve so he could front money. The deal was he took seventy percent and we took thirty. He wanted me to find people to buy the other parcels — again, he'd front the money. People who could never be traced back to him. I did. They never spoke to anyone but me."

"The friends you made in rehab?"

"Right. The problem was Egon. Once the money came through — I mean, once Wade Properties anted up — Egon wanted to keep a larger percentage. He badgered me and kept at it — he could be really nasty, especially if he had too much to drink. He couldn't stay off the booze. He cut out drugs, but he couldn't shake the sauce. I got sick of it so I told him it was Craig. He buttonholed Craig. Craig cussed me out, but he knew that Egon would be back time and time again. So he killed him. I left. Figured I'd be next."

Pete leaned back in his chair. "Do you know why Craig killed Oliver Hitchens?"

"He told me someone at work was getting nosy about Horseshoe Estates and a future project, which Craig felt would net even more money. He blew the pumps to scare people about the water supply. He thought it would divert Oliver. Didn't. He told me some things, but not everything. As I said, he'd done this over the years in small ways, using college friends, people out of the SSRM loop, not his immediate friends. But now he was trying to do it big, just in case the environmental groups and the ranchers upended everything. Craig wanted to own water rights in Bedell Flat before it became even more difficult. Sooner or later, he believed SSRM would have to utilize this overlooked area. He'd made so much money on Horseshoe Estates he was getting arrogant."

"And Oliver knew this?"

Teton frowned. "Oliver figured out that Craig was going to try to buy up rights in Bedell Flat. I don't know what else he knew."

"Did he ever mention Sam Peruzzi or Friends of Sierra?"

"He hated Friends of Sierra. Craig didn't name names. Look, I've told you all I know. I stole a car, but buying land on a tip-off isn't a crime."

Pete stared at him coldly. "You must have suspected he'd killed Oliver and maybe even the Friends of Sierra member, Sam Peruzzi."

"I didn't want to know. Egon's death woke me up."

After questioning Teton, Pete called Mrs. Peruzzi to tell her he'd found her husband's killer and he was dead. He said it might never be proven but he was sure it was Craig Locke.

Then he called Sergeant Evans.

After informing him about Craig Locke, Pete remarked, "Sorry I can't give you five minutes in the cell with him."

"I hope the bastard suffered."

"Sergeant Evans, he did. The two dogs protecting the jogger brought him down and ripped his throat out."

"Then there is some justice in the world. Give those dogs a steak on me."

"Will do."

"Something bright." Pete handed a bouquet with tiny orchids and pink roses to Mags, and a dramatic one with birds of paradise to Jeep.

"Let me put them in vases." Jeep took them both as she headed for the kitchen.

"Excuse me. More presents." Pete dashed outside, returning with two T-bone steaks from the supermarket.

"Supper?" Mags took the steaks.

"These are from Sergeant Evans in Susanville, for Baxter and King."

Jeep had just walked back, one large vase in hand, which she placed on the hall table. She saw the steaks in Mags's hands.

"Rewards for our heroes," Mags said.

"Perfect!" Jeep took the steaks and hurried back to the kitchen to put them in the fridge.

Pete hugged Mags again and kissed her. "I am so glad you're all right."

She hugged him back. "I am but I'm still in shock. That fast, Pete, it happened so fast."

Solemnly looking up at the handsome fellow, Baxter said, *"I knew."*

Pete bent on one knee, rubbed the dog's head. Then King came back from the kitchen and he petted him, too.

"Well, I think I found the Russian and his killer." Once he stood, Mags took Pete by the arm and walked him into the den.

She showed him the close-up of Remington's drawing. Showed him again the bracelet of colored square bones on her wrist.

"Sure looks the same. He has more beads." Pete put his arm around her shoulder. " 'Course, he hadn't lost his bracelet in what might have been a fight to the death."

"I think our Russian is Sergei Makharadze. Prince Ivan Makharadze, his brother, originally led the Cossacks in Buffalo Bill's show in 1892 or 1893. When the Prince returned to Georgia, Sergei signed up to replace him. Everyone else I've managed to track, but I find no mention of Sergei after 1902. Before he signed up with Buffalo Bill, he was posted to Persia, what they called Iran then."

"Looks like you found two killers." Pete kissed her cheek.

"I can't prove that Major James Plunket did it, but he and Colonel Wavell were in close touch. Wavell, if the online information is correct, ran a web of military intelligence. Remember, Great Britain and Russia were still at odds over what we now call Iran and Afghanistan. In other words, both men were spies and I guess Sergei found out something important — what, we'll never know. But our country was developing more sophisticated weapons as were the Germans, English, and French. The First World War was the first war with machine guns. Perhaps that was it as the U.S. really advanced the science of armaments, spurred by what we endured during the Civil War, the first war where railroads were used. I just don't know."

"You make a good detective, know that?" He kissed her again. "Every time I think of Craig lunging for you, I don't know." Pete couldn't express himself. "I just know I don't want to lose you."

Baxter loudly added. *"She's safe as long as I'm with her. Don't worry."*

Preceding Jeep, who could be heard coming down the hall, King came over and licked Baxter's head. *"For a city dog, you're okay."*

Jeep appeared at the doorway, beverages in

hand. "Let's celebrate. Funny, isn't it? No matter how smart we are, fate steps in." She looked down. "Or dogs."

AFTERWORD

On March 10, 2010, about two hundred women who had served as Women Airforce Service Pilots received the Congressional Gold Medal, the highest civilian honor given by Congress.

Three Nevada pilots: Julia Bartlett of Reno, Dorothy Ebb of Gardnerville, and Madge Moore of Las Vegas were among the honored. Were she flesh and blood, Jeep Reed would have stood with them.

Deanie Parrish, eighty-eight, of Waco, Texas, said the women had volunteered without expectation of thanks. "We did it because our country needed us," Parrish said.

Nine hundred or more of the WASPs have passed away. Thirty-eight were killed in service. Still considered civilians, "the flygirls" were not entitled to the pay and benefits given to men.

Of the two hundred still living, no attempt

is being made by Congress, as far as I know, to correct this oversight.

ACKNOWLEDGMENTS

Ms. Carol Lloyd, a Red Rock resident and professional researcher, helped me enormously. Apart from her formidable and speedy skills, she's good company.

Ms. Patricia Hodges, M.D., also provided a wealth of information. A graduate of Washoe High School, and then the University of Nevada at Reno, she knows the territory. Her recollections and understanding of Nevada politics proved invaluable.

Special thanks to Marion Maggiolo of Horse Country, Warrenton, Virginia for alerting me to the presence of Cossacks in America. A woman of high intelligence and energy, she continually delights me with new ideas.

Mr. John Schafer, MFH, who owns a casino in Virginia City, shared his insights on Nevada history and its current economic condition. He and Mr. John Edwards invited me and four other ladies to high tea, which was a wonderful way to learn just by listening to these people. We ladies would have been happy to simply sit and look at the two aforementioned gentlemen as they are rather handsome.

I couldn't have written this book without the help of the above people. I hope I have the opportunity to abuse them again, too. What fun they all are.

ABOUT THE AUTHOR

Rita Mae Brown is the *New York Times* bestselling author of the Mrs. Murphy mystery series (which she writes with her tiger cat, Sneaky Pie) and the Sister Jane novels, as well as *Rubyfruit Jungle, In Her Day, Six of One, The Sand Castle,* and the memoirs, *Animal Magnetism* and *Rita Will.* An Emmy-nominated screenwriter and a poet, Brown lives in Afton, Virginia, with cats, hounds, horses, and big red foxes.

www.ritamaebrown.com